Earthy Delights

'You're in my house now,' said Anthony. 'And I call the tune.'

'Is that so?' Rosemary answered. Her body jerked as he slapped her on the arse, then thrust his finger into her wet panties.

'You're defiant. All the better,' he purred, then abruptly let her go, raising his fingers to his nostrils and sniffing her scent. 'Ambrosia. Nectar for the gods.'

Rosemary pulled down her skirt and rearranged herself. 'Mr Selby,' she announced in icy tones, loathing him, 'you have a strange way of treating a guest.'

Earthy Delights

TESNI MORGAN

BLACK
lace

Black Lace novels contain sexual fantasies.
In real life, make sure you practise safe sex.

First published in 2000 by
Black Lace
Thames Wharf Studios,
Rainville Road, London W6 9HA

Typeset by SetSystems Ltd, Saffron Walden, Essex
Printed and bound by Mackays of Chatham PLC

ISBN 0 352 33548 3

Chapter One

She had never considered herself a sexy woman, not even in the early days with Terry.

Not, that is, until she walked into the greenhouse and spotted the bare torso and neat, denim-clad bottom of the new assistant. A spasm of lust, such as she had not experienced for years, shot straight to her pussy and gave it a squeeze.

Wow, she breathed to herself.

Wow, he certainly was.

He grinned across at her, a boyish, open grin and said, 'Hello. I'm Scott.'

'Ah, yes. I've read your CV,' she said, resisting the urge to fluff up the sides of her hair. In body speak this was a dead giveaway. She lowered her hand and took his outstretched one, adding, 'Pleased to meet you.'

His handshake was firm, his palm warm and dry. Electric shocks shivered through her.

'You're Rosemary Maddox, aren't you? I've seen you on TV,' he said, and she could feel herself blushing under his frank regard.

'That's right. My partner, Terry Veney, interviewed you for the job.' It was silly to let this young man get to her. Gone were the days when she was shy and retiring.

'I think you'll find I'm qualified,' Scott said. 'Did my

1

time at horticultural college and have worked on several projects since.'

'I know,' she answered briskly, withdrawing her hand, which he was still holding. She could feel the heat of him, and the barely concealed sensuality of his touch. 'Terry told me. We're well staffed, but need someone to stand in for me when I'm away filming.'

'It'll be a pleasure,' he said, smiling widely. His teeth were American movie-star white and even, contrasting with his sun-browned skin, but the rest of him was rough trade. Cropped dark hair, the hint of stubble, a thin, angular face, and deep-set blue eyes hedged with unfairly long, curling black lashes.

'Has Terry shown you round? I've only just got back from Kent. That's where the programme's filmed, mostly. Though we do the occasional outside slot, if the venue's interesting.'

'I know. I'm a fan,' he said and the look in his eyes made her clit throb. A moment later, her panties were damp. This boy shouldn't be let loose on the streets, she thought. He's dangerous and far too full of himself.

No, it's me, she decided, pulling back. I'm knackered. It's been a long week. Michael's so pernickety. Oh, I know he's a fine director, but Jesus, we're only making a poxy gardening series, not the prequel to *Star Wars*.

'I'm glad you enjoy it,' she said, sheer nerves making her speak louder than necessary.

'*In Your Own Backyard* is great TV. Who thought of it? Was it you?' he enthused, and she couldn't stop glancing at his large, capable hands; she wanted them on her breasts and then drifting down past her navel to her sex.

'Michael Pendelton came to see us after we'd won a medal at the Chelsea Flower Show,' she said, words tumbling out, glad to talk. Anything to avoid the draw of that muscular bronzed body stripped to the waist in the humidity of the hot-house. 'He brought the head of Ace Productions with him, said Ace wanted to make a programme for the amateur gardener, and asked if we might be interested. Terry wasn't, but I was. A year on and the ratings are still soaring.'

'Most men watch it because of you,' Scott said, leaving the trays of seedlings he had been tending and inching closer to her. 'It's that dark, exotic, gypsy look that gets them going. Makes them think of hay fields, and country frolics, the open road and freedom.'

'I hope not,' she said sternly. 'It's an educational thing. We have lots of letters from women.'

'Dykes, I expect. I'll bet most of the mail addressed to you is from men,' he teased. 'Retired blokes and suchlike, who want to see that gap at the tops of your thighs and how your jeans cut into your crotch as you work.'

'That's not true. I think you're very rude,' she snapped, turning away from him, fully conscious that she was wearing exactly that – a pair of faded denims so tight that the seam pressed between her lips.

Her T-shirt was white and had the programme's logo printed on it; her lacy bra glimpsed through. This was normal working gear for her, but Michael had been quick to spot its potential, and that of her clear complexion, positive attitude, sepia-coloured curls and green eyes.

Scott shrugged his wide shoulders and she found herself yearning to lip the little hollow by his collarbone and tug at the fine dark hair that sprinkled his chest. He smelled of the fresh young sweat that was trapped in the tufts at his armpits.

'I didn't mean to offend you,' he said. 'I think you look fabulous. It really doesn't matter, Miss Maddox. It's whatever pleases the viewers, isn't it? That's what pays the bills. Am I right or am I right?'

'You've a cynical way of looking at it,' she replied, convincing herself that he was arrogant and she didn't like him.

What did his opinion matter anyway? He was a beginner, and she part-owner of half a dozen propagating houses even bigger than this one, and several acres of land that had been transformed into nurseries. There was a large shop where everything connected with cultivation

3

could be purchased, besides wooden and cast-iron out-door furniture, sheds, loggias, ornamental ponds, statues and fountains. A café had been opened last year where customers could take a break from browsing. Plants Galore was fast becoming a household word among gardening enthusiasts.

'I'd like to be working with you soon,' Scott said, smiling down at her.

'Fancy yourself on TV?' she challenged, wondering if this was the reason he had been chatting her up.

'If it meant being with you all day and every day.'

What a charmer! Thinks he's God's gift, she concluded and went out, closing the glass door behind her. It won't wash with me, boy. But there was mayhem in her belly and the need to be satisfied. Terry should be in the office. Maybe she'd just enter unannounced and rip his pants off!

Jesus, but she's something else. Scott Bradbury whistled soundlessly and addressed the box of sturdy little plants he was about to prick out. An evocative word that had sprung to mind as he struggled with an erection that simply refused to lie down.

She was even more attractive than when on screen. What a body. That sort of super-fit shape brought about by exercise as part of the daily routine, rather than faddy gym workouts.

Older than him, of course, maybe approaching thirty, but he had always found mature women more exciting than girls of his own age. They knew so much. Their eyes and body language spoke of experience. Their confident voices teased him and made his cock twitch. They had a certain bossiness, too, which enthralled him, rousing strange desires – the need to serve them and have them punish him if he didn't do it properly. He liked women in uniform – nurses, traffic wardens, female horse-riders wearing jodhpurs and hard hats, and carrying crops.

His first lover had been a college lecturer. He was

4

eighteen at the time and she was forty. He was eternally grateful for the things she had taught him, not the least of which concerned female sexuality and the importance of the clitoris. In the lecture-room she'd worn calf-length dresses, modest and high-buttoned. In the bedroom she strode around in leather, flourishing a whip. Scott had never looked back.

'You're mad,' his best mate had said. 'Kinky, that's what you are. A dirty perve.'

'You don't know what you're missing. You should try it sometime,' he would retort.

'Not me. I'm a man of simple tastes,' his friend assured him, but Scott had noticed that he thumbed through any fetish magazines that might have been left lying around and would linger on some pages.

The greenhouse was exceedingly warm, with the sun blazing down on its glass. The plants threw off heavy odours and their leaves were beaded with moisture – just like his cock. There was no one about; it was Scott's second day there and, confident of his abilities, they had left him to his own devices.

The other employees were a mixed bunch: a couple of elderly men; a middle-aged one who fancied his chances as foreman; two girls fresh from college; a lad who hadn't attained the right A levels to enter those hallowed halls of learning but who had been taken on as an apprentice. He did the lowly jobs around the nursery, much of it concerned with mulch and the compost heap. Scott had met them all in the canteen during lunch.

He had settled in, congratulating himself on his success. He'd worked on a commission since finishing the horticultural course, obtained through brazen cheek on his part. He remembered how he had gone along to a stately home in Somerset where the owner wanted a parterre laid out. Several established landscape architects had been there with their flash cars and laptops, but he had arrived in a borrowed banger, looked the site over, noted down measurements on the back of a used envelope, gone home and spent two days and nights working on sketches. He had submitted his ideas and, to his astonishment, they had been accepted.

This had opened the door.

The next step had been to gain further practical experience and no one was better qualified to teach him than Rosemary Maddox and Terry Veney. Both were prize winners and their innovative, beautiful designs were uncontested. And she was a television personality, with all the clout such a position brought in its wake.

She was one hell of a looker, too, and if he knew anything about women, she already had the hots for him. What was the matter with Terry? he wondered. Wasn't he coming up with the goods?

Scott was uncomfortable. The heat, his thoughts and the close fit of his jeans were arousing him. He retired to the far end of the greenhouse where he could hide behind thick, lush vegetation. Leaning against a shelf, he reached down and massaged his cock through the denim. It pulsed, already rock-hard. He liked the look of it swelling behind the zip. The tip brushed against his waistband. The smallest movement on his part caused delicious friction.

He wished Rosemary was there to see it.

He undid the metal button and let the zip slide down slowly, watching his cock emerge from his dark, wiry pubes. He held it, stroked it and rejoiced in its thickness and length.

'You've got a whopper,' his teacher–mistress had said at her first viewing. 'That's a tool to be proud of, Scott. No, don't touch it till I say you may. You're a very naughty boy. Bad manners in bed are unforgivable. Get down on your knees and suck me.'

She had implemented every syllable with a blow, her cane whacking his bare bottom. Scott had been shown not only how to pleasure a woman but also how to enjoy submission.

Now he fondled himself and thought with pride of her compliment. Several women had complained that it was too big, hurting them when he drove it home. Most were intrigued. How would Rosemary react? He was longing to find out.

He undid his belt and his jeans slid lower down his hips. He wore no underpants and his hairy belly showed. He could smell himself, a rich aroma of sweat and genitals and the shower gel he'd used that morning. He straddled his legs and dipped a hand into the open fly. Reaching below his upward-angled cock, he cupped his balls, massaging the scrotal sac. He groaned quietly. It was exciting, but not unbearably so.

He wanted to hurry in case someone came in, yet wanted the sensation to last for ever. He had done this hundreds of times and knew better than anyone how to bring himself to the edge and then hold off, pressing firmly at the base of his cock to prevent it spurting.

He enclosed his shaft, fingers rubbing the stem, thumb circling the top. It was a deep, fiery red and he rolled his foreskin up, squeezing it together so that only the slit showed, then letting it slide back to form a ridge round the helm. Moisture seeped out and he spread it round his aching tip, sensation mounting until he knew he couldn't last much longer.

Oh, fuck it! he thought, reaching that plateau from which there was no return. It was just too good. He pumped himself vigorously, then stopped for a precious moment, letting the feeling die back. He repeated this once again, and again, but it was too much. He rubbed harder, his touch rough, enclosing the helm with the foreskin at every upward stroke, then pulling it down. His cock jerked; orgasm was a breath away. Another frantic pump and his seed boiled up and out of him. He came into his hand in spurts, moaning and convulsing, his eyes closed, his head flung back.

The world righted itself. The contractions lessened. His cock sagged and he wiped it on a tissue, then returned it to his jeans and zipped up.

He left the greenhouse and strolled to the double doors at the entrance, then looked across to where the house stood. It was a solid Edwardian mansion and this had once been the kitchen garden. The office was inside and that was where Rosemary would be right now, reporting to Terry.

Rosemary loved every inch of the place, recalling the thrill when she and Terry had first got together, deciding to pool their futures and their resources and go house hunting. Sutton Close had been the second property they had viewed and they'd looked no further. The price had been right, the spacious grounds unbelievable. Plants Galore was born.

She mused as she walked towards it, part of her brain engaged with Scott – his tanned body, his crinkled nipples, his tight arse, the promise of his prick. She wanted to phone her long-term friend and agent, Melanie, and tell her about him.

It was Melanie who never shirked from asking pertinent questions, like, 'How come you and Terry haven't married?'

'I don't know,' Rosemary had replied, annoyed at having to address this issue. 'I can't really explain it. Somehow, as the years have slipped by, everyone seems to have forgotten that we're not. There have been no children to legitimise, no real reason why we should upset the status quo. Financially, everything has been worked out. We're the sole beneficiaries of each other's wills. No arguments, no discord. People say we're the perfect couple.'

'It strikes me that you've never been in love with him, or he with you,' the forthright Melanie had commented.

'That's not true. We were ... are in love, I mean,' Rosemary had protested, then succumbed. 'Oh, all right, I have to admit that I've a dreadful feeling we're drifting apart.'

'Then leave him.'

As she approached the office, Melanie's sensible advice rang in her ears, and she heard her own terrified answer: 'I can't. There's too much at stake.'

'Bollocks! I can hardly keep up with the demands on

your time. You've money of your own. Sell the business and split the proceeds.'

I can't do it, Rosemary wailed to herself as she pushed open the door and walked in. I'm afraid of being alone. I need Terry, even if it's only as a security blanket, like my Bye-bye, that tatty old shawl I refused to be parted from until I was about to go to secondary school.

She stopped on the threshold as if turned to stone. Terry was there all right, but so was Belinda Parker, their whey-faced secretary. They were close together but sprang apart guiltily when they saw her.

Rosemary had never liked Belinda. She was just too efficient, her tits were too big – an enviable 40C cup – and she adored Terry, almost genuflecting in his presence. Now her cheeks were flaming, and there was an air about her, the unmistakable, giveaway glow of a woman who has just been fucked by the man she loves.

Terry had turned his back to Rosemary but she could see that he was fumbling with his flies. 'Didn't expect you quite so soon,' he mumbled.

'I can see that,' Rosemary said heavily. 'Have I interrupted something?'

'A meeting. We're discussing finance,' Belinda butted in, and Rosemary didn't like the way she was fronting her up. Bold as brass, in fact, whereas normally she was a mouse.

'Like where you two are going for your honeymoon and how much it's going to cost?' Rosemary couldn't resist this jibe, but she was hurting inside. Ten years of her life had just gone down the tube. OK, Terry might be boring – in bed and out – but they'd had a lot going for them – once. It stuck in her craw that this simpering doormat should profit from her hard work.

And the house? Her beautiful house that she'd worked so hard to restore and furnish. What would happen to it if she and Terry broke up? No doubt, Belinda would fill the nursery wing with babies as plain and downright insipid as herself. You're just being catty, Rosemary reminded herself miserably. Why can't you be happy for them?

'We need to talk,' Terry murmured unhappily.

'I think so.'

'Shall I go?' Belinda piped, gazing at Rosemary with round eyes, which were half scared, half defiant.

'Yes, darling. I shan't be long,' he said gently, and a knife stabbed Rosemary's heart as he leaned over and kissed Belinda before she scurried out.

'Well, well. Mr and Mrs Hamster,' Rosemary scoffed. 'You suit each other.'

'Sarcasm is the lowest form of wit,' he retorted, still having trouble with his cock, which refused to rest quietly in his trousers.

'Fuck off!' she snarled.

'I want to tell you about Belinda and me,' he said, perching on the edge of the desk in an attempt to look nonchalant. 'It's not something that's happened overnight.'

'Ah, so it's been going on behind my back for a long time, has it?' Christ, I sound like the rotten script of a soap opera, Rosemary thought. This can't really be happening, can it? And oddly, now that there could be nothing more between them and part of her was glad, she ached with desire for Terry, wanting to have him again. Just once more, for old times' sake, perhaps. Whatever was causing it, she was creaming the satin crotch of her panties and her nipples hurt as they chafed against the lycra lace bra.

She looked at him, seeing the brutal truth of a man approaching mid-life crisis, with thinning sandy hair and a lantern chest, a man who smoked too much and worried too much and didn't take care of himself. And, while noting all this, she still yearned to lie across the desk, pull down her jeans and have him fuck her as he'd just fucked Belinda.

Night after night she had lain at his side completely bored. Now she burned for him. What's wrong with me? she wondered. Is it because someone else wants him?

10

Am I viewing him through Belinda's eyes, or is it just a case of dog in the manger? I don't want him, but I'd rather no one else did either.

How bitchy and selfish can you get? I didn't know I had it in me.

'I'm sorry, Rosie,' he said, his voice choked. To her dismay, she saw that his mild grey eyes were moist. 'You're away so much these days. I feel kind of left out. I couldn't do what you do, in front of the camera, but it's made a big difference to our relationship.'

'I thought you were happy about it. The business is doing so well, isn't it?' she said, pushing the conversation when she knew it was going nowhere.

'Orders are pouring in and everyone is talking about Plants Galore,' he enthused, using this as a red herring to divert her from his infidelity, maybe even to excuse it in some dim-witted, muddled way.

'Well then,' she said, wondering what on earth she meant. Nothing was well at all, it seemed.

'Belinda's been a brick, coping with the rush,' he said, as if in mitigation, his voice ringing with pride.

'So she should. She gets paid enough.'

'She's worked really hard. Over and above the call of duty.'

'Good old Belinda, ready and waiting to step into my shoes.'

'It's not like that. She isn't like that. Neither of us want to hurt you.'

'Oh, Terry! What a load of shite! Hurt me? I'll bet neither of you gave me a thought when you were at it. Where did it happen? Here, in the office? In the back of the car? Not in my bed, I hope. I don't think I could stomach that.'

'It wasn't in your bed, and anyway, I always looked on it as our bed,' he protested, his weathered face flushing.

'Mine. Ours. What does it matter? I suppose you want me to leave the business?'

'It might be for the best,' he conceded gloomily.

11

'You'll buy me out, and the house, too? Or shall I make you a handsome settlement so that you're the one to go?'

'I really don't mind, though we could remain in partnership. Whatever you want, Rose.'

She could see Belinda hovering about in the outer office. She was wearing beige and it did her no favours. Dun-coloured hair strained back and held in place with girlish slides, glasses with tortoiseshell frames and – her only claim to fame – those massive breasts. Did Terry get off on sucking them? Did she suck his cock and swallow his come? Were they into fellatio, with her under the desk like a president's whore?

'I don't think we should work together any more,' Rosemary said coldly. 'Get your lawyers on to it.'

'What will you do, if you decide to leave?' He seemed genuinely concerned.

Having trouble with your conscience, Terry? she thought acidly. Then she said, 'Oh, I'll be OK. I'm on TV, or haven't you noticed? The series will run for a long time, so they tell me. And I can always buy another house and set up a nursery in opposition.'

'You wouldn't do that, would you, Rosie?' he quavered, and she took a sour satisfaction in seeing that he was almost regretting this move. They both knew that if she went Plants Galore would soon fade into the background.

She came nearer to him and stood close, hoping that if Belinda peeped through the glass panel she'd shit herself with worry that they might be getting together again. Shooting her hand down, Rosemary grabbed his balls and squeezed them.

'Watch me,' she said.

The moment she stalked out of the office, shutting the door with a crash, Rosemary made up her mind to seduce Scott.

It wasn't 5.30 p.m. yet. He was bound to still be there.

The sun was lower now but it was still hot. The breeze had dropped and the earth baked in the stillness. Damn all men! Rosemary swore to herself. If it wasn't for them I'd have gone straight to my room, got out of these jeans and into a bikini and plunged into the swimming pool. The thought of it almost turned her from her purpose – cool water, wavelets of her own making, a few lengths before lazing in the shallow end, a tall glass of iced fruit-juice to hand.

Later, she promised herself. When the pool's lit up from below and the moon sails across the sky. Maybe lover-boy will join me. After all, Terry can hardly complain if he does, not after what he's been doing with Mrs Hamster, née Miss Mousekin.

The glass of the main greenhouse glinted crimson. It seemed to beckon. Rosemary turned the door handle. A swampy heat hit her, redolent of growing, fecund things. She could almost hear the plants engaged in their single-minded urge to reproduce. They used any means at their disposal – perfume, nectar – in order to lure insects to carry their pollen, even if it meant the stupid little creatures died in the attempt. They, too, were following their instincts. Victims of Mother Nature. Just like humans.

At first she thought it was deserted, then she saw Scott. He was packing up and getting ready to leave. He stopped what he was doing and stared across at her. He seemed taller, browner, more flagrantly virile than ever; his blue-linen collarless shirt was unbuttoned to the waist. It matched his eyes.

They didn't speak. Words were superfluous. They moved towards each other and Rosemary's blood pounded as he pulled her up against his warm body. He lowered his face to engulf her mouth.

The touch of his lips filled her with such passion that she couldn't breathe for a moment. It was as if she had never been kissed before – as if this was her first time. It brought out the teenager; the naive girl; the virgin. She felt the balance of power going askew. She was no longer the boss. He was taking charge.

He pressed his tongue against her lips, opening them. Rosemary's insides clenched and her clit throbbed. How long? Oh, God, how long had it been since she felt like this?

Young man, beautiful young man, making her whole again, stripping away the tight control, the pretence, the icy hardness. She wanted to sing and shout and rip off their clothes, to have him take her in as many positions as found in *The Kama Sutra*. Without stopping his exploration of her mouth, his hands skimmed her waist, then caressed the under-swell of her breasts. He's taking too long, she thought impatiently. I want him now.

She was so aroused that she could think no further. Nothing must stop this. Nothing.

She had a quick vision of the camera crew bursting in and recording every raw moment. Then she imagined Michael including it in a late-night showing, uncensored, on Channel Five. That would put the cat among the pigeons!

But there was no one about, only her and Scott. He lifted his head and smiled down into her face; his bright eyes shone. Gently, his tongue caressed her lower lip, first the corners, then the pouting middle section. She moaned and did what she had wanted to do since seeing him for the first time. She slid her hand down between them and cradled his bulge.

Scott stepped back, still holding her lightly, and let her examine him. 'D'you like what you feel?' he asked, amused.

'Oh, yes,' she gasped.

'Would you like some more?'

'Yes.'

'Yes what?' His voice was crisp.

'Yes, please.'

'That's better, Miss Maddox,' he replied, teasing her but without malice. He unzipped his fly.

She drew in a breath as his cock leaped out, curving and brown-skinned. It was bigger than Terry's, bigger than any other lover's, though her experience was limited and she had been almost a virgin when she met Terry. She palmed it, and Scott's excitement communicated with

14

hers, her fingers acting like lightning conductors. She wrapped her hand round him and moved it up and down. His cock expanded another inch. She gulped, impressed.

What would such a huge thing feel like inside her? Would she be able to take it? There was only one way to find out.

His hand was under her T-shirt, working its way up to find and hold one lace-covered breast. The expensive, under-wired creation was suddenly too tight. Her nipples wanted the roughness of his work-hardened fingers on them. Terry's hands had been rough once, but now he sat in an office all day. Rosemary felt the sudden need for a man of the soil.

The jungle-green surroundings, dripping with moisture, filled her with the desire to be naked. She tugged at Scott's belt, letting him know of her urgency.

'All right, all right,' he soothed. 'Don't worry. There's plenty of time. I've been left to lock up; everyone else has gone home.'

'No audience then?' She was almost disappointed, wanting to flaunt her new-found sexuality, and brashly advertise the fact that she was about to fuck this fine young stud.

He laughed quietly. Even this was charged with masculinity, the sound of the hunter assured of his prey. 'You're a show off,' he said.

'I think you're right.' He must be, she concluded. She had taken to the cameras like a duck to water, with no shyness, awkwardness or hesitation; on-screen she was supremely confident, in a way she never was in her off-screen life.

Playing to the gallery, Melanie called it.

Melanie! Good God, what would she think of all this? Probably demand a slice of the pie. She liked men; the younger the better.

Dazed with lust, Rosemary protested when he disengaged his crotch from her fingers, but only momentarily. With an arm looped across her shoulders, his hand

15

dangling down to brush her nipples through her clothes, he took her over to a pile of pallets. They were the height of a bed.

'Now,' he said, his attitude changing, the gentleness gone.

His fly gaped, and she wormed her hand inside, finding the hotness of his groin, and weighing the fullness of his balls. He released himself long enough to unlace his trainers and strip off his jeans. The shirt came next and she was staring at every inch of his muscular body. He was a near perfect specimen.

He spread sacks on the improvised couch and then lay back, watching her as she undressed. Suddenly self-conscious, she wished she had organised their first mating to take place under different circumstances – in her bedroom, perhaps, with subdued lighting. But then her nostrils responded to the pungent perfume of Star-Gazer lilies and waxen stephanotis, hoops of jasmine and sprays of honeysuckle, and she knew she'd rather be there than any place on earth.

There was something crude, almost primordial about it. This man. She hardly knew him, but when he said, 'Down,' she advanced on her knees towards him.

He was playing with his cock, his thighs spread wide, his balls resting on the sacking. With his free hand buried in her hair, he drew her closer. She was between his legs now, her bare breasts tickled by his pubic thatch. She breathed in his scent. It was strong and musky, stirring her senses.

She clasped his rod, feeling it pulse in her hand, then her lips encircled the cap, and her tongue tasted him. She sighed, drawing the length into her mouth, sucking steadily and hearing him groan. It gave her a feeling of satisfied discomfort at being stretched to comply with a demand she could hardly meet. Her cheeks ached, her jaw, too, as she mouthed him. His pleasure was almost as sweet to her as her own, a coil tightening inside her.

The intensity of his need taking charge, she worked his cock. Her hair straggled forward, in the way, but he

16

simply pushed it back and held it there, his lips pouting, his eyes heavy-lidded. She thought he would want to orgasm at once and she prepared to milk him. His pre-come mingled with her saliva, and she lapped at his stem, concentrating on the sensitive underside.

His fingers digging into her scalp warned her to remain still. His cock throbbed but did not shoot, and he slid it from her. 'There's another way I want to try,' he said. 'Sure, I could easily come in your mouth, but we'll do that next time. Tell me what you want me to do to please you.'

'Don't you know?' she whispered. Was it possible he was so ignorant?

'I want you to talk to me about it. Show me. Touch yourself.' As he spoke, he reached for her breasts, his thumbs circling the nipples.

'I can't. I've never . . .' she began, but he silenced her.

'You masturbate, don't you?' he said and, though she couldn't see his face, she guessed that he was smiling.

'Yes,' she admitted.

'Do it for me,' he ordered.

Terry had never wanted her to do such a thing. She took her pleasure secretly when he wasn't about – in the bath, in hotel bedrooms. She loved to play with her clit, watching herself sometimes in the mirror, seeing her pink slit opening, shining, and that sliver of flesh ripening between her lips.

The sweat beaded her body as she thought of it. It was impossible to stop now. She sat beside Scott on the pallet, making herself comfortable so that she might savour this unique experience. She had often daydreamed of a man watching her bring herself to climax, but had never done it before.

Half sitting, she opened her legs and parted her outer lips, relishing the crisp feel of her bush. Her finger found her wetness. She glanced at Scott to make sure he was looking.

'Go on,' he said huskily. 'Bring yourself off, then I'll lick you out.'

Using her other hand, she held her flesh apart. Her clit protruded. She touched the head with delicate wet strokes. Shivers of desire ran through her body, gathering in her epicentre. Forgetting Scott, she closed her eyes, focusing on the fantastic images behind her lids. She didn't want anything to disrupt her climb to the peak.

She felt his hand on hers, and then the warmth of his breath as his mouth hovered above her mound. 'Oh, I don't want to stop. I must have it,' she moaned.

'Let me help, please,' he said and, lifting her finger away, replaced it with his tongue.

The feeling was so acute that it resembled pain. She writhed against his mouth, lifting her hips, pressing herself to him. Orgasm flowed through her, the sensation so intense that she blacked out for a second.

It didn't stop, not at once. Scott sucked her gently, prolonging her climax, taking her down carefully, stage by stage.

With his hand resting on her belly, he lay beside her, admiration in his eyes. 'Now what d'you want?' he asked.

'You,' she said firmly, and folded a hand round his cock.

His smile widened and he reached for his crumpled jeans. 'Put this on for me,' he said, handing her a condom.

She opened the packet and drew it out. Not a pink one, as she had expected, but black. She wasn't familiar with condoms. She and Terry had never used them. She was on the pill and they had trusted one another. A misplaced trust, as it turned out, she thought wryly. Does he pop one on his dick when he's about to plug the hole of his little furry friend? Does Mrs Hamster insist, in case he's caught something nasty from me? I'll bet he's told her I'm a tart.

She sat over Scott, his cock swaying slightly from side to side. Here goes, she thought, and tentatively started to roll the rubber over the glans. She heard him grunt, and felt the cock jerk as she covered it to the base, then leaned back to admire her handiwork. Somehow, that shiny black covering added to its fascination and gave it a sinister aspect. It seemed more than a human appendage. It could have been a hand-carved lingam, a plastic dildo, a vibrator. Rosemary had never tried sex-toys. It was like a sunburst in her head to realise that she could do so now – she could do what the hell she liked.

But, just for the moment, there was a living, throbbing thing, attached to a strong, lusty man. He kneeled each side of her, parted her legs and eased his ebony-wrapped prick into her. Though she was so wet, it was a tight fit. He rocked his hips, and an inch more of him slid inside, then another. Now she could feel him butting against her. Far from hurting, it was blissful. She clenched her muscles round him.

'You're wonderful,' he whispered, and leaned forward to brush his lips against her cheek and her mouth. 'I knew you'd feel like this.'

He gripped her ankles and placed them on his shoulders, then held her buttocks and lifted her higher against him. She felt him plunging deeper into her. Though she'd had an orgasm, this was an added bonus, the feeling of him pounding at her forcefully, selfishly, taking his pleasure.

He dug his nails into her buttocks, threshing in and out, his hips pistoning until she felt him erupting inside her. He slumped down, covering her body, the canvas sacking rough against her back and shoulders. His hands released their crushing grip, but continued to smooth her buttocks.

He raised himself on one elbow, staring down at her and smiling. Passion satiated, she decided that he was too conceited by half, and almost regretted that she'd now given him something to crow about.

'I don't intend to be a notch on your bedpost,' she said, but was aware of his fingers insinuating themselves between the crack of her bottom, the middle one pressing against her anus.

'Would I?' he asked innocently, his voice as bland as milk.

'Yes, you would.'

'Not me, Miss Maddox. Not where you're concerned. When are we going to do it again?'

He was quite unrepentant and Rosemary couldn't suppress that bubbling feeling of wellbeing. There were a dozen reasons why she might live to regret fucking him, but just for now, she felt warm, wet and desirable, and immeasurably glad that she'd done it.

Chapter Two

She fumbled for the phone on the bedside table, and Michael's crisp voice rang in her ear, when she answered. 'Rosemary, can you come in this morning?'

'What? Why?' she asked, surfacing from a muddled dream. 'It's Saturday.'

'We need to talk about that roof-garden conversion,' he replied. 'I'm on the boat.'

'Can't it wait until Monday? I've been planning to veg-out by the pool.'

'It could, I suppose, but there're a few snags to iron out. Anyway, I want to see you. Can you leave Terry behind?'

The timbre of Michael's voice always made her shiver, and when he was being dictatorial on set she came out in goose pimples. Power was an irresistible aphrodisiac.

'It seems like I'll be going most places without him from now on,' she said.

'Oh, what's happened?' His tone changed, becoming sharper.

They'd worked together for months and she had been aware of the chemistry between them from the onset. So far, she had merely flirted with the idea, fencing round the indisputable fact that they were destined to make love.

'I'll tell you when I see you,' she promised, and the tears were close. She needed a shoulder to cry on.

'Right. The river's looking great today. How about lunch? I'll cook you something special.'

After putting down the receiver, she sat and brooded on her future. This is how it would be from now on – she'd wake alone.

What were the words from that 70s Joni Mitchell song *My Old Man*? 'The bed's too big, the frying pan's too wide.'

Funny how nostalgic you can get once the man in your life is no longer there. He was a nerd, but she hadn't realised she would miss Terry quite so much. It's not a proper miss, she decided resolutely, more a habit.

She threw back the duvet, dragged on her towelling robe and padded down to the kitchen. It was empty. Robert had gone to visit his lover. Rosemary missed his gossipy chit-chat. Though an airhead, he was her house-keeper and general factotum. He kept a finger on the pulse and would have undoubtedly clocked Scott. There was no sign of Terry or Belinda. She hadn't seen them since that confrontation last night and imagined they'd sneaked off to Belinda's poky little flat to play house or burrow or whatever it was rodents like them lived in.

Good luck to 'em! she thought dourly and stomped back to bed carrying a cup of tea and the post. Not much of interest. Sweepstakes scams; Get Rich Quick competitions; a Wish You Were Here postcard from friends holidaying in Tuscany.

The house was too quiet, though there was activity outside. Saturdays and Sundays were when the punters flocked to the nursery to make their purchases. Extra staff were usually called in. She could have been down there, signing autographs and encouraging the public to part with their money.

'I can't be bothered,' she said rebelliously, going into the *en suite* bathroom and spinning the dolphin-shaped taps.

Would Scott be working? And if he was, did she really

22

care? I'm not going looking for him, she thought, sinking down into the cast-iron tub and fixing her mind on plumbing. Showers were invigorating, a boon for those in a hurry, but there was nothing quite like a self-indulgent, leisurely soak in foamy scented water. Cleopatra had the right idea when she bathed in asses' milk, attended by hunky slaves.

Rosemary daydreamed of Scott in a tiny white linen kilt and golden manacles, hair ruffled and curly, à la Greek. Yummy, she concluded and looked along the half-submerged length of her body, admiring the clean curves of her legs and the contrast between her sun-kissed skin and the frothy bubbles. Her pubes were darker when wet, forming a neatly trimmed triangle. She played with them, parted them, exposed her pink slit. She thought of Scott again, and a pleasurable sensation warmed her.

She reached for the mobile and pressed Melanie's home number. All she got was the answerphone. Of course, she was away for the weekend, shagging her latest acquisition, a garage mechanic she had picked up when having her car serviced. Now he was servicing her.

Bleakly, Rosemary realised how few real friends she had. There were no brothers or sisters and her parents were divorced. Her father lived in Australia and her mother had married an archaeologist and was digging a site in Peru. They hardly ever contacted her. She thought she was used to being a loner, but apparently not.

There were advantages to this, of course, and she opened her thighs and swifly brought herself to a climax. Comforted by the feel of her own fingers that never let her down, she finished her ablutions and got out of the bath in better spirits, thinking about Michael and wondering if today would be the day they'd get it together.

Why not? She was a free woman now.

She took her time deciding what to wear. Though appearing on TV in sensible CAT boots or sport sandals hefty enough to take it when she was wielding a spade, pretty under-things were one of her weaknesses, second only to chocolate. But now, she thought, having shafted Scott, sex might become *numero uno*.

The drawer of the tallboy gave up its secrets; rows of silk and lace panties, bras and suspender belts in matching sets. They ranged from white, through to cream, beige, coffee-brown and black, with blue, red, apricot and green ones thrown in for good measure. None were sensibly substantial.

Was she expecting to show Michael her knickers? The thought kept popping into her head and she smiled as she stepped into a brief violet pair cut high at the sides. She twisted round to look at her rear in the dressing-table mirror. This was how Michael would see her, perhaps. She waggled her bottom provocatively and the sight made her dewy.

She could not resist running her hands over the satiny material and the smoothness of her skin, then reaching up to hold a breast in each palm. It felt incredibly good. Is this what men loved to do, exciting their cocks by handling a woman's breasts? She could understand it, her own feeling so delightfully soft yet firm, hinting at abundance and completion.

She had never owned a peep-hole bra or split-crotch panties, and decided it was high time she did. For whose benefit? Scott's? Not necessarily. Michael was keen. Time to let my hair down, she thought, and she posed in front of the mirror, seeing wisps of pubic hair poking out at each side of the narrow silk gusset. She lifted one leg and rested her foot on the stool. The material just about covered her mound, clasping its fullness like a loving hand.

The sun was streaming in at the window, presaging another hot day. She wouldn't wear a bra, just a simple yellow crop-top that darkened her tan. And for the lower half? A full Indian cotton skirt with a brown background. When she stood in front of the light her legs showed through.

She slipped on a pair of gold toe-post sandals, then sat down to engage in the ritual of applying cosmetics: an

almost meditative procedure. After cleansing and mois-
turising her skin, she added a thin layer of base, a touch
of blusher and a light dusting of powder. A firm believer
that the eyes were windows on the soul, she brushed her
thick lashes with a mascara wand, and added a smear of
green shadow to the lids. Her naturally wing-shaped
brows needed hardly any pencil.

Her damp hair took on an ebony sheen, curling around
her fingers as she scrunched it upwards; she then hung
her head down and gave it a whoosh from side to side,
as instructed by Gary from the studio make-up
department.

She painted her lips a poppy shade, hung hoops in her
pierced ears and finished off with an Aztec necklace. She
plumped up her pillows and shook the duvet straight,
remembered she hadn't used any perfume and rectified
this with a generous squirt of her favourite, which was
too heavy for summer but who cared? Then she ran
lightly down the stairs.

She avoided the garden centre where Scott might be,
and went into the double garage. Her Golf looked a bit
lost without Terry's Mercedes parked next door. Refusing
to think about that, Rosemary got in the car, revved up
the engine, slipped a cassette into the player and left
Plants Galore to the accompaniment of the Triumphal
March from *Aida*.

Fuck 'em all, she thought. At least she could play her
favourite music without someone moaning that it was
boring. Terry liked Country and Western. No doubt
Belinda liked it, too, or if not she'd pretend she did. The
same would probably go for orgasms. Terry wasn't too
hot in the sack. Rosemary had often faked it. Now it was
Belinda's turn. I'm never going to fake it again, she
vowed.

She drove into London via Hammersmith Bridge. The
traffic was steady, not as thick as a weekday, but busy
enough. This was Michael's first floating home and he
had been angling for her to visit it for ages. He'd told her
the mooring alone was ferociously expensive, and the

boat itself had cost a bomb. He had sold his town flat to pay for it and considered it to be worth every penny. It was frightfully up-market, of course. Anyone who was anyone lived either in a converted wharf-side factory apartment or a church that had been de-consecrated, or on a narrow boat.

Rosemary arrived on the dockside complex and, following Michael's instructions, drove along the quay to where black and white gates proclaimed that this was Oldgate Marina. An officious-looking man in a navy-blue uniform and peaked cap, waved her to a halt. She immediately dubbed him Captain Pugwash.

'Can I help you, miss?'

His meaning was clear. What he really meant was: 'What are you doing here? Are you a terrorist? Have you come to blow up the joint?'

She gave him the benefit of her wide smile, crinkled her eyes at him and replied, 'I'm invited to lunch on Michael Pendelton's boat, the *Daisy May*.'

'Identification, miss, if you please,' Captain Pugwash insisted.

Not responsive to my girlish charms? Perhaps he's gay, she thought, too long at sea with his jolly Jack Tars. 'Will this do?' she said, and handed over her driving licence.

He squinted at it and then at her. 'Don't I know you from somewhere, miss?'

'Quite possibly,' she answered, a trifle weary of the question, which cropped up frequently, in the supermarket, the book shop, the bank. 'Do you have a television set?'

'Oh, yes, miss. Wouldn't be without it.'

'Then perhaps you've seen *In Your Own Backyard*?'

'Of course! You're Rosemary Maddox. Well, fancy meeting you! Wait till I tell the wife. She'll be thrilled.'

'Keen gardener, are you?' Rosemary asked, hoping he wouldn't keep her chatting all day.

'Oh, yes, Miss Maddox. Dead keen. And I've picked up so many tips from you. I never miss your show.'

'Thanks,' she said, and she meant it.

26

She had never quite got over the thrill of fame and popularity, and it was satisfying to know that she really did help people add that little bit extra to their lives by growing things. A very basic need, it seemed, harking back to the days of the hunter–gatherers. Were it no more than a window-box, or a pot-plant in a high-rise tower block, contact with the earth was therapeutic.

The gates swung open and Rosemary waved goodbye to Captain Pugwash, and swept through. She found the *Daisy May* at anchor in line with other boats, large and small. They all had one thing in common; each was immaculate, with gleaming brass fittings and neat paint-work. There was nothing shoddy or down-at-heel about this flotilla.

Michael was doing his Old Salt routine, wearing a yachting cap and pacing the deck with a cheroot clenched between his lips. If the security guard had been Captain Pugwash, then Michael was a swashbuckling pirate-king.

'Hi, there,' he called out and held out his hand to help her climb aboard.

'I thought you'd be chewing tobacco, not smoking it,' she said, returning his peck on the cheek.

'That's for deep-sea sailors, I believe,' he said, squeezing her hand. 'This was a grain barge, once used for travelling along the canals.'

'It's huge,' she commented, admiring the length and the bottle-green paint.

The bargemen's utensils, kettles and coal scuttles, pans and buckets, had been restored and enamelled and hand painted with cabbage roses. They were filled with an abundance of petunias, geraniums, cascading aubretia and fuchsias, as kitsch as the patio of any suburban semi-detached.

Rosemary knew all about this. Michael had picked her brains and she had supplied the plants and a member of her team to set them up.

'They've come on well,' he said as proud as if he'd produced them from seeds planted in John Innes Potting Compost No.2. 'Thanks, Rosemary. There's a sort of tacit rivalry among we bargees as to who'll put on the best display. I reckon I've won, hands down, and I'm the new kid on the river. I love watering them and smelling them and sitting out here in the evening, admiring them. There was no room to grow anything in the flat, other than mustard and cress on somebody's damp face flannel.'

'I'll bring you some herbs. Dill, thyme and mint. They sprout like weeds and you can pot them up, then add them to your cooking,' she said, marvelling at the change in him. Gone was the crabby, critical director. Now he seemed almost human.

'I'd like that,' he said, his glance like a warm caress. 'Who knows? Maybe one day I'll get myself a cottage in the country and turn truly rural.'

'I can't see it happening,' she replied with a laugh. 'I've never met anyone who's such a townie.'

'I may surprise you.'

The space was restricted and Michael was a big man. She was conscious of his closeness as her breasts brushed his arm while he led her to a small table shaded by an awning. It was cool there; the river breeze was refreshing, the sounds from the other boats reassuringly normal, and the company of this knowledgeable man was highly enjoyable.

Rosemary unwound as he poured her pungent red wine. They ate salad and tuna pasta with crusty garlic bread, and crunched into the most heavenly olives stuffed with almonds, anchovies and peppers.

He sat on the bench beside her, never pushy, simply attentive, and she thought him the most distinguished of men, with his craggy features and close-cut hair sprinkled with grey. He was casually dressed in top-of-the-range sportswear: a sweatshirt, deck shoes and a pair of jogging bottoms. These were loose-fitting, but somehow underscored his generous sexual equipment unfettered by jock pants. His forearms were sinewy, and his body in good shape. She knew he worked out several times a week and had his own personal trainer.

As she crossed her bare legs under the flowing skirt,

she felt her crotch pressing against the flat padded seat. Her knickers were damp. It wasn't just the wine and the sunshine and the lazy feeling of peace. It was Michael's presence that was making her wet.

He went into the galley and returned with apricots and ice-cream, laced with Cointreau. 'You're spoiling me,' she protested, giggling like a girl.

'Just give me the chance,' he murmured, and awareness tingled down her spine. He had never spoken to her like that before; so soft, so kind. 'You need spoiling. You look a little peaky, my dear.'

'Oh, damn. What you really mean is that I'm looking old.'

'I don't mean that at all. Let me put it another way. You look stressed.'

'It's Terry,' she said, finishing her pudding and picking up her re-filled wine glass. 'Seems that he and Belinda have been getting down to it. I think wedding bells are in the air.'

'How sweet,' he answered ironically. 'They've been in the air for me twice and neither marriage lasted. All I'm left with are colossal maintenance demands and monumentally large boarding-school fees for the kids. Highly overrated pastime, getting married.'

'Try telling that to Terry. He won't listen. Too influenced by Belinda.'

'She of the big tits?'

'That's right.'

'And you mind?'

Rosemary was possessed of the sudden hunger to part his legs, undo the ties of his jogging pants and give him the best blow-job he'd ever had. Instead she sat there, pressing her thighs together and saying, 'Not as much as I think I should. We've been together for nearly ten years. It's like a bereavement.'

'But you're not absolutely devastated?' he said, his breath tickling her ear, spiced with the orange liqueur. He slid an arm behind her along the back of the bench.

'No,' she admitted. 'It's been going nowhere for a long

29

while.' She found it hard to form the words. Her tongue felt too big for her mouth. Something to do with the alcohol, she suspected. 'How much have I drunk?' she asked. 'I'll be over the limit.'

'Then I suggest you stay here,' he replied, placing a hand on her bare arm. She could feel him trembling.

'Did you do this on purpose, Mr Pendelton?' she said severely. 'Trying to seduce an innocent maiden?'

God, I am drunk, she thought. Definitely hazy, yet nothing can dull the fire in my pussy. He's a bloody attractive man.

He caught her arm and she had neither the will nor energy to draw away. 'I've always wanted to make love to you,' he said. 'Right from the day I saw you at the flower show. But you were with that dull twat, Terry.'

'I know, and I've wanted you, too,' she said. What was the point in trying to deny it?

His arm moved to clasp her shoulders. She leaned into him, liking the feeling, hearing the steady drumming of his heart beneath her ear. He placed a hand under her chin and lifted her face to his, his lips brushing hers, lightly at first, then delving deeper, his tongue tasting her teeth and the soft cavity of her mouth. Rosemary sighed and gave herself up to him.

She surrendered to pleasure, her arms lax at her sides. He was so large, so powerful a man, and she could feel the heat and hardness of his cock pressing against her. He touched her breasts while he moved his mouth down to suck at the tips through the thin yellow fabric. Two wet circles appeared where his lips had been. He lifted the fabric and pushed it up and over her breasts.

Just for a moment, she was possessed of bourgeois panic. One of the people from the other vessels could be getting a ringside view. She tugged her crop-top down. The wet patches clung like a second skin to her nipples.

Michael laughed and smoothed a hand up her leg. 'There's no one about. It's siesta time. Why don't we go below if you're worried?'

Rosemary stood up unsteadily, bracing herself on a

brass rail. It was a wonderfully still afternoon. The narrow boats swayed gently, and a family of moorhens scudded along, the chicks following their little black mother, heads bobbing. The City of London shimmered under a heat haze in the distance, and the sound of traffic was muffled. Saturday, a day of rest, a day for shagging after lunch somewhere secluded and far from the madding crowd.

'OK,' she said, and followed him.

The steps ran down into the main stateroom. The ceiling was so low that he had to stoop a little, but the furnishings were luxurious; thick carpet, deeply cushioned lockers, beautifully crafted woodwork, and all the advantages of technology.

'I didn't realise there would be so much room,' Rosemary exclaimed as, his fingers linked with hers, he took her on a tour.

'This is the bathroom, the guest cabin, the kitchen and utility area,' he said. Then he opened another door and said, 'And this is my cabin.'

The bed was large, situated beneath the opened portholes. She sat down on it. A deliciously cool wind ruffled the damp curls at her forehead. She watched Michael. Even in the dimness she could see his erection distorting his trousers. He moved over and joined her on the bed. His hand slid up her leg and under her skirt. He found the edge of her panties.

'I hoped you weren't wearing any,' he teased. 'I've been trying to figure it out all afternoon.'

'Bloody cheek!' she said, and could not resist loosening the drawstring of his trousers and slipping her hand inside. The cock shaft was thick, the cap denuded of foreskin. 'I never can make up my mind which I like best. A cut or uncut male,' she went on dreamily.

'You've had so many, I suppose?' he replied, mocking her gently.

'Maybe,' she said, and palmed his smooth flesh and felt it quiver. This excited her. There was no turning back.

He freed himself, kicked off his shoes and dropped his pants to free his cock. The sweatshirt came next. He was well built, with silvery dark hair furring his chest and scrawling down past his navel to thicken at his groin. She took nothing off, lying back with her skirt rucked high and her nipples like cones against the wet circles. He was naked, she was clothed. It made her feel wantonly wicked, a loose woman indeed.

He kneeled beside her and she grasped his shaft again, rubbing it and rejoicing in his gasp. He leaned over and rimmed her ear with his tongue and then pressed the tip of it inside. He petted her nipples and the combination of tongue and fingers made her shiver. Scott had been fun, urgent, youthful and different, but Michael was seducing her with panache.

'Oh, yes,' she whispered, as he continued to caress her ear and then found her mound, pushing aside the violet knickers, stroking and tickling, spreading the wetness that escaped from her sex.

His finger slid inside her – a strong, large finger that aped the motion of intercourse. He pumped it in and out, and his thumb found her clit. She sighed her pleasure into his mouth, and he kissed her lips, then her breasts, nuzzling at her nipples, never relaxing his attention on her bud. She moved into him, clinging with her arms around his neck, her face buried in his clean-smelling flesh. She was so hot. The sweat broke out in her armpits and she tore off her top and wriggled out of her skirt. Naked, she returned to his arms.

It wasn't simply what he was doing with an expertise that told her he had had many women, but more the way he worshipped wherever he touched. She could forget his wives and probable mistresses. Just for the moment he loved her, wanted her, and no one else but her. At the very point of orgasm, he held her off the bed with a hand between her buttocks, widening her and sinking his fingers inside.

She came in a welter of sensation that shocked from her toes to her head. It didn't stop there, either. Michael kept up the rhythm on her clit, lightly this time, until the tension was released again and she cried out. Then he held her close, kissing her mouth and nestling her wet mound in his hand.

'Now,' she muttered fiercely, locking her legs round his waist.

He chuckled and kneeled over her. She took his cock and rubbed it against herself, then guided it in. He thrust, went in deeper, then held still before withdrawing. He reached in the locker for a condom. So calculating, she thought, as she watched him break open the packet and roll the latex up his length. He had expected this to happen.

But the chill generated by so deliberate an action passed quickly when he lay on his back and drew her down on top of him. Her breasts swung over his face and he sucked them in turn, then lifted her body so that her crotch took their place. She braced herself, knees each side of his head, bearing down on his tongue as he stuck it inside her to lick her juices before he slid it up to flick her clit.

'Oh, Michael,' she sighed, her eyes closed and her head back.

He held her bottom with both hands, keeping her steady, then sucked her clit hard between his lips and tongued her in a short, savage burst. She came again, her body pulsating. He moved her sharply down and positioned her over his prick, then impaled her with a single thrust of his muscular hips. She grunted as he fucked her. It was a good feeling, a feeling of fullness close to bursting.

She circled her pelvis, plunging downwards until his pubic hair mingled with hers. Fists resting on either hip, she pumped and gyrated. Glancing at him, she saw his face screwed up in ecstasy and felt him twitching and exploding.

Later, when they were dressed again, she remembered the purpose of her visit. 'What's all this about the roof-garden?' she asked, enjoying the feel of his arm around her waist. 'Or was it just a blag to get me here?'

'No, but I was rather hoping to kill two birds with one stone. We'll discuss it later. Let's go on deck. It's sundowner time. The hour for gin and tonics.'

From outside, the building was an ugly, red-brick Victorian warehouse. But the view made up for it, the River Thames like a Turner landscape or one of those mystical and obscure Monet paintings of London seen through a peasouper. Rosemary stood and looked at it for a moment; it was early morning and foggy and she could hear the distant sound of ship's horns, the muffled traffic, the stir of a city awakening.

The team arrived in vans; camera and lighting crew, gardeners and their paraphernalia. So much equipment was needed for even the most modest shoot, and this wasn't modest by any means. Michael was in control. He rolled out of his car, lit a cigarette and proceeded to issue orders.

The morning had not yet heated up and Rosemary huddled into her fleece. She had brought Scott along with her, a hopping-with-excitement Scott, thrilled beyond measure at being on location. Michael didn't look too pleased, but she ignored this. It was no use him getting possessive. Just because she'd bunked up with him on board the barge didn't mean he could start getting ideas that they were an item.

She had spent Saturday night on the *Daisy May*, got up early and been home in time to sun herself and swim. Then when she heard Terry and Belinda return to the house and start pottering about in the kitchen while he prepared dinner for his Mousekin, she had dragged Scott inside. Leaving wet footprints, solid as an otter's spraint, leading from the pool, through the hall and up the stairs in the direction of the bedroom, she'd shagged him senseless, making sure the door was ajar. She'd amazed herself by the noise she could make if she put her mind to it.

Revenge was sweet.

I feel fine, she thought, and strode through the plate-glass doors to the area designated as a garden. The building was four storeys' high and this luxury apartment was at the top. She had yet to meet the owner. So far, Michael had consulted with him, and been given a frontdoor key.

'Hi, there,' drawled her co-designer, unfolding his long, thin legs and rising from a deckchair. 'Had a dirty weekend?'

'Not exactly,' she responded warily. Though admitting that Jonathan Flynn had talent, his meteoric rise to stardom needled her, as did his patronising manner.

Michael, however, had insisted that he take part in the show; not always, but when he felt the inclusion of this charismatic individual would up the ratings. Jonathan had his own programme. There he bewitched the audience more by his presence than the stunning use of emulsion and fabrics with which he transformed interiors. He was also a wizard at performing the same miracles outside, his daring ideas and startling colour concepts blending in a most remarkable way.

He cast an eye over Rosemary and then shifted to Scott, who was clinging to her like the proverbial limpet. Jonathan's glance sharpened.

'My new assistant. Scott meet Jonathan Flynn,' she said coolly.

'Welcome aboard, Scott,' Jonathan said, with a wave of his hand.

Rosemary wasn't yet easy in his company as he'd only turned up on site once before. But having studied his proposal for a section of the project, she had agreed this was precisely what was required. It was harmonious, and would leave her free to concentrate on the shrubs and water feature.

Though wanting to keep this rival at a distance, her nipples were puckering. Jonathan was just too handsome and he knew it. His shirt sleeves were rolled up, showing tanned forearms. The collar was open around his throat where pale gold chest hair gleamed invitingly. He wore form-hugging white linen trousers, and his hair was tawny with blonde streaks, styled to look shaggy and casual. For some reason she couldn't quite name, probably her incurable romanticism, he reminded Rosemary of the early nineteenth-century poet and rake, Lord Byron.

And I've always been a sucker for that mad, bad and dangerous to know peer, she admitted to herself. No wonder the Jane Austen-type maidens treated him like a rock star, writing him letters and offering their all. What is it about the bad boy that's so appealing? Scott looks like an amiable puppy in comparison. And haven't I heard through the grapevine that Jonathan, in common with the long-dead Byron, jumps on both buses; isn't he blatantly bi? This made him even more intriguing and the tingle in her nipples fired down to her cunt.

'So, it's to be cobalt-blue decking?' she began, struggling to keep on course.

'And fencing,' Jonathan reminded, smiling at her in a way which let her know he was aware of the effect he was having on her hormones. 'And lots of ornamental grasses. What d'you think of my idea for the barbecue? A hollow base with coloured glass-brick walls, lit up from inside.'

'Impressive,' she agreed, wishing he wouldn't step any nearer. She was already titillated by his aftershave, something spicy with exotic undertones, and the way his trousers fitted as if he had been poured into them. His small bum made her palms itch. 'At least the owner hasn't asked for Feng Shui,' she went on. 'Seems to be into minimalism, though, according to the decor. Has he approved of the plans for out here?'

'He certainly has,' said a voice behind her. A ghost from her past materialised without warning

'Neil!' she croaked, her mind whirling.

He grinned and came over to take her hands and kiss her lips. 'That's right, Rosemary. Jesus, how many years is it?'

'I don't know. Ages. I didn't realise we were working for you,' she stammered, memories pouring in.

Neil Kemble had been her first serious boyfriend and his the first cock to succeed in breaching her virginity. She could feel her face flaming. Now he was dressed in a summer-weight suit, every inch of him proclaiming that he was 'something in the City'.

'I asked Michael not to mention my name. I wanted to surprise you.'

'You've done that all right,' she replied, trying to turn it into a joke while cringing with embarrassment inside. 'You haven't changed much,' she went on, and it was true, he hadn't, still burly, still ruggedly handsome, a little heavier.

'And neither have you, Rosemary, only to become more gorgeous,' he said smoothly.

Oh, yawn. What a worn-out chat-up line, she thought. A lick of fair hair fell over his forehead in a way she recalled vividly. But where had all that pent-up emotion gone? It seemed incredible that she had once imagined herself in love with this man.

'I'm sure that's not true,' she said, struggling to be calm. 'I'd like to think I've matured. I was green as grass back then.'

'A lot of water's passed under the bridge, Rosemary. You're famous and I'm doing OK. Got my own computer company. Maybe we can go on from where we left off,' he suggested, almost aggressively confident.

'If I remember rightly, we didn't part on the best of terms.'

'We were kids. We're a bit wiser now. Are you married or anything? I'm not.'

'I'm single,' she replied, and it was painful to have her solitary state proclaimed aloud.

'I'd like to take you out,' he persisted. 'What about dinner one night? We've a lot of catching up to do.'

'I'll have a look at my planner,' she said dismissively, then turned to Michael who was deep in discussion with the chief cameraman. 'Can we get on? There's so much to do.'

Uncomfortably sure that Neil was watching her, she took off her fleece, put herself in the hands of Gary from make-up, then gathered the crew around her. Each knew his or her particular task. The terrace had to be paved, with selected areas covered in bright pink gravel, and Jonathan's decking needed to be installed. Rosemary worked on the trickle fountain, setting the pseudo-antique basin in place, inserting the pump, covering it with mesh and then pebbles, and having the water cascade from the hands of a stone goddess.

Shots had to be done over and over again until Michael was anywhere near satisfied, and the afternoon was well advanced before he even considered stopping. The roof was a sun-trap and Rosemary could feel her face, shoulders and arms turning coppery brown. Jonathan was grumbling because sweat was ruining his make-up, and Gary was in a fret.

'Right. That's it, everyone,' Michael said at last. 'Same time tomorrow morning.'

'I'll be a little late. I'm bringing over shrubs and plants,' Rosemary reminded.

'Good girl,' Michael answered absent-mindedly. He was always totally absorbed when on a shoot.

Scott came from the kitchen for the umpteenth time, carrying a tray filled with polystyrene cups of tea or instant coffee. The crew groaned with relief and passed round cigarettes, then attacked a tin of shortbread biscuits and packets of crisps.

'Are you doing anything tonight?' Jonathan asked Rosemary, sipping his tea delicately as if the cup was made of bone-china rather than plastic.

'Oh, Christ, I haven't thought that far yet,' she said, slumping down near the newly erected decking that formed a platform at the end of the terrace. There it was screened by a six-foot fence. Jonathan's fingers were stained bright blue. There was even a smear on his shirt.

'I'm having a few friends round,' he vouchsafed. 'Care to come along?'

'All I want at the moment is a shower,' she said. 'Then I'll decide on the evening. I may opt for feet up in front of the telly.'

'I hear you've left Terry,' Jonathan remarked from the shade of a potted palm tree.

'What is it with you all? Does it make you feel better if someone else is in the mire?' she snapped, irritated by the endless round of studio tittle-tattle. It was as well that they didn't know about Scott and Michael, but it wouldn't be long. 'I've given him the elbow, but I'm still in the house and we own the business jointly.'

'A tad touchy, aren't we?' he commented, smiling like the Cheshire Cat. 'Awful time, a break-up. I know, dear, been there lots. You might as well hang out with me for a while. Here's my address and mobile number.'

'Are you ready, Rosemary?' Scott interrupted, glaring at Jonathan.

She smiled at his rather touching macho manner. 'Yes,' she answered and got up. The gusset of her shorts felt sticky, digging into her cleft, too tight for comfort, but she liked the sensation.

She drove, and London in the rush hour had become Dante's *Inferno*, filled with honking horns, poor air quality and road rage. 'You should've let me drive,' Scott scolded.

'I enjoy the challenge,' she answered, shooting him a sideways glance. During a hold-up at traffic lights, she rested her hand on the inside thigh of his worn jeans and worked her way upwards.

'Rosemary! For fuck's sake!' he protested, but without much conviction.

'Precisely,' she murmured.

The lights were a long time changing and she managed to cup his bulge, before the car moved on at snail's pace. It gave her the chance to fondle him. There was something about faded denim, worn threadbare in places, especially round the fly where the male package rubbed against it constantly. Rosemary realised she had missed that. Terry had opted for chinos of late, no Levis for him. But Scott, ah, Scott made up for it. She could feel that familiar ache welling inside her and she almost over-ran the junction.

She drove off the motorway and on to a country road. 'I'm glad I don't live in town,' she said, gently removing her hand from the heat of his crotch.

'I disagree,' Scott said breathily, easing his cock with one hand and putting the other one on her bare knee. 'I'd like a flat like Mr Kemble's. It's great. And I'd like his car, too. Always wanted a Jag.'

'Where do you live now?' she asked, the surface of her brown, rounded knee responding to the touch of his warm hand. The hairs rose all over her limbs and, though she knew she smelled ripe, she didn't care; she needed sex.

It occurred to her that she had never before shown any interest in where Scott went when he left Plants Galore. She had presumed he must have a life beyond the nurseries, but he'd offered no details and she hadn't asked. They simply met, grabbed at each other, and fucked.

He reddened under his tan, and dug his fingers into her knee, then walked them up to where the tight fringed hem of her cut-offs sawed across her thighs and into the crease between. 'I live with my mother at the moment,' he said gruffly. 'But I'm looking for somewhere of my own.'

Rosemary made no comment, imagining him at his mother's kitchen table eating breakfast before he left for work. The box of cornflakes, the buttered toast. Would he have marmalade, peanut butter or jam? Just for a moment he shrank to child-size, a little boy under mother's jurisdiction. Is this why he liked *her*? Did she in some way resemble the matriarchal figure?

She swung into a lay-by and switched off the engine. 'Where's your father? Is he there, too?' she asked, turning to him.

'No, just Mum and me,' he answered, a little sheepishly.

She felt an uprush of concern and this troubled her. She had no intention of becoming seriously involved with him. It would have been better had he remained more or less anonymous. She had all the information she required on a need-to-know basis. He was a competent gardener and a good shag. Why complicate the issue?

'She wants to meet you,' Scott blundered on, making her feel even more of a bitch. 'I've pointed you out to her on the TV and told her I work for you. I'm sure you'd get on.'

She didn't know what to say to that, so she squirmed out of it by leaning across and kissing him. This immediately diverted him, as she had known it would.

She took her lips away, looked at him quizzically and said, 'Here in the car, or shall we get out?' Then she reached into the glove-compartment. She couldn't be sure he carried a condom, despite the bravura of the jaunty black ones he'd used with her to date. Now that she had ventured into the stormy seas of casual sex, she had realised it was vital she had a packet of three about her person at all times. She'd bought them in the supermarket, guiltily slipping them into the trolley between a tube of toothpaste and a bottle of shampoo.

Now Scott's bewildered expression made her laugh as she handed one to him. 'We can't do it here, can we?' he asked.

'Why not?' she answered, filled with that exhilarating element of control. 'There's not much room in here, I grant you, but I'm sure we could manage.'

'With cars going past?'

'Oh, well, if you don't want to,' she said carelessly, and made to turn back to the steering wheel.

'I didn't say that. You're the one with the reputation at stake, not me.'

He was on her, holding her arms firmly against her body, then pushing his hands under her T-shirt. The interior of the car was ridiculously small for such an

41

awkward and space-consuming act as fucking, but Rosemary was so excited that this was of no consequence. While he put on the rubber, she reached under the seats and let the backrests slide down till they were almost horizontal, pressing against those at the rear.

Scott put a hand between her legs and massaged the narrow gusset of her shorts. The early evening sunshine fell through the windscreen on to his cropped head. She embraced it with both palms, rubbing the stubble backwards and forwards. It felt like silk under her fingers. He found the fastening and unzipped her, pushing the shorts down about her knees. She kicked off her sandals, lifted her legs and freed herself, panties peeled away. Now she was naked from the waist down. There was something intoxicating in knowing that any passer-by could glance in and see what they were doing.

Their love-making till now had contained an element of tenderness, but this was fierce. Scott lifted out his erect cock, then covered her with his hot young body and plunged it in her. Her clit spasmed hungrily, denied contact, and she pushed her hand over her mound and used her middle finger to rub herself. He pulled back so that he could see what she was doing and watch the stem of his cock as it pushed in and out, gleaming wetly in the sunset glow. Her orgasm was beginning to thunder in the depths of her belly, her finger moving faster as she felt the hardness of his balls tapping against her thighs with each inward thrust. The car seat was diabolically uncomfortable, digging into her spine, but she opened herself wider to take in every last inch of him.

She came, her pussy tight around his cock and he bent his head, his mouth on hers as his body shuddered and he spent himself.

A steady stream of homeward-going cars rumbled past, and soon Scott disentangled himself from her. Rosemary clicked up the seats and put on her shorts but didn't bother with her knickers. These, she tucked into the pocket of his denim shirt, teasing him.

'Better take them out before Mummy pops it in the washing machine,' she warned.

Scott frowned and slouched low on his spine. Her loins contracted and she wanted him again when he held the silky bundle to his nose and sniffed, saying, 'I'll keep them for ever, just like this, Rosemary. Unwashed and filled with the smell of your sweat and your piss and you.'

Terry was in the office when Rosemary let herself into Sutton Close. He had obviously been listening for her, bouncing through the door and blocking her path.

'What d'you want, Terry?' she asked abrasively. She still felt warm from Scott's love-making and needed time alone to relive it.

'You're making a fool of yourself,' he rapped, his face flushed and hair untidy.

'Pardon me?' Rosemary stared him right in the eye, arms akimbo.

'That young man you're fucking. Scott Bradbury. I've a good mind to give him the sack.'

'You'll do nothing of the sort.' She was really angry now, unable to believe that he could suggest it. 'Ha! You've got a nerve after what you've been doing with Belinda.'

'She's not ten years my junior,' he retorted nastily.

'So what? Are you jealous, Terry, jealous because he's young and handsome and everything you aren't?' she scoffed. Then she went to push past him. 'Now, please move. I've had a hard day.'

'You'll be sorry,' Terry muttered, but the determination in her eyes made him give way.

'I don't think so. What I do and who I do it with is not your concern any more,' she answered loftily, as she mounted the wide curving staircase, adding over her shoulder, 'I've an appointment with my solicitor and you'll be hearing from him shortly.'

Chapter Three

'Childe Roland to the Dark Tower Came,' he murmured as he mounted the stairs to his eyrie at the top of the house.

It amused him to quote so respectable a poet as Robert Browning. There was nothing at all respectable about *him* and, as he unlocked the room above his private apartment, excitement tingled down his spine and focused in his groin. He could feel his cock hardening. He opened the door and clicked on the light. The room's atmosphere enfolded him. Here he was alone. No one would disturb him.

He liked to fancy that in olden days he might have been feared, with people pointing the finger and muttering about the Black Arts. Thank God for a more enlightened age. Not exactly civilised, perhaps, but enabling him to follow his urges and do pretty much as he liked. He went over to the workbench and straddled a stool. Then, with the delicate fingers of an expert, lifted up the small china head he had recently fired.

He examined it critically, the tension in his nerves mounting, his cock firming up inside his black trousers. He could find no flaw. The head was perfect in every detail. He had already added the hair – real hair – *her* hair. He had been lucky to lay hands on it but, in his experience, most men were venal, and the studio stylist had not been above taking a bribe, when told that the clippings were for an ardent fan.

The man's sardonic smile deepened. Once upon a time it was thought that hair and nail parings could be used in magic spells against one's intended victim. Maybe this wasn't so very far from the truth, though he didn't intend to harm his Adored One.

He held the head closer to the light. Yes, the face was an exact replica of hers. It was undoubtedly his best piece of work. He took up a fine sable brush and dipped it in a jar, then added just the merest whisper of additional colour to the smooth cheeks.

The face, arms, hands, legs and feet were made of porcelain, and he had sculpted the original clay moulds. The body was of wood, lovingly carved himself, and he had made the garments in which he would dress the doll. Everything was almost ready to be assembled.

His plan was coming together and he laid the head aside and pulled a loose-leaf file towards him. Numerous cuttings were pasted on the pages and he flipped through them, pausing now and again to compare the doll's face with photographs of the original. This wasn't enough, and he rose, going to a shelf full of videos. He selected one, holding it for a moment. He turned it over and over, enjoying the feel of it with as much relish as the sensation of his bare helm rubbing against the inside of his trousers. He switched on the monitor and slipped the tape into the slot.

He sank into an armchair, which was positioned where he could view the best. The introductory music was cheerful, the voice-over jolly and informative. Its very banality made him excited. His breath shortened. He reached down and touched his cock, stroking the shaft through the fabric. It ached for release.

His eyes narrowed. There she was, addressing her unseen audience. A first-class presenter, she had the easy manner of someone who knew her job inside out. Her voice was melodious and she projected it well. Obviously she had been coached somewhere along the line.

He sat upright in his chair, nails scratching at the swollen balls between his legs, and up the cock distorting his fly. He didn't unzip, enjoying the tightness of the enclosure, his fingers tracing the rigidity and picking up the heat. Dampness spread from his helm and formed a wet patch, darker even than the blackness of his chinos.

He watched her, his tongue creeping out to moisten his lips. Everything about her sent sparks to his nerve ends. Her hair was dark with mahogany highlights and her eyes were green. Her skin was sun-browned, owing nothing to the fake-tan bottle. Her small waist and flat belly were emphasised by the close fit of her denim cut-offs. There were no two ways about it: they were very brief. His eyes fixed on the fringed hems at the tops of her thighs, and the way the material cut into the division of her bottom-cheeks and the plump lips of her sex.

His fingers moved faster over his prick. It had been difficult carving genitals on the doll's wooden torso. He'd be able to do better once he had seen hers, measured them, inspected, tasted and fondled them.

His cock surged against the zip, but he didn't set it free, continuing to massage it with long strokes, sometimes giving it a squeeze. The front of his trousers became more damp. He didn't take his eyes from his video goddess, thinking: She must get hot and sweaty working like that. What did she smell like? Was her personal odour seaweedy, or did she give off the perfume of herbs, or of the earth itself? Would there be stains on the crotch of her panties? Had she been fucked during the making of the programme? As he thought of this, he could no longer resist opening his trousers, lifting out his heavy cock and grasping it.

She seemed to be staring at him, her eyes filled with interest, as if she was really watching him masturbate. The camera zoomed in on a close-up. He felt he had only to reach out to touch her. He'd push a finger inside her shorts and play with her pubes. Her bush was bound to be dark, crisp and curling.

He knew he was acting like a star-struck boy. All the lovers he had had during years of sexual activity meant nothing compared to this. He'd never even met her, his fixation tantamount to voyeurism. It was so easy. He could act out his fantasies at any time simply by calling her image up on the screen. This was almost enough, but not quite.

Now she was moving and her breasts lifted slightly, the tips stone-hard beneath the bra and vest. He groaned, imagining her naked while he smoothed scented oil over her skin, between her breasts, round her nipples, down and down, to circle her navel and anoint her cleft. She'd sigh as he found her clit and massaged it to orgasm.

The need burned in him like an insatiable thirst. He held his prick, working it hard, the cap a deep, angry purple dewed with cream. Now she was walking away from the camera, her hips swaying. Beautiful arse. Had it ever known the whip? The sight and the thought kick-started his cock and he spurted in a rush, filling his hand.

Totally spent, he allowed the final spasms to die, then wiped his fingers, rearranged his trousers, glanced again at the doll's head, and crossed to his computer.

Not long now, he told himself. It was almost time.

The sun sank lower and the decking turned dark blue in the shadows slanting across the almost unrecognisable flat roof. Rosemary straightened, pushing her knuckled fists into the small of her back. She'd been having trouble with the fountain and had stayed on after everyone else had left. Scott had wanted to help, but she had sent him home in the van.

The quiet hour spent alone had grounded her. The past days had been hectic, but adjusting the pump, making certain that the water cascaded at just the right speed and angle, had set her firmly on course again. This was what she was happiest doing, working with plants, turning a derelict site into a beautiful garden. She always imagined it to be like a canvas on which she painted a scene as she saw it in her mind's eye, but using greenery, flowers, water and earth instead of brushes and paint. Neil's stark concrete roof had been no exception. With valuable help from Jonathan she had transformed it into an exotic paradise plucked from the tropics and set down in an airy space overlooking London's Docklands.

The late sunshine beat hot on her head as she stood admiring her work, but she was critical, too. The job was nearly finished. A few last-minute adjustments tomorrow and the film could be wrapped. Jonathan was already planning the end-of-shoot party at his gaff, as he modestly put it, though everyone knew he had a remarkably palatial home.

There would be a few days' respite and then that slave-driver, Michael, would be calling a meeting to discuss the next project. There was very little let-up; programmes were scheduled months ahead. This present show would not be screened until well into next year.

Rosemary arched her spine and worked her shoulders, her muscles protesting. I need a holiday, she decided. A break from all this. A break from Terry and allied problems. I'll phone Melanie, see what she can arrange.

'How's it going? I didn't expect to find you doing overtime when I got in from the office. Not that it isn't a lovely surprise,' Neil said, stepping out between the double glass doors. He was barefoot and his hair and chest were wet. He had a towel knotted around his waist. She envied him the opportunity to shower.

'I didn't know you were here. There was something I needed to see to,' she replied, switching her eyes back to the trickle fountain. The longing to immerse herself in water was paramount. She needed her pool with a greedy want that rivalled sex. 'I'm off now,' she added.

'Must you go?' He came closer.

She could smell the sharp scent of the soap that had laved his skin and mingled with the hair of his chest, belly and that musky area at his crotch. Rosemary remembered how it had once been between them.

Sweaty, ham-handed necking. His scruffy room (he had been the fourth member of a house-share). His fumbling ineptitude when it came to actually doing it.

'Yes, I must,' she said, but as she stared at him, she was aware of the sultry heat of the evening, the sense of isolation in this tiny green island perched on high, and a reckless drive to dip a toe in the sexy stream and find out if his technique had improved.

'Won't you have a drink first?'

He was smiling down at her with that little-boy-lost charm which he had always been able to switch on. He was a part of her past. She had been too busy to keep in contact with it – apart from Melanie and the obligatory Christmas card to ex-student female friends, now mostly married with a clutch of children. Sometimes one of them sent her an e-mail if they wanted to chat about her show. But Neil? For some reason she had shoved him to the back of the queue.

She knew why, of course. They'd made love, if you could dignify those awkward, unsatisfactory couplings with this term. She'd lost her cherry and he had been jubilant, completely unaware that though he had reached an orgasm, she was left frustrated. Too shy to tackle him about this or even to bring herself off in front of him, she had taken to faking it. When he finally found out, he'd been furious, calling her a bitch. She had hated him for months, feeling worthless, convinced that the break-up had been her fault. Now she wondered how it would be if they tried again.

She knew Scott would be waiting for her. So what? She didn't owe him a thing. And she had the ignoble desire to score points off Terry. She sensed that Neil could be a whole heap of trouble, but this made it all the more intriguing. Curiosity killed the cat, and she was willing to risk one of her nine lives.

'I won't drink alcohol. I'm driving. But cranberry juice would be great, if you have any,' she answered, and stood quietly waiting until he returned with a tray. A beer for him and a glass of burgundy-coloured fruit extract for her.

He placed it on the round cast-iron table and motioned her into a chair. The dark green metal was cold against the backs of her bare thighs, and the carving chafed as she moved to cross her legs. To her astonishment, Neil reached over and prevented this by placing one of his large hands on her knee.

'No, Rosemary,' he said levelly, a hot look in his pale blue eyes.

'What?' she bridled, trying to tug her leg away but knowing she didn't really want to. He was being masterly and this surprised her.

'I said, don't cross your legs,' he reiterated, his fingers digging into her flesh. 'I want to see the way your shorts cut into your crack. Can you feel the seam rubbing your bumhole?'

Rosemary was momentarily stunned. Her body responded; her clit began throbbing; she felt that glow from within that made her wet. Her mouth parted in aroused wonder and she said, 'You never talked dirty like that before.'

He chuckled, and his free hand came to rest on the sizeable bulge raising the towel crossing his lap. 'Times have changed. We've changed. I've learned a lot and so, I imagine, have you. Looking at you, I don't think you're the kind of woman who's satisfied by the average swift poke.'

'That's where you made your mistake before,' she said, lust churning inside her at the sound and look of him. 'You never took the time to make me come.'

'I didn't know how. I do now. I can play any game you want, bind you, massage every inch of your body, or put you across my knee and spank you. We could try it all,' he suggested slyly, and the towel gave up the ghost under the strain, falling open over his thick pale cock.

She remembered it of old. Its size was average, but its present hardness impressed her. It curved back up across

50

his belly, the head bumping his navel. It was alive, a sensate thing that would impale her like a spear, heedless of her pleasure, blindly seeking its own. This is what had happened years ago, but Neil had said he'd changed. He might have done, but what about his rampant cock?

'Spanking? I don't know about that,' she demurred, while his hand moved from her knee and gently stroked her cheek.

'You've never done it? But you've wondered what it would be like?'

'Maybe,' she admitted, acknowledging to herself one of her secret fantasies. A strong male who'd stride into her life and take her over. He wouldn't be above administering a spanking if she displeased him. She shivered and wanted Neil to move his fingers down between her legs where he would find her hot clit.

'I remember the movies you liked, Rosemary,' he said softly. 'Costume dramas with lots of swordplay. A swashbuckling hero. You're a romantic, yet you couldn't wait to be dominated.'

'Why didn't you try it, then?' she challenged. 'Why did you make love so boringly?'

He shrugged, then said, 'I didn't know a damn thing. It wasn't till after I'd lost touch with you that I learned how to excite a woman. Then I went to fetish clubs and got a taste for it.'

Rosemary's brain could hardly take in what her ears were hearing, but he had grabbed her attention. 'You, Neil?'

'You'd better believe it, and in the many ways I can pleasure you. I can light a candle and drip wax over your breasts or push ice-cubes up your pussy. I can lick creamy dessert out of your arse. I can cram your cunt full of squashy fruit then slurp the juice, and yours. Oh, yes, Rosemary, I've grown up. D'you want me to demonstrate?'

Cornered, she didn't know what to say. She glanced round her nervously. The area was secluded now, the fence and tall palms blocking the view from other apartments. Her mind shot up defences; she didn't really care for Neil much. He'd been a bitter disappointment in the past. Why get involved with him? Yet her body had answers to all the sensible reasons why she should pick up her belongings and head for her car.

It was her body that was making her rash, urging her to throw away caution and let passion take over. He turned in his chair so that he was facing her, his wide-spread knees encompassing hers. He stared into her eyes, and his hands came up to cup her breasts, thumbs revolving over the hard nipples. She lowered her lids, head tipped back as spasms of pleasure shot through her breasts, a hotline to her clit.

There was no longer any doubt about the outcome of this. Rosemary could no more stop herself than cease breathing. Her senses remembered his personal smell, the touch of his big hands, the way his eyes burned and his full mouth pouted hungrily as if he would feed on her. She wanted to turn the clock back, and once more experience the emotions that had thrilled her then. Young love. First love. All the newness and excitement of a sexual encounter. This was impossible, yet she strove to catch the faintest lingering echo.

Neil stood, dragging her up with him.

He was much taller than her, and bulky. Naked, too, the towel was long gone. His erection pushed against her, a serpent seeking a nest. His head blocked out the sky as he kissed her, fleshy tongue devouring hers, exploring, tasting, mastering her mouth till she was limp and breathless. So far so good. But what of his promises?

He sighed between her lips, then slid his hands up her back, lifting the T-shirt where it clung stickily to her spine. With blind, adept fingers, he unhooked the fastening of her white bra. The air played on her sweaty naked ribs as both bra and shirt rolled up until her breasts were exposed. Neil looked down.

'Gorgeous tits,' he murmured. 'They're bigger than they were. Implants?'

'No, all my own,' she answered, gasping as he pinched her nipples, making them stand out.

'Then you must have had a baby.'

'No babies,' she said and pushed both bra and top higher so they lay like a band across her chest.

'I wanted you to have mine.'

This shook her. 'Did you? I never knew you cared so much.'

'There's a lot about me you don't know. They've known pleasure, haven't they, these tits of yours?' he went on, eyes heavy-lidded as he admired them, caressing and flicking, tweaking and kneading till the pebble-hard tips darkened to rose-red. He lowered his head and licked each in turn.

Then, giving her no time to protest or even think, he sat on the step of the decking and she was over a pair of thighs that felt rock-solid beneath her. With a hand thrust under her, he unzipped her shorts and hauled them and her panties down, and her naked backside came into view: two splendid mounds of sun-tanned flesh. Somehow she felt more vulnerable than if completely naked, the T-shirt round her chest and shoulder-blades, the shorts down to her knees. His cock was jumping against her side as he pressed her into his lap. It wet her, a trickle of pre-come inching across her waist.

This is weird! she thought. What am I doing here – on my own set, as it were, on Jonathan's decking, on a roof? Dear God, shall I ever be able to view the programme without remembering this?

She wriggled, appalled by the undignified picture she presented to the evening sky. She'd never been spanked, not even for fun. Spanking had been taboo in her parents' house. They'd been happy to spare the rod and spoil the child. Yet the very strangeness and forbidden aspect of it added to the dark glow of excitement. Her whole body seemed to be on fire. As she lay over Neil's lap, unknown sensations were rising, a confusion of desire and shameful humiliation getting mixed up with a tingling anticipation.

She could hear his uneven breathing and guessed him to be as excited as she. His hands smoothed her bottom, parting the cheeks and caressing the crease, then moving between the tight bud of her anus, and then between the fluffy lips of her pussy. He dabbled a finger in her and spread her juice over her clit. She moved forwards to meet that slippery touch and he gently massaged her for a moment. She was on the point of coming. A few more strokes would bring her the ultimate bliss.

His other hand was so soothing over her buttocks, but this changed abruptly. She heard the rush of air and the sudden slap of his palm against her skin and she winced as the blow burned and heat spread over the whole area. His slaps beat on her like a steady rain. She squirmed, moaned, protested, but he paused only to massage her reddened cheeks and dive a finger into her, keeping pressure on her clit with his thumb.

The pain of her punished arse became intense. She could smell his sweat and arousal, could feel the iron stiffness of his cock. She was agonised and wildly excited. She had no point of reference, nothing to relate to in the churning sea of this new experience. She hurt like never before, yet it was familiar; wild, primitive, the haunting memory of a dream, or perhaps a previous incarnation.

How impossibly strange that it should be Neil, her long ago lover who should introduce her to this world. Did she like it? She didn't know, yet every time he stopped, she screamed inside, 'More! Give me more!'

'You're enjoying this, aren't you?' he said huskily, while she sobbed and the tears ran down her face, dripping on to the decking. *Slap!* 'I knew you'd be into the scene when I first saw you on the box. Oh, you were bossy, all right. Very much Miss Controller, but I could see beneath that crap. What you needed was a thorough spanking, because you're a dirty little slut who begs to be kept in her place.' *Slap! Slap!*

'No. I don't. Honestly! Oh, please stop!' she yelled.

'Not yet. You've not had enough. Tykes like you need to be made to suffer.'

His finger dug into her tender parts, forcing a yelp from her. Then his thumb continued its heavenly friction on her bud. She no longer knew what she wanted, only that the pleasure should go on and on till she exploded.

He spanked her harder and her bottom seemed bathed in fire. Then he suddenly stopped, tumbled her from his knee and on to her back. Her rump hurt where it touched the wood and she swore at him. She was tangled in her shorts and panties, but he tugged them off. Now she was naked, apart from the clothing across her chest and her substantial sport sandals.

God, I must be a lewd sight! she thought, and fresh juice trickled from her.

He kneeled over her, pulling her arms above her head and pinioning her wrists with his hands. The look in his eyes did nothing to reassure her. It seemed that he hated as much as desired her. Was he settling an old score? Whatever his motive, it didn't matter. Rosemary was too far along the road to self-destruction to stop now.

He nudged her thighs apart with his knee and then lowered himself on to her. She arched her hips to meet him. His cock was so stiff that it needed no guidance to find her, the bulky stalk easing in smoothly.

She opened her eyes and stared up into his. 'Aren't you forgetting something?' she demanded. 'I hope you're not going to be so selfish as to leave me unsatisfied.'

'Don't worry. That was just a little tester. I wanted to see if it fitted as sweetly as it used to.'

He withdrew and put his mouth where his cock had been. Rosemary lay supine, feeling him suck her stem and draw it out, then his tongue tip playing over her fully exposed clit.

'Which side d'you favour? Or is it here, or just above where it pokes from its hood?' he looked up to ask.

'Oh. There! Yes, that's just right,' she moaned, her two hands resting on the insides of her splayed thighs, spreading herself for him, unfurling every fold, giving him the glistening pinkness of her labia.

'That's lovely,' he said, pausing to examine her. 'You're

like some exotic flower, and you taste delicious. I want you to enjoy this. I'm going to give you the best climax you've ever had.'

Rosemary was too riven with pleasure to be surprised at his expertise. He used his tongue superbly, focusing on her clit and, at the same time, he reached up to finger her nipples. She could feel the sensations rising from the tips of her toes, up the backs of her legs and gathering in her groin. She grabbed him each side of his head, holding him steadily to his task, urging him on with frenzied movements of her hips. She was totally abandoned, every part of her open to him, and his tongue played over her cleft, sucking at her, then letting go, driving her mad.

'Don't stop!' she begged.

He chuckled. 'You want it awfully badly? Then ask me nicely.'

'Please,' she implored, hovering on the edge of climax.

'Please, Neil,' he reminded, giving her clit the tiniest flick of his tongue.

'Please, Neil,' she repeated, agreeing to anything in her extremity.

She moaned in pleasure as he settled down to a steady, regular licking that lifted her higher and higher. With a shrill cry she peaked in a welter of delight. He held her there lightly, till each spasm passed, then he dropped her down gently, his fingers taking the place of his lips.

'Give me your cock,' she grated.

'Patience,' he cautioned.

When he was ready, she stared at his cock draped in slippery, well-lubricated latex and imagined it filling the ache inside her. She wanted to get fucked. That much was certain.

She spared a glance at the darkening sky. The sliver of crescent moon that had hung, ghostlike, over the city all day, now shone brightly. The air was heavy with the sweet perfume of tobacco plants and night-scented stocks. The lights had come on automatically, shining like glow-worms on walls and amidst ornamental pots. The breeze caressed her skin and she shivered with the thrill of making love out of doors where water trickled and her beloved earth was close, its aroma redolent of fertility. And, astoundingly, against the distant hum of traffic, a nightingale began to sing.

'My neighbour has an aviary,' he explained, and it was as if the bird had been hired to add to the sensual atmosphere.

She lay flat on her back, scooting her hips forward with her knees bent over the step of the decking. Neil kneeled below her, angling his cock and pressing the plump head of it to her. Sighing with relief, she lifted her legs and hooked her ankles over his shoulders, giving him greater access.

He slid in another inch and groaned, his eyes shut as if he wanted to concentrate every iota of sensation and direct it to his cock. The knowledge of his longing for release made her want to come again. She eased up further so that his cock plunged deep. She matched her rhythm to his as he withdrew and lunged, in and out. The wet sound of flesh on flesh complemented that of the miniature waterfall.

'Oh, God . . .' he muttered, increasing his pace, his hips driving like pistons and his cock gaining momentum.

She knew he was going to come, and that she wasn't quite ready to, but it didn't matter. She was already fulfilled and this pounding cock inside her was just what she needed to round it off. 'Come on,' she whispered urgently. 'That's it. Fuck me. Do it!'

He pumped and bucked, his breathing ragged, then, with a strangled snarl, he let go. She felt his cock thicken and twitch and his final jerks as he came. He collapsed on top of her, his face buried in her shoulder, his hand in her hair. She rested, his weight pushing her down against the planks, then he stirred, rolling to one side, withdrawing carefully.

He smiled across at her as she sat up. 'Let's do it again.'

She shook her head. 'Not tonight. I really must get back.'

'No disappointments this time?' he asked. She wanted to wipe the smug look from his face. He hadn't been *that* good.

'No,' she said, pulling down her bra, easing her breasts into it and hooking up, then rearranging her T-shirt. She reached for her thong and shorts and stepped into them.

He leaned on one elbow and regarded her. 'I meant what I said about babies,' he announced, flaxen fringe falling over his brows. 'I haven't married, Rosemary. Must have been subconscious. I was waiting for you.'

'Thanks!' she replied, a touch acidly.

'We'd make a fine pair,' he went on. 'Me with my business acumen and you with your career. I'd like being married to a celeb.'

'Fancy featuring in *OK!*, do you?'

Now she was getting annoyed. Blokes who chatted her up simply because she was a TV personality got right up her nose.

He smirked, preening a little, and she thought how ridiculous he looked with the full teat of the wrinkled condom dangling from his cock. 'Well, it wouldn't do my business any harm,' he admitted.

'Forget it. I'm not interested in the marriage stakes,' she cut him off abruptly. 'Once this job is over, I doubt we'll see each other again.'

'That's a shame,' he said, and she could tell he didn't believe her.

He stood up, taking off the condom and tossing it down on the tray by the glasses. He clasped her under the elbows and drew her close.

'I'm serious, Neil,' she warned, not even bothering to free herself.

'Why? I've a lot to offer,' he questioned, and behind that bland smile she caught a glimpse of the real man – quite ruthless when it came to getting his own way.

'Blame ambition. I'm a career girl,' she hedged, wanting to put him off without offending him.

'You were with someone, though?' he persisted, pulling her hard against him so that she could feel the firm, packed muscles of his chest and belly.

'It's ended, and I'm enjoying being free. Now, please, let me go.'

'I won't give up,' he said, and draping his loins in the towel, he accompanied her to the patio doors, across the vastness of the shining teak floor and into the hall.

'That's your choice,' she said as he let her out. 'I've enjoyed this evening. Let's not spoil it.'

She went towards the lift, aware that his eyes were boring into her back. It gave her an uncomfortable feeling. She was relieved when she stepped into the elegant glass and iron cage, out of his sight.

Melanie had just finished when the phone rang. 'Shit!' she muttered and was inclined to let the answer service pick it up when she heard Rosemary's voice.

'I'm here. What can I do for you?' she said with remarkable composure, considering that her lover's cock was lodged somewhere inside her and she'd just enjoyed a very satisfactory orgasm.

'Oh, Mel . . . where have you been? I've been trying to reach you for days. Didn't you get my messages?'

'Hmm? What? Sorry, I didn't get in till late last night and was too preoccupied to check on them.' Melanie pushed back her honey-blonde fringe and wriggled down under the duvet. George stirred and curled against her back, his cock slipping out.

'I must see you. God! What's happening to me? Terry's shafting Belinda and I've been acting the alleycat. I need a break. It's work, work, work . . .'

'And fucking, by the sound of it,' Melanie put in dryly. 'Jesus God, slow down, will you?'

She clasped the rough-palmed hand of her latest lover, holding it steady on her breast while she tried to concentrate. Rosemary sounded in a state, and the last thing her agent wanted was anything that was going to rock the boat. *In Your Own Backyard* was a winner and long may it continue.

Business considerations apart, she cared for Rosemary, adopting the mother-hen role, although they were around the same age. But Melanie was streetwise and Rosemary had led a backwater existence, until comparatively recently. Playing about with nature, cocooned in the gentle and lovely world of creative gardening was a far cry from the cut and thrust of the entertainment industry where Melanie fought for the rights of her clients.

'Can I see you?' Rosemary persisted, and Melanie's sharp ear picked up on the hint of tears. So Terry had been dipping his wick elsewhere, had he?

'Don't know when. I'm chock-a-block. Can you get into the office at lunchtime and we'll share a sandwich? That's the best I can do.'

'Thanks. I'll be rather grimy but no matter. Finishing a roof-garden, and that's part of the problem, or rather its owner is.'

'You're talking in riddles. See you at one. Bye now.'

Melanie replaced the receiver and wriggled round to face her companion, bleached-haired, dark-eyed, stunningly pierced and tattooed George, the car-mechanic. In the sobering light of satiety, she wondered if she was bonkers or what, encouraging such a scruff. It's my upbringing, she decided, his robust prick falling neatly into her hand, still latex covered. Melanie never took risks in that department. Rich, well-brought-up girls kick against the traces and take up with the most unsuitable blokes. How nice to be able to blame it on your background or parents or what-have-you, never taking any responsibility for your own actions.

She gave George's cock a squeeze. It responded, leaping to attention with the alacrity only found in the young male. Pity, she mused. Women get more sexy as they grow older, but men definitely go off it. It would never enter George's head to take Viagra, but several of my colleagues are talking about, if not already swallowing, it.

Life was a paradox, but a most enjoyable one and she loved every minute of hers.

George pushed a hand between her legs and paddled a finger in her wetness. She was tempted to yield, but a glance at her wristwatch made her throw back the duvet and swing her long legs over the edge of the mattress.

'Not this morning, Georgie boy. I've got to work, and so have you. Come on, I'll race you to the shower. And I mean for a wash, not soaping one another all over like bad actors in a porn movie.'

'Aw, that's tight. Can I see you tonight?' he mumbled, running a hand over his shorn head.

'No, darling. I've commitments. Anyway we've been together all weekend and more.'

'I know,' he grinned, lean, muscular and naked. 'It was wicked. I could go on shagging you for ever.'

A compliment in one way, for she was years older than him, but Melanie looked at him, her head to one side. No, he didn't exactly fit into her beautiful bedroom, all antique furniture and drapes, every item painstakingly collected, nor into the house itself, an inheritance from an aged relative. Oh dear, she thought, recognising the feeling. Time to say goodbye to George, I fear. Playing with the gypsies in the wood is over for a while, and I must get myself sensibly on track.

Even as he did his best to interest her while she showered and he leaned against the tiled walls and watched her, her mind was streaking ahead to the meeting with Rosemary. Instinct told her that she'd missed a trick through being away. She didn't like the sound of what Rosemary had said one little bit. It was essential the status quo be maintained. Anything that happened in Rosemary's private life was bound to have a knock-on effect on the programme, the big book offer that was hanging in the balance, the web site, the personal appearances on American TV and radio under negotiation. In fact, the whole shebang.

Even when George soaped his hands and rubbed them over her streaming wet breasts, following the trail of suds across her navel and glossy pubes into her crack, she still wriggled away, her agile brain focused on her friend's predicament.

Unabashed, George took her rejection with a philosophical shrug, and used his soapy fist as a sheath for his hard cock. Leaning against the shower stall, he soon forgot her, grunting his way to orgasm. Melanie went back to the bedroom and began today's power-dressing.

Tall, willowy, always up to the minute without being absurd, she had fought hard to climb the ladder of recognition in her field. Studying management, the media and psychology had equipped her for her chosen profession. Bumping into an old friend who was already established as a theatrical agent had been fortuitous, for he had asked her to join him. Despite opposition and snide remarks to the effect that she had slept her way into becoming his partner, all untrue as he was a closet gay, she had earned their respect, and now had a sizeable and prestigious clientele.

Oh, Rosemary, what have you been up to? she thought. You're my star.

Ignoring George, who now appeared in combats, a T-shirt and trainers, she applied her make-up and got into a pair of baggy pants and matching silk blouse. She picked up her shoulder bag, keys and cigarettes.

'Come on, George,' she said brightly. 'I'll drop you off at the garage on my way to work.'

Chapter Four

Rosemary climbed the stairs to the second floor of a chrome and concrete, glass and high-tech office complex near Chelsea Wharf.

She felt decidedly out of place; untidy curls escaping from Gary's pinning several hours before; make-up mussed by a morning working in the heat. No time to change. Michael had ordered her back at 2.30 p.m. Her shorts were creased, her crop-top grubby. The viewers would love it, convinced she was a toiling, hands-on sort of a gal. True enough, though she did have a team of helpers off-camera.

Her bare legs were impressively tanned, as were her arms, and any part of her that had been exposed. This pleased her, giving her that I've-just-returned-from-a-trip-up-the-Amazon kind of look, the sort her mother must have acquired by now. Not that I'll ever know, her thoughts ran on. She never even drops me a postcard; not so much as a Peruvian nose or a shrunken head.

She straightened her spine and out-stared a couple of immaculately dressed blondes who swept past, wearing horn-rims, French pleats and an air of importance, files tucked under their arms. They're probably only secretaries, she thought with uncharacteristic cattiness. It wasn't fair, but since being stabbed in the back by the perfidious Belinda she viewed this breed with a jaundiced eye.

She paused outside a door which bore the legend: 'Wesley Brown and Melanie Hart, Theatrical Agency'. She hoped the women would see her. They did, and started whispering, their supercilious attitude changing. Did they recognise her? She rather thought they did. Look on, she addressed them mentally. I hold a show together. *In Your Own Backyard* is a vehicle for my talent. I've even got an Equity Card to prove it.

Good God, I'm turning into a diva, she realised with a start. I never used to behave in this high-handed manner. It's only happened since I found out about Terry's disloyalty. Now I'm getting too full of myself, flattered by these new lovers, though the sensible part of me knows they're only in it for themselves. If I don't watch it, I'll become a thoroughly nasty person, dictatorial, arrogant – and afraid. Probably end up in a rehab centre, fearsomely expensive and tucked away in the country but, nonetheless, a hospital for junkies and alcoholics.

Having mapped out her imaginary future and depressed herself even more, she found Melanie in her sanctum. The sight of her down-to-earth friend steadied Rosemary, dragging her back from the abyss.

'What's been happening with you, Rose? That whacky telephone call. It threw me,' her friend carolled from the other side of a wide desk.

The room was air-conditioned, a place of light – a working place where Rosemary could get into working mode. And Melanie's steady voice was so reassuring – forthright, amused, with a cynical edge. She was a rock, a tower of strength, a tough lady who protected her clients' interests fiercely. No one got away with a dodgy deal when she was in charge. She went through the small print with a tooth-comb.

Rosemary slumped down on a red velvet couch and leaned her head against the cushions. 'You'd never believe it. First off, Terry and I have split.'

'Congratulations,' Melanie remarked, pouring coffee

and bringing it over to her. 'You should have given that creep the push months ago.'

'Easy for you to say. I couldn't. It needed something like finding him fucking Belinda,' Rosemary replied, and tears choked her throat.

'No regrets,' Melanie said, offering a beringed hand. 'You mustn't even think of patching it up.'

'I'm not,' Rosemary brought out defiantly. 'I've gone through hacked off and come out the other side. No man, and certainly not him, is ever going to crap on me again.'

Melanie's golden-brown eyes regarded her seriously. 'I'm glad to hear it,' she said, crossing one silk trousered leg over another and waggling her bare toes in the stylish mules. Her green nail lacquer sparkled. 'But I've a feeling that you haven't told me the whole story yet.'

Rosemary sat up abruptly, feet planted on the varnished floorboards, hands on her knees. 'I think I've gone mad!' she exclaimed. 'I'm shagging everything that breathes. Well, every male thing.'

Melanie grinned and handed her a cheese sandwich, then settled back to eat her own. 'Tell me more,' she encouraged.

'Well, there's Scott, a new assistant at the nursery.'

'Young?'

'Oh, yes.'

'And gorgeous?'

'I think so,' Rosemary said and laughed. Her spirits were reviving at Melanie's pertinent questions and her fingers tingled at the remembrance of Scott's balls in her hands and his cock in her mouth.

'Then you should be rejoicing.'

'He's on the rough side.'

'So what? You should see George.'

'Let me guess. The garage mechanic?'

'Right on, and he's as common as muck. It doesn't much matter when they're shagging you, does it? I've never before had a guy with a cock ring through his foreskin. It adds an extra dimension to penetration. As for the bolt in his tongue! My clit's jumping at the thought of it. What a sensation!'

Rosemary's imagination supplied potently stimulating pictures. 'But it's not only Scott,' she confessed, feeling her cheeks growing hot and envying Melanie's insouciance. She knew she had a string of lovers, not all male, for she appreciated female sexuality, too.

She'd never been propositioned by Melanie and she was glad about that. Sex complicated relationships and one often lost close friends once that boundary had been crossed. It was impossible to go back to the time before passion intruded. Not that she didn't find her attractive. Melanie was hard to ignore, so tall and graceful, with her superb dress sense and her hair cut short and bouncy and swept back behind her ears.

'Come on, Rose. Don't keep me dangling. Who else have you been knocking off?' she asked, her eyes shining teasingly. Yet there was sympathy as well, the understanding of someone who had been there, done that and got the T-shirt to prove it.

'Michael,' Rosemary confessed, a vision of him in the nude springing to mind.

'Not Michael Pendelton, the ogre himself? My dear, how could you? Was it like bedding an iceberg?'

'No. He was rather sweet, as a matter of fact.' Rosemary experienced a pang of guilt, knowing that there was no love lost between her agent and director. Melanie was always trying to get a better contract and a larger fee for her, while he protested that it wasn't down to him and she must tackle the powers that be.

'Wonders will never cease,' Melanie commented. 'Is he big? Is he circumcised? Did he make you come?'

'Yes, yes and yes, but you're not to repeat any of this.'

'Would I?' Melanie protested. Her eyes were wide between mascara-spiked lashes and she'd pressed her hand to her heart.

Melanie always indulged in the most exquisite shirts; subtle, colourful, mix and matching with innumerable skirts and trousers. Made of finest silk, they were some-

66

times diaphanous, her small breasts crowned by prominent dark nipples. Today Rosemary could glimpse no trace of a bra. Yet Melanie never looked tarty; these tops were as much her trademark as the perfume she wore, her toffee-coloured hair and her slim, graceful feet.

'Who else have you been shagging?' Melanie continued, and her hand dropped down to where her palazzo pants draped her belly and disappeared into her fork. She cupped her mons, then eased the fabric away from her pussy lips as if all this talk about men was getting her juices flowing.

'We're doing a roof conversion and the owner is a bloke we knew at college. You might remember him. Neil Kemble,' Rosemary answered, aware of the beautiful woman seated beside her, but aware in a way she had never felt before. It wasn't envy or plain admiration. There was a smouldering, desirous quality that made her hot inside.

'I do. You were thick as thieves once. He came across as a right dork, too cocky by half. Has he improved?' Melanie asked, and her red-glossed lips lifted knowingly, as if she guessed at the monumental changes boiling within Rosemary and gave them her seal of approval.

'I suppose so,' Rosemary said uncertainly. 'He's rich now, and influential, and into kinky sex.'

Melanie wriggled against the crimson plush. 'Sounds fun,' she giggled. 'How kinky?'

'He took down my knickers and spanked me.' As she put it into words, Rosemary felt again the heat and pain of his blows, the fury of her orgasm and the way her buttocks had stung for hours afterwards.

'Is that all? Not too kinky. You found it shameful but exciting. You liked being dominated. Wanted him to go on doing it. Was this your first time?'

Rosemary cast her a glance and nodded. Had her friend hidden depths which she hadn't revealed? She didn't seem in the least outraged by Rosemary's submission, and this was odd coming from someone who was so obviously an independent female.

'And all this has happened over the last week.' Rosemary's breathing was ragged. She could feel moist heat at her crotch as she dwelled on each highly charged episode.

'Good on you. Stop worrying. Take it as one in the eye for Terry – let him know that you can put it around, too. As long as it's not interfering with your work. It isn't, I hope?' Melanie stabbed her a shrewd glance.

'Not really. But I do feel tired. Is there any chance I might be able to get away for a couple of weeks? Southern Spain, perhaps. I've always felt at home in Andalusia.'

'Home is where the heart is,' Melanie said. 'And it's plain as day where your heart lies. It's with those bull-fighters and flamenco dancers in their cock-hugging pants.' Then she raised her finely arched brows and pulled a dubious face. 'Can't see Michael agreeing to a vacation. He has another proposition lined up which you'll hear about in due course. Sooner rather than later, I think.'

'What is it this time?' Rosemary's heart sank at the prospect of going straight from the roof job to another gruelling stint in some as yet unknown venue: a dull plot needing a face-lift; a cottage with a water meadow that would benefit from taming; a garden-share scheme organised by inner city flat-dwellers in a rare outburst of community spirit, and funded by the council.

Melanie shrugged her thin shoulders and helped herself to another sandwich; she was one of those irritating people with a fast metabolism who never put on an ounce. 'Who knows, dear? Michael is a law unto himself.'

'You can say that again,' Rosemary sighed. 'You know he called in Jonathan Flynn on this last job?'

'He's Wesley's pet, but yes, I did know. How do you get on with him? Well, I hope. We don't want him going into one.'

'I've had to bite my tongue. He's inclined to take over, but no match for Michael. I'm going to his soirée tonight. An end-of-shoot celebration.'

Rosemary was looking forward to seeing him in his own environment. He hadn't stopped flirting with her for an instant. This had aroused her body, dampened her panties and titillated her curiosity until she was bursting to find out if there was any truth in the rumours concerning his love life.

'You fancy him?' Melanie asked, lighting up a cigarette.

'Who wouldn't? He's like an eighteenth-century dandy come to life. Beau Brummel or someone.'

'The Marquis de Sade is probably nearer the mark,' Melanie said, blowing smoke rings. 'You'd like to fuck him?'

'Yes, but I wouldn't give him the satisfaction of knowing it.'

'Ah. So he's not on your list, as yet?'

'I've enough with the other three,' Rosemary declared. Yet she wondered – had she? Why not go for gold? See just how many she could clock up.

'You might be surprised at what he can do,' Melanie replied, and her eyes went dreamy. 'He really is a bundle of fun.'

'You've slept with him?' For some unearthly reason, Rosemary found this shocking. It was as if a Sunday-school teacher had admitted to being on the game.

She knew Melanie was of liberal habits. But Jonathan? Somehow it was hard to imagine them together, locked in sweaty, bed-rolling sex. Hard to imagine him spurting, losing control of himself, gasping as he fucked, yelling as he came – he who always appeared to be master of any situation.

'Not exactly slept, but did plenty of other things.' Melanie took a drag at her cigarette, then inhaled smoke through her nostrils. 'Never judge a book by its cover. He may look like a fop, but he's built like steel, and his stamina is amazing. Inventive? Oh, yes. Wesley's over the moon about him and we'll both be coming to the bash.'

'Scott will be there. Most of the crew are invited,'

Rosemary put in, and as she saw Melanie grind her stub into the brass ashtray and stretch her body sinuously, she regretted having to endure an afternoon of heat and Michael's irascibility. She'd much rather stay there, sharing confidences and basking in the sensuality that hung round her friend like a wicked aura.

'It's a quarter to two,' Melanie said, reverting to business mode. 'Off you go to work. Lucky old you. I've a load of boring people to see, as well as that chap from the publishers who're featuring you in their magazine.'

'I haven't seen the photo proofs yet,' Rosemary complained, swinging her long-handled bag over her shoulder. 'Are they OK?'

'Ducky, they're knock-'em-dead gorgeous. Shots of you in various stages of undress . . .'

'And lots of planting and pruning know-how?' Rosemary's professional pride surfaced. She had no desire to turn into a garden shed pin-up.

'Of course, and a few pictures of you in the obligatory wellies,' Melanie said with a smile as, an arm looped over Rosemary's shoulders, she saw her to reception. 'I'll meet you at Jonathan's. Wes'll be with me. He may even wear a frock.'

'I'm too tired to go out,' Rosemary said to her reflection when she eventually reached home.

'You've promised Scott,' her image answered. 'Can you face his dejected puppy look if you let him down? He wants to socialise with the top guns.'

'Bugger!' Rosemary exploded.

She knew it was true, and she'd told Melanie she'd be there, to say nothing of that itch which was urging her to challenge Jonathan on his home ground.

'You've got to do it. "On with the motley" and all that.' The sweaty-faced woman in the mirror stared back at her and gave no quarter.

Rosemary swept the hair off the back of her neck, lifting it for coolness. The mirror-woman did the same. 'Lord, but you're a mess,' Rosemary murmured.

'Then do something about it,' sneered her alter-ego.

'To hell with you,' Rosemary snarled and tore off her clothes, tossing the soiled garments into the wash-basket. Naked, she marched into the *en suite* bathroom.

She had come to terms with loneliness now, relieving her feelings by chucking Terry's clothes into the hallway and shouting that if he didn't take them away, then they'd end up in the dustbin. Now she had the bed to herself and admitted that it had been a long time since she wanted him in it, and would have rather scrubbed floors than made love with him. What a state to be in! In a way, Belinda had done her a favour.

She was about to step into the shower when the cordless phone buzzed. Frowning, she picked it up. 'Hello. Who is it?' she said automatically.

There was silence, yet she sensed someone was there. There were jokes made about 'heavy breathers', but this was real. She went cold, goose-bumps raising the fine down on her arms. Then, into that taut silence while she pressed the instrument to her ear and waited, came a click. Whoever it was had rung off.

She dropped the phone as if it had scalded her. If this was a joke, then it wasn't funny. Someone had used her private line, which was ex-directory and given to few. Who?

Nobody, insisted common-sense. A faulty connection, that's all. Have your shower and get on with it.

Of course. That must be it. Stop being so jittery, she told herself, but before operating the power-shower she ran into the bedroom and turned the key in the lock, scenes from the classic Hitchcock film, *Psycho*, dancing on the dark side of her mind.

She gave a long-drawn sigh as the water flooded down. It was blissful and she leaned back against the tiled wall and let it play all over her, then took up the jet and guided it to her breasts. Drops of water hung from her crimped nipples and then joined their fellows coursing over her belly and into the thicket covering her

71

mound. She angled the jets, and squirted perfumed gel into her palm and spread it over her body.

Starting at her throat, she slid her hands over her chest and cupped her breasts, the gel slipping and sliding under and around the fullness. The lather creamed her ribs and cruised like a slow-moving avalanche across the tiny disc of her navel. She reached down and walked her fingers into the wet swathe of hair forming a wedge on her pubis. Pulling gently at it, she parted her slit, exposing the shiny pink labia. A dull ache spread across her lower belly, an ache of expectation and desire.

She caressed the sensitive area just above her bud. It swelled in response. She frigged it lightly, soapy there, wonderfully slippery. Indulging herself in pleasure, she was able to forget the troublesome phone call. In that trance-like state leading to orgasmic euphoria, she closed her eyes and thought of nothing but the magical contact between her finger and her clit. It excited her to feel how swollen it was.

It was a divine invention, vastly superior to the pleasure organ of the male, and her enjoyment was extreme, urging her to rub herself faster. The ecstasy came in a rush, reaching every part of her as the spasms spread.

'Oh, oh,' she sighed, her legs shaking, her finger easing off.

Coming to herself, she finished showering and, wrapped in a towel, pattered back to the bedroom. Time was running on, and she had promised to pick Scott up. She hurried over her preparations, liberal with the body-lotion, deciding against garter belt and stockings. It was just too hot. A cream lace panty and bra set from her collection would do, and a swirling-skirted white strappy dress. It was sleeveless and had a heart-shaped bodice fastened with tiny ball buttons. High-heeled sandals completed the outfit, along with a leather clutch bag and floaty Eastern shawl. Leaving make-up to the minimal, except for the eyes which she painted liberally, she combed her hair with her fingers, as Gary had taught her, and nodded at her twin in the mirror.

'Will that do?' she asked aloud.

The image nodded, and said, 'It's all right. Pity about the nails. You've got hands like a navvy.'

'Thanks a bunch!' Rosemary retorted, rising from the dressing-table stool and snatching up her car keys. 'I do happen to work for a living, you know. Gardening plays havoc with a manicure.'

'Tut! We are scratchy tonight, aren't we?' mocked her reflection.

'Piss off!'

Rosemary reached the door and lifted a hand to the light switch. She jumped violently as the phone started to ring. She stood there petrified, then ran out of the room, followed by the phone's shrill insistence.

'Cor, this is better than going down the pub or watching TV,' Scott opined as Rosemary wheeled into the gravelled drive.

She nodded, impressed despite herself by Jonathan's present address – a large Edwardian house on Highgate Hill. Detached and set back from the road, it was surrounded by trees and mature gardens, and the curving drive ended in an adequate parking area already filling up with private cars, and vans bearing the *Backyard* motif.

She found a vacant space and switched off the engine, then sat there, staring into space. 'Did you phone me earlier?' she said suddenly.

'Me? No. Were you expecting me to?'

'No,' she answered, and believed him.

Why should he do such a thing? His hand came to rest on her knee, fingers warming her through the thin cotton. Perhaps it had been a wrong number after all. But deep inside her, she knew that her first, fearful instinct had been right.

There were steps leading up to the open front door and Rosemary mounted them, walked into the spacious hall and followed the sounds that led her to the rear; she could hear chatter, laughter and a falsetto male voice singing madrigals. He was accompanied by a lute.

On a wide, paved terrace, Jonathan was holding court. Rosemary thought he looked like a Turkish potentate surrounded by slaves and sycophants. He was even dressed for the part – full striped trousers – a lavishly embroidered djellaba open over his lightly furred chest, and a turban at a rakish tilt on his handsome head.

She found herself melting into lubricious lust. All the resentments she had harboured against the temperamental designer were instantly erased by the longing to join him on the cushion-strewn divan, dip her hands into his pants and become acquainted with his private parts.

He looked directly at her and, though continuing a conversation with Michael, it was as if no one else was there. The lines of his gracefully positioned body were lean, and his skin solidly tanned. He must have spent much time abroad, or lolling out there in that sun-trap of a garden. Mesmerised by the outline of his cock resting against his thigh under the loose pantaloons, she could see that it was thick, bordering on erect, and knew this tribute was for her.

Melanie waved from her perch on the balustrade. The skirt of her simple, crinkled crêpe dress opened when she moved, showing an expanse of brown leg and a flash of silk-covered triangle.

'Hello, Rosie,' she said, and her eyes shot to Scott, appraising him and measuring him. Rosemary took him over to be introduced.

It wasn't only Melanie who wanted to get to know him better. Wesley, Melanie's chubby partner, stood up and kissed Rosemary's cheek, but his attention was obviously on her companion.

'Nice to see you again, honey,' he drawled in his Bostonian tones. He smiled at her vaguely, pushed his spectacles up to his brow and regarded Scott with mild blue eyes, then said, 'And what d'you do? Are you in the entertainment business?'

'He's a gardener, like Rose,' Melanie put in. 'Isn't that right, Scott?'

'Yes, Miss – eh – Hart,' Scott mumbled, eyes darting to Rosemary, pleading that she help him out. She didn't. You wanted this, she thought cruelly. You wanted the chance to mingle with these people.

'Call me Melanie,' her agent said, and her hand came to rest on his bare forearm.

'And I'm Wesley. Melanie and I work together,' the American butted in, his face and balding head carrying an all-year-round coppery tan. He wore Bermuda shorts and a golfing shirt, neither of which did him any favours but his confident air out-weighed this.

Rosemary knew him to be as hot off the mark as Melanie. Set him in his office clad in a business suit and with his business head on, and producers and actors would tremble in his presence. He had that hard-edged way of trading, and frequently popped over to the founder branch in New York. There was another in Los Angeles. Many were the famous names on his books.

Yet here he was, giving the come-on to Scott – that handsome, healthy, well-developed young stud. Rosemary took the opportunity to murmur to Melanie, 'I had a heavy breather on the phone this evening.'

'How unpleasant! I thought your number was protected.'

'It is. I don't know how he got hold of it.'

'Or her,' Melanie reminded crisply.

'I think it was a him. Maybe I imagined it,' Rosemary back-peddled, feeling foolish.

'If it happens again, then shout, "Fuck you, wanker!" Or blow a police whistle into the receiver. Deafen the sod!' Melanie advised.

'I will, but I expect it was a one-off,' Rosemary said without conviction.

She could see that Melanie wanted to get back to Scott, so she left him to her tender mercies and sauntered over to speak with Michael.

He was talking to the camera crew. They were a laconic

lot, dropping in on their way home, still wearing the clothes they had sweated in all day. No one showed that they were impressed by Jonathan's mansion. They sat about, munching canapés and downing bottled beer, while the ones elected to remain sober and drive settled for Coke or coffee.

'All right, Rosemary?' Michael asked, grinning at her, leaving his tyrannical persona on the set. 'It's in the can, dear. I'll work on it next week, so you can do what you like.'

'I've a couple of church fêtes to open, where I'm to judge the flower show,' she replied, being careful not to appear too intimate with him in front of everyone. Not that it mattered much, apart from leaks to the newspapers, always hot to jump on anything sleazy.

This was one of the prices of fame. She could no longer go where she liked or with whom she liked. There might be a member of the paparazzi lurking under a stone somewhere, wanting to make a quick buck out of someone else's personal life.

'Such appearances are a bore, but necessary any way you slice it. It endears you to your public.' Then he moved closer, his bare arm pressing against hers, his voice lowered. 'When are you coming down to the boat again?'

'I'll let you know,' she whispered, pulse throbbing as his large hand stroked the inside of her wrist.

'Don't leave it too long before you pay me another visit,' he advised, and she was aware of the sheer power of his personality. He was like a juggernaut, crushing all that stood in his way. He had her number, but surely he'd have no need to terrify her with sinister calls?

'I won't,' she promised.

'Rosemary, come here,' Jonathan called. 'My dear, how gorgeous you're looking.'

She left Michael and weaved between groups of people helping themselves to snacks and talking shop endlessly. Nothing else existed for them save the day-by-day dramas and traumas of behind-the-scenes television.

'I could say the same about you,' she said, and he patted a space beside him, encouraging her to sit. She hesitated fractionally. The outcome of any close contact with him bordered on the inevitable.

'We've not had the chance to get together,' he went on, his hazel eyes keen behind his lazy pose.

'Working as a team is pretty together,' she said, fully aware of his inference and the way his body leaned closer to hers on the opulent, silk-covered couch.

'Not what I have in mind, sweetie. I want to show you my house. Will you let me give you a guided tour?' He stood up, his djellaba floating around him, taller than ever in his high, swathed turban.

'Before you go, I'll say goodbye,' Michael put in.

'Are you off?'

'Yes. Things to catch up on. Phone me, Rosemary,' Michael went on as he bent his head to kiss her lightly.

'I will.'

'And don't do anything I wouldn't.'

'Right.'

'He's jealous,' Jonathan remarked as he slipped a hand under the crook of her elbow and took her to where a Jacuzzi bubbled in the conservatory. It was hot there, lush and green and the madrigals continued, relayed through a further set of speakers. That celestial, passionless voice sent chills down her spine.

'I don't usually go for baroque music,' she said. 'But this is wonderful.'

'My taste is eclectic, but the sound of a counter-tenor is something else. Did you know that in Italy, in the old days, a boy with a lovely voice would be castrated before puberty to preserve it?' he asked, his eyes caressing her.

'I did know, but had kind of pushed it to the back of my mind. I prefer symphonies and opera, something full-bodied . . .'

'With balls, in fact,' he said, smiling slowly. 'Well, here we go. I had no idea you loved music. Maybe we can go to Covent Garden together. The critics are raving about the quality of the productions since it re-opened.'

Thoroughly relaxed now, Rosemary was delighted to have found someone on her own wavelength. Everything about the decor pleased her, too.

'I'd like that,' she enthused. 'And all this is just perfect.'

She spread her arms wide. The mosaic floor, the large black bath set in Islamic tiles and rimmed with gold, all smacked of its owner's sybaritic approach to life.

'I'm getting there,' he said with mock modesty, and the light streaming from the coloured glass in the cupola formed a halo round his head. 'I've worked my rocks off. I wasn't born to luxury, but Jesus Christ, I enjoy it and was determined to get it.'

Her respect for him took an upward climb. Under his flamboyant façade, there was a clever man who had exploited his artistic flare and spectacular good looks, a talented man, who had slogged it through art school and become as professional as herself when it came to his work.

'We're more alike than I thought,' she said, idling a finger through the tepid water. Then she took the bull by the horns, asking, 'By the way, you didn't ring me this evening, did you?'

His peaked eyebrows shot up. 'No. I don't know your number. Why?'

She shrugged. 'Oh, it's nothing. Just someone trying to get through.'

'It wasn't me,' he averred and his fingers joined hers in the water. 'Want to try it?' he suggested, and she thought: to hell with it.

'Looks tempting,' she said. 'But I don't have a bathing costume.'

'Does that matter? I don't mind, if you don't.'

His smile and eyes challenged her. She was never one to refuse a dare.

She bent and gripped the hem of her dress, then pulled it over her head. The warm air touched her skin, making her nipples lift the fragile lace bra. She was tempted to retain her high-sided bikini briefs, but knew that if she did she'd either have to drive home bare-bottomed, or

78

wear wet ones. Neither alternative appealed, so she took them off.

At that moment, Melanie walked in. 'Hey, you haven't taken long to make yourself at home,' she said. 'It looks absolute heaven! I'd like to join you but Wes and I have offered to take Scott out to dinner. Is that kosher with you, Rosie?'

'Of course. I don't own him,' she answered. 'Just look after him, that's all. He's like a babe unborn. He doesn't need corrupting.'

'He may not be as innocent as you suppose,' Melanie returned, trailing a finger over Rosemary's peaked nipples. Then she turned to Jonathan and said, 'The rest of your guests are leaving, too. There's talk of finding the nearest pub, I gather. You know what they're like, never happier than with a pint in their hands. And that's the women! No, seriously, they're off.'

'I'll go and say goodbye,' he announced. 'Don't move, Rosemary. I shan't be long.'

When he came back, Jonathan leaned lazily with one elbow supported on a painted iron column. What he saw pleased him. Rosemary certainly was a beautiful woman with her lithe limbs, heart-shaped face and her hair floating on the water.

'You look like Rossetti's *Ophelia*,' he said. '"Her clothes spread white and mermaid-like",' except that you're naked.'

'How flattering,' she murmured. 'I've always wanted to be a Pre-Raphaelite lady, all long, swan-like throat, saintly expression and masses of Titian hair.'

He had been planning luring her into his lair for some days, and had very nearly lost that jealousy which had kicked against appearing in her show. But Wesley had convinced him that, just at the moment when his career was peaking, he couldn't be overexposed. His name linked with Rosemary's would be profitable all round.

Did he want her? Cementing their relationship off-screen would do no harm. But did he really desire her?

He stood and looked down at her as she lay in the deep, black marble pool.

'Shall we play a little?' he asked softly. 'Will you trust me?'

The question of passion no longer existed. Though Jonathan sometimes needed basic, uncomplicated sex with men, he also appreciated the softness, the smell and the mystery of a woman's body. He considered himself lucky, able to know the sensual enjoyment of both. Tonight, his cock quivered as he imagined stroking Rosemary's clit. Would she come quickly? Or, if he touched her there, would she suddenly decide she'd had enough and demand to leave?

She lifted her lids and looked up at him, her green eyes questioning. 'Play, Jonathan? What sort of game did you have in mind?'

He took a white silk cord and, holding it out, said, 'I think we'll begin with this.'

So delicately that she was hardly aware, he looped it round one of her wrists and fastened it to a ring embedded in the marble near her head. Another followed, then two more binding her ankles, spreading her legs and exposing her thighs and mound as the bubbles frothed and ebbed.

He saw her expression change to one of apprehension as she tugged at the cords. 'Don't be afraid,' he soothed. 'I'm not going to hurt you. Far from it. You'll experience nothing but the most exquisite delight.'

He left her for a moment and changed the CD to one of a harpsichord playing a sombre pavanne. It was like a time warp, the setting ageless. They could have been back in the seventeenth century with himself a member of King Charles II's debauched court, where razor-sharp wit, elegance and profligacy rubbed shoulders.

I should have been born then, he thought, concentrating on the music and seizing the spray. He directed the warm, pulsing jets over her body, starting at her toes, going up the curves of her legs, and along her thighs to land on her sex. There he paused, letting the nozzle dance in time to the galliard which had taken over from the stately measure. He pressed it against her clit, toying with it, hearing her gasp, and seeing how her body arched against the restraints as the pleasure mounted.

He shrugged off his robe and dropped his pants, kicking them aside. He could see the proud curve of his cock, the helm purple under the pressure of his lust. He could see the blush of arousal suffusing her chest, neck and face as the warm jets dashed against her mound. She lifted it high, imploring him to give her release.

She moaned in protest when he withdrew the chrome head. Water streamed over her breasts, the nipples as ripe and succulent as cherries. Letting his mouth take over from the jets, he leaned across and fastened his teeth on one, nipping and licking, tasting the unique flavour of her skin and the scented water. Her sighs became groans and her pelvis thrashed, expressing her impatience for anything that wasn't associated with her clit.

'What is it, Rosemary?' he said above the hissing of the jets. 'What do you want me to do?'

'Touch my clit,' she implored, no longer controlled, reduced to a wild thing, randy as a cat on heat.

'Like this?' he murmured, the blood converging in his groin, thickening his cock even more. He let the jets beat against her pussy relentlessly, driving faster, then sucking back, to form into a rushing wave that thrashed her clit.

Her yells told him that she had come in a torrent of sensation, and he was tempted to make her do it over and over again. He knew he could. Instead he dropped the jet and stood above her. He opened his legs as she sighed and jerked amidst the tumult of bubbling water. Taking his cock in his hand, he worked the foreskin back and over the helm, feeling that hot tingling in his balls, keeping up the smooth strokes that became faster as orgasm took over.

He gave a loud bark as his seed fountained, once, twice, thrice, falling like creamy rain on Rosemary's face and breasts.

* * *

81

She woke into Stygian darkness. The phone was trilling. She grabbed it up and, at the same time, switched on the bedside lamp.

'Have you been a naughty girl tonight, Rosemary?' said a husky, foreign-sounding voice.

'Who is that?' she quavered, disoriented, as she gripped the receiver frantically. 'Is it you, Scott? You, Mike? Or Neil? Jonathan, this isn't funny. Get off my line.'

'It isn't any of them. I'm a friend concerned about your welfare,' the voice answered.

I was right. It *is* a man, she thought.

'Why are you ringing me at this ungodly hour?' she demanded, unable to keep her voice steady.

'I wanted to talk to you. I know what you've been doing and where you've been doing it,' he continued softly. 'Tell me what it felt like when you came, Rosemary. Describe it to me. Did your clit throb? Did your cunt convulse? And your nipples, those lovely, lively tits, did they go hard?'

'I don't have to listen to this!' she shouted, outraged yet furious with herself because those obscene words made her loins clench. 'Go away, and don't phone me again!'

She pressed the OFF button, and lay there trembling. His words still reverberated in her ear and, just before she'd cut the connection, she had heard him laugh, a mocking, knowing laugh that seemed to understand and approve of her dirtiest fantasies.

Chapter Five

Rosemary was convinced she was being stalked. Paranoia, she lectured herself sternly. It didn't work.

There was nothing she could put a finger on; just the uncanny feeling that she was coming under close scrutiny. The phone call had terrified her, sending her adrenalin into panic mode. This was no flight of fancy, no scenario dreamed up late at night. The stark reality of it had come as an icy shock. This had given way to heat, making her sweat in her bed, sending shivers down her spine and thickening her clit.

That voice. A foreign intonation, though probably a fake. He had emphatically denied being one of her lovers, but then he would, wouldn't he? He'd be hardly likely to admit it?

Though busy – a radio interview and an appearance on a morning chat show ahead of her – she had wrestled with the problem throughout the week. Who would be warped enough to do this? Scott and Michael were unlikely candidates. Neil? Maybe. He had shown aspects of his character which made her remember why she had left him in the first place. Jonathan? A strong possibility.

Her session with him in the Jacuzzi had proved that his sexual predilections were, to say the least, unusual. There had been no penetration. He'd merely brought her to climax, then ejaculated over her. After this, he'd calmly offered her a towel and shown her the rest of his extraordinary house.

The flamboyant, idiosyncratic decor stunned the eye and nourished the libido. There was a predominance of crimson, purple and gold, silks and velvets, swags and *trompe l'oeil*.

Then, in complete contrast, he'd served her sushi and fragrant herb tea in a Japanese room with sliding, paper walls. Plain to the point of austerity, its only ornamentation was a screen delicately painted with chrysanthemums and views of Mount Fuji, a netsuke collection, a low table and flat red pads on the floor for seating. A recording of the samisen, which Jonathan explained was a three-stringed, guitar-like instrument, provided background music. The occasion was strangely formal.

She had driven home, completely baffled.

Then had come the phone call, followed by silence until one night after Scott had just left.

She was lying in bed, luxuriating in the aftermath of his loving. She'd almost asked him to stay, uncharacteristically reluctant to be alone, but had thought better of it. He was almost too devoted to her, and had fiercely denied that anything had gone on between him and Melanie.

Melanie had confirmed this earlier, saying, when Rosemary rang to tell her about the call, 'Scott's in love with you. What a babe! I had no luck with him and neither did Wes.'

'Shall I report those nuisance calls to the police?' Rosemary had asked anxiously.

'Only if they're bugging you. Are they?'

'What do you think?'

'I don't know. You might be getting a kick out of it.'

They'd run through possible suspects, then Melanie had suggested Terry. It was true that Rosemary had seen her solicitor and the partnership was in the process of being dissolved. He had agreed to let her buy him out, but every time they met the atmosphere was vile. The normally mild-mannered Terry was a very angry man. But would he have the nerve to bug her like this? It didn't seem to be his style, even if he was prompted by Mrs Belinda Hamster. Rosemary wouldn't put it past her to be vindictive.

Another option sprang to mind. Supposing it was a member of the public who'd become obsessed with her? This wasn't unusual, a cross celebrities had to bear. It was nasty, though, to realise that someone, somewhere, used you to fire his sexual extravaganzas, dreaming steamy dreams and masturbating while leching over your photograph. Her skin crawled and she felt like retiring from the limelight. Privacy seemed a pearl without price just then.

But – and it was a big but – she couldn't deny that Melanie was right. It was a terrific turn on, a secret – one that she was ashamed to own – but there nevertheless.

She wished she'd insisted that Scott remain. Apart from anything else, once was not enough for her. Linking her arms behind her head, she gazed up at the ceiling. It had a central rose and coving rich with acanthus leaves. Not anywhere near as grand as the plasterwork gracing Jonathan's house, but of a similar period. She mused on him. He was busy again, planning his next series.

She missed him, missed Michael and the crew. Grumble though she might, labelling him an insensitive slave-driver, she was addicted to her work, miserable if there was a lull. Neil had left messages on the Plants Galore answerphone, but she had ignored them, telling Fran, her secretary, that she was out to Mr Kemble. She had appreciated the lesson he had taught her, tingled at the memory, was hot to repeat it but with another master.

She replayed the scene in her head – she sprawled over Neil's knee, his hand chastising her bare rump. She was aroused again. The piscine smell of sex wafted from her, and she stretched voluptuously, then rolled her nipples between thumb and forefinger. She was tempted to go across to her dressing table, open the drawer and take out her vibrator, long, thick and of variable speed. She'd recently bought herself this lifelike black one, superbly moulded in latex with veins running along the shaft, and a helm with a retracted foreskin. Its performance had been a revelation.

In a minute, she told herself, first I'm going to enjoy a slow, leisurely finger-fuck. Her bud was swollen. She roused it even more, circling and teasing the ardent little head. She was wet from shagging Scott, and slid two fingers into her slippery channel. There was nothing quite like natural lubrication; baby oil and KY Jelly weren't quite the same. In and out, slow, easy, with her thumb keeping up that sweet pressure on her clit.

Her heart skipped a beat when the cordless phone beeped. She kept as still as a rabbit menaced by a stoat. The machine would pick it up. All she had to do was wait for Fran's tinny recorded message. She couldn't. She fumbled for it.

'Rosemary Maddox speaking,' she said, grinding the smooth ivory instrument against her ear, her sex wet, her mouth dry, her heart pounding.

'Ah, sweet Rosemary. I thought for a dreadful moment that you were asleep. I know your boyfriend left not long ago.' It was the same voice as before; husky, accented, rasping along her nerves and reverberating down that hotline to her clit.

'How d'you know? Have you been spying on me?'

Cold dread settled on her. Was he lurking in the grounds, using a mobile? The house was isolated, surrounded by the gardens, the greenhouses and the shop. There was no one else around for half a mile or more. Except Robert, and he'd be unlikely to hear her if she screamed, tucked up in the housekeeper's quarters.

The stranger chuckled, and lowered his voice to a whisper, 'Don't be scared. I know everything you do, every move you make. I watched you on *Rise and Shine* yesterday morning. A rubbish programme, but you were great.'

'Who are you?' she demanded, scared, thrilled,

offended that this phantom menace had the power to play fast and loose with her emotions.

'It doesn't matter – yet. I'm here to tell you what to do.'

'How d'you mean?'

His voice was deep and eager. He sounded excited. 'If not asleep, then were you playing with yourself when I phoned? Scott's a good-looking bloke, but you could take half a dozen men, I'll bet. Isn't that so, Rosemary? You'd like a crowd of them watching you. Like they do when you're on the TV, but this would be more intimate. You'd arch your breasts, then open your legs and show them everything, bare yourself from cunt to arsehole, and take their dicks into every orifice.'

'You're disgusting!' she snarled, but her hand crept down to explore her lips, parting the dark hair and working along the wet folds.

'Then why don't you hang up?'

Good question, she thought. Why don't I?

The truth was she couldn't resist talking to this faceless, nameless man. Her nipples ached; her bud thrummed and she had never been more excited. That old movie, *Strangers On A Train*, she thought. The storyline had been spot on. It was so much easier to talk to a total stranger. Confession time. 'Hear me, Father, for I have sinned.' Priests, doctors, total strangers on a plane or a ferry, or, like now, along a telephone line.

'You can't put the phone down, can you?' he continued in that dark, velvety tone. It touched her as intimately as if he'd put his cock inside her. 'You want to know what I'm going to say next. You're willing to obey me. Longing to submit.'

'You're very sure of yourself,' she said, screwing up her courage to defy him, yet carrying on this raunchy conversation. She plunged a finger into her cleft, moving slowly, caressing it, relishing the feel of the saturated, engorged lips.

'Oh, yes,' he answered.

'I suppose you're going to try and convince me that

you're handsome and rich and that I really should meet you?' she said scathingly.

'No,' he replied, ice-cool. 'Tell me a story, Rosemary. Tell me what arouses you. Talk about it, and while you're talking, masturbate. I want to hear your voice go wobbly when you start to come. Now, start. Talk to me.'

'Why should I?'

'Because I said so.'

She wanted so much to deny him, but found that she couldn't do other than obey. 'I'm lying on my bed, sort of propped up by pillows.'

'What are you wearing?'

'Nothing.'

'And what are you doing with your other hand, the one that isn't holding the phone?'

'It's between my legs,' she whispered, laved with heat from loins to brow, a blush warming her cheeks.

'And what are you thinking about?'

'I'm remembering something, an incident at college.'

'With a boy or a girl?'

'Neither. It was with a flower.'

'Go on. You're making me horny as hell,' he urged, and chuckled. 'Are you stroking yourself? Do you want to come? Not yet. I'll tell you when. First, I must hear more.'

'Be fair. You haven't told me what you're doing. Are you holding your cock?' She couldn't believe she had just said that.

'Yes. I'm sitting comfortably with my tackle out, stroking my balls and running my fingers up to my knob. It's nice and slippery, a real boner.'

'And where is this?' she managed to ask, trying to be crafty though the scene he conjured tightened her inner muscles like coiled springs. Her fingers settled into that magical rhythm which would soon bring on her orgasm.

'I'm not saying. It will be useless to try and trace this call, by the way. You won't be able to do it. Now, get on with the story.'

She edged into her vulva and circled it, her fingertips

sensitive to the ridged walls. Her clit pulsed greedily and she withdrew, trailing fresh dew over it. As she lightly massaged the tiny bump, so she let her thoughts drift back.

'One of the lecturers had a passion for exotic blooms, the wackier the better,' she began. 'She raved on about the Venus Fly-Trap and the Pitcher Plant, those insectivorous things who thrive on living organisms. She was fey, around forty and eccentric, but she knew her stuff. For some obscure reason, I was one of her favourite students. She interested me, with her long fingers and fine-boned face. A pretty woman, in an other-worldly, witchy kind of way.'

'Was she gay?' he broke in, and his breathing was heavier. She imagined his cock to be twelve inches long, thick-stemmed and meaty, the purple glans emerging and retreating through his fist.

'Maybe. I never heard anything about a husband or partner. Her name was Rita Holby, and she wore flowing retro skirts and Jacob's fleece cardigans, hand spun and knitted by herself. She had hennaed curls that corkscrewed to below her waist. When she talked about her beloved flowers, her face lit up, her eyes shone and her lips quivered.

'"Their reproduction system is mind-blowing," she would say, pacing through the enormous hothouse with me in tow. "We'll come here at dusk and I'll show you."'

'And did she?' he enquired dreamily. 'Are you fingering yourself?

'Oh, yes,' she gasped, slowing her reaction by rubbing the folds each side of her clit, avoiding the ultra-sensitive tip, wanting to make the feeling last for ever.

'Good girl. My cock's fit to burst, hot as Hades, but I can hang on. I know how to delay orgasm. I'm a master at it.'

'Is that all you're master of?' she asked, her tongue cleaving to the roof of her mouth, so thirsty she wanted to break off and fetch a drink of water.

'Silly question. Isn't it obvious that you're my slave

and I'm your master. Proceed with your tale, but don't stop playing with your pussy.'

Rosemary swallowed hard, patting her slit, toying with it, keeping climax at bay. 'We went there one evening. It was summertime and the nights were warm,' she said, breathing fast. 'She opened the door with her own key. We weren't supposed to go in there except under supervision. The plants were so rare, you see, so valuable. I can remember the smell, a heady perfume rising from each blossom, and the air heavy with moisture. The sound of water dripping, the eerie sight of Spanish moss hanging in trailing strands from the branches of trees, grey as ghosts in the twilight.'

'It spooked you, made you shiver ... made you think of graveyards and vampires, and bloody kisses on your neck,' he murmured. 'Were your panties damp? Did you want to touch yourself, like you're doing now?'

'How did you know?' She stretched her legs wide under the duvet and raised her pelvis, using her fingers to hold her lips apart while thumbing herself.

'I've already said. I know everything,' he repeated, his voice like honey dripping in her ear. 'Go on.'

'Rita was flushed. There were little beads of sweat on her upper lip. I could smell her musky odour. I doubt she used a deodorant or shaved her armpits. We reached one of her favourites, an enormous tropical lily. It had thick, fleshy leaves and a great, waxen trumpet of a flower. To my amazement, I heard her talking to it. Her voice was squeaky and excited. "Come along, my beauty," she said. "How lovely you are. How proud and noble, and that orange stamen – why, it's positively glowing!"

'Then she turned to me. "Look, Rosemary. Have you ever seen anything so gorgeous?"

'It was lewd, reminding me of a man's prick – not that I'd seen many, mind you, but by then I wasn't a virgin. I couldn't very well say this to Rita, so mumbled something pathetic about the marvels of nature.'

'Describe it to me in detail,' he ordered, and she could imagine his enormous cock jerking under his touch.

'It was a bit more pointy than a penis, and it stood up stiffly from among the death-white petals. I was reminded of the Devil's Stinkhorn, but it lacked the horrible stench. Its scent was overpowering though, sweet, narcotic, stronger at night, beguiling insects to rub against it and carry away pollen on their legs. An aggressive, male thing, concerned only with flaunting and flirting in the interests of procreation.'

It was hard to concentrate on what she was saying with two fingers thrust inside her and another drumming on her pleasure organ.

'Just like a man, then,' he rasped, and she could almost see his hand flying over his cock. 'What did she do next, this tutor of yours?'

'Oh ... I can't ... I want to come so badly,' she whimpered.

'Not yet. Slow down. Stop rubbing yourself,' he commanded. 'If I can hang on with this enormous stonker, then so can you.'

Moaning, she withdrew all pressure from her cleft, resting her hand on her plump, furry mound. 'Rita acted strangely. I think she was a little crazy. Anyway, she leaned over the plant, urging me to watch closely. Still talking to it, she gently slipped her hand into the trumpet and grasped the stamen. "There, my precious," she crooned. "I'm going to massage you, till you puff your pollen all over me."

'And that's exactly what she did. I shall never forget the weirdness of it, or the intent expression on her face as she gave the lily a hand-job. Whatever she was doing, it worked. Pollen spiralled into the air, a cloud of spores containing the plant's genes. She collected some and transferred it to the beautiful female of the species, standing aloof in a large pot close by.

'"There, Rosemary," she said, and she was trembling. "That's how we do it."

'"You're midwife to dozens of baby lilies," I joked, not

knowing where to look. It was embarrassing. She was obviously high on this botanical manipulation. I think you may be right about her being a lesbian, because she swayed towards me, and I thought for one awesome moment that she was going to kiss me.'

'Would you have minded? Are you into women? I like the idea of you enjoying sex with one, tongues entwined, breasts pressed to breasts, divine limbs wound round each other, cunny rubbing against cunny.' There was a new, vibrant timbre in his tone, and Rosemary wondered if he was about to spill over.

'I've never made love with a woman,' she said, and thought of Melanie and how desirable she seemed lately.

'Tell me more about Rita.'

'There's nothing much to tell. I left her with her flower, and she could hardly wait to get shot of me, her hand already up under her skirt before the door had closed.'

'It left you horny. You wanted sex.'

'I did. I went to my room and flopped across my bed, then undid the zipper of my jeans and cupped my pussy. I came in two seconds flat.'

'Did it satisfy you?'

'Partly, but I was restless. I wanted a man. So I wandered out into the moonlight. The garden was hushed, the stars spangling the indigo sky. The smell of damp earth was intoxicating, still warm from the heat of the day.'

As Rosemary took that journey back in time, her own touch made her quiver. She left her cleft to concentrate on her nipples, squeezing her breasts together so that she could palm both at once. At the same time, she pressed her thighs tightly against one another in an attempt to keep pressure on her needy bud.

'What happened? Did you meet someone there, under the moon, beneath the rustling branches, with maybe an owl hooting or bats swooping from daytime roosts in old bell towers?' His voice called up irresistible images, and that liquid, melting feeling took over, her middle digit returning to her clit.

'I bumped into him. I didn't know he would be there. He stared at me, his face pale in the gloom, the glint of a gold sleeper against his black hair. It was Lee Penna, the handyman who helped around the college. I'd already noticed him. It was hard to avoid his eyes, deepset in a swarthy face. They said he lived rough, in a beat-up caravan, and was from Romany stock. He'd done time, they said, gone down for causing an affray. He wasn't young, getting on for fifty, and his eyes were hungry as a wolf's whenever he looked at we girls.'

Dear God, I haven't thought of Lee for years, she realised, fingers frantic as she stroked and poked at herself, the strong smell of female arousal in her nostrils.

'And you did it with him?' the voice prompted.

'Yes. We didn't speak, just came together. I could feel the shape of his dick through his cord trousers as he held me to him. His hands were rough, scratching my nipples. He smelled of beer, of the raw passion of a man seeking a mate, making me forget college and caution and anything sensible. He was strong and ruggedly handsome, with a thick moustache that tickled me when he went down on me. "Give me your minge," he muttered. "Let me taste it. There's nothing like the smell and flavour of a woman's cunt."'

'You lay with him on the earth? You're a pagan, Rosemary,' the dark voice of temptation whispered down the telephone.

'I did. Oh, yes,' she gasped, and her fingers became Lee's tongue, flicking over her clit, fondling, stroking, bringing her closer to the edge. 'He turned me over, kneed my legs apart, kept his finger on my button and thrust into me from behind.'

'Up your arse?'

'No, I've never done that. In the usual place. He held me tight, on his knees behind me, thrusting and thrusting, his teeth at the back of my neck, like a stallion nipping a mare.' She could hardly form the words, keeping up a constant massage on her clit as contractions radiated through her.

The listener chuckled and said, 'Not had a prick in your lovely little hole? You've never been buggered? Joys to come, Rosemary.'

She hardly heard him, imagining Lee sucking at her breasts, his fingers swirling round her shaft and tormenting her aching clitoris. He was palpating it with a feather-light touch, and she reached the highest peak of exquisite sensation, orgasm rippling through her, then breaking in a great wave. She couldn't contain a cry.

'Ah, you've come. That was naughty. I didn't say you could. Was it good?'

She couldn't speak at first and collapsed against the mattress. 'What about you? Have you come, too?' she asked breathlessly, her heart slowing, the tumult inside her beginning to fade.

'No. I'll reserve it till later. It was your pleasure that concerned me. Good night, Rosemary. You will be hearing from me again,' he said, and then the phone went dead.

Rosemary stared at it, unable to credit what had just taken place. She placed the instrument on the nightstand, shocked by her own behaviour and devastated by his abrupt departure. She had no more idea of what he looked like or his intentions towards her than on that former occasion, only now it had gone much, much further. Like a creeping evil, he was invading her soul.

He put down the mobile and turned his attention to his partner in crime and long-term paramour. She lay face-down over a specially designed bench, wrists and ankles tethered to rings on either side, her hair streaming like a golden river, obscuring her face and dripping to the floor.

He studied her. From her shoulder-blades to where two delectable dimples indented her pelvis just above her bottom cheeks, she was laced into a blue satin corset, wasp-waisted and excruciatingly restrictive. In front, her full breasts bulged over the lace edging, ground against the bench by her weight and the strain of the handcuffs bolted to the metal rings. But it was her rear that

94

enthralled him; those twin white globes criss-crossed by scarlet weals, the tops of her wide-spread thighs, the dark blue fishnet hold-up stockings, her silver shoes. The heels were so high they made her calf muscles bulge. Her crack was exposed, the crinkled amber mouth of her anus, the pink purse of her shaven sex, the lips parted to display the underside. He could see the gold ring piercing her clit hood, and the sparkling diamond dangling from it.

He ran a finger up that inviting slit, dabbling in her juice and sniffing it, then transferring it to his mouth. 'Yes. That's mine,' he murmured, reverting to his normal, public-school voice, dropping the phoney foreign accent.

He had been lying when he told Rosemary he was masturbating. In reality, he had been pumping his cock into this gorgeous woman. Before he phoned, he had stimulated himself and his lover by thrashing her. Now he positioned himself behind her again, slipping his length into her welcoming cunt.

'Oh, do it, please, sir,' she whimpered.

He stopped, and drew his cock from her pulsating depths, his control superb. 'What right have you to speak?' he said frostily.

'None. I'm sorry,' she murmured, her flesh shaking, the light dancing on her striped rump.

'Submissives have no rights, have they?'

'No,' she agreed, writhing on the bench in a vain attempt to find relief for the frustration that had been building while he was on the phone.

He grabbed up the whip, the haft in his hand and the lash trailing. He let the tip dangle across her crotch. She cried out and raised her hips as high as she was able, given her restraints.

He smiled, thinking: Lord, but she's eager. Rosemary will be the same once I've tamed her. All women are sex-slaves deep down and adore being mastered, despite the furore about equality. It's been inbred for centuries. A strong man means protection for them and their brats. It removes responsibility. They don't have to think for themselves, letting their lord and master make the choices.

He threw back his arm. The whip sang. He thrilled to hear the leather whacking her bare hinds. She yelped and threshed. He struck her again, the red latticework on her buttocks augmented by fresh lines. He didn't use his full strength, tantalising her with the fear of something more intense. Her struggles aroused him. His dick was painfully enlarged, his balls tense in their hairy sac. He was tormenting himself as much as her, prolonging the agony till the last possible moment when a mighty orgasm would explode from within him.

He started to flog her in earnest, covering her backside with fiery strokes. Then he threw the whip aside and plunged his fingers into her liquid heat, spreading her essence up her crack and anointing her anus. He opened her, greasing the pathway to heaven. When he judged her ready, he slowly and carefully mounted her, easing his prick into her tight hole, feeling the resistance, then the relaxing of her sphincter as she accepted him. He knew she was anxious lest she miss her climax, and slid a hand beneath her, finding her clit and rocking it till he felt her shudder and the sudden clenching round his cock.

Now he could let go at last, the serpent fire roaring down his spine and discharging itself in a massive convulsion that left him gasping.

She was prone beneath him, and he stroked her hair sleepily, then moved, unlocked the cuffs and helped her to her feet.

'It's going to happen just like I predicted, darling,' he said. 'Rosemary Maddox won't know if she's on her arse or her elbow.'

'There's something for you,' Fran said, poking her head round the study door.

She was like a breath of fresh air, with her spiky burgundy hair ablaze with fanciful clips, her PVC skirt brief to the point of indecency, and her nails, long as dragons' claws and painted a metallic peacock-blue. It was a wonder she managed to use the computer keyboard.

'There usually is,' Rosemary sighed, having decided to forget her nocturnal caller and get down to pressing business.

She had been putting off proofreading the book she had written about the art of bonsai trees and the Zen Garden. A specialist subject, but one which she had undertaken after consulting with experts. Her publishers had wanted it, jumping on the Feng Shui bandwagon. Coupled with her name, this should prove a winner if it hit the bookshops around the middle of November. She had already taken part in a Christmas Special to be screened on Boxing Day.

'It could be more fanmail,' suggested the bright-as-a-button and loyal to a fault Fran. She had taken it upon herself to be not only Rosemary's aide, but her minder as well. 'But it's quite big. Could be a bomb,' she continued and she held it with the tips of her fingers, grimacing.

'Who is going to bother to exterminate me?' Rosemary laughed.

Fran shrugged her bony shoulders under the white fishnet vest, her tiny breasts concealed by black lace cups. 'I dunno. The Society for the Prevention of Cruelty to Bonsai Trees? The Guardians of Television, who want to bring about the downfall of a load of old cobblers? You tell me.'

Rosemary took the manila envelope from her, studied it and said, 'This didn't come by post?'

'Hand delivered,' Fran replied, a grin on her red slash of a mouth. 'Came via a messenger-boy on a motorbike. He looked positively edible in his leathers. I wanted to sink my teeth into his teeny little tush.'

Rosemary had a gut feeling about the letter. She was aware that Fran was dying of curiosity but she wanted to open it in private. There was too much happening lately, too many mysteries. This package was a continuation. She felt it in her water.

She tucked it into her bag and said, 'Hold the fort here, will you? I shan't be long.'

On reaching her bedroom, she ripped open the padded envelope and drew out a neatly framed photograph protected by bubblewrap. She frowned as she examined it. The photo was of a bronze and green figurine, and pure Art Deco. 1925 vintage, the original would be a most valuable piece if it came up for auction. A collectors' item for those who were willing to pay a high price for erotic statuettes. It was beautiful and explicit, and Rosemary grew hot as she focused on it.

The woman depicted seemed to live and breathe, the jaw-length bob so reminiscent of the period brushing her cheeks. Supremely haughty, her eyes were heavy-lidded, her lips rolled into a pout, her chin lifted defiantly. She was wearing a flapper dress with a ripped top, the narrow shoulder straps yanked down and baring a pair of firm, round breasts with jutting nipples. The short skirt had been reduced to a fringed rag, drawn around her tightly, outlining her belly button, and pushed up so high it barely covered the apex of her thighs. She stood on a plinth with her legs apart, wearing court shoes and stockings upheld by garters. It was as if she was alive; she was wilful and arrogant, with her arms behind her and hands clasping a riding crop.

Rosemary put the photo down on the bed, and opened the folded sheet of paper that accompanied it. Inside was a printout, saying, 'I want to see you dressed like this, Rosemary.'

'So can you help me, Inspector?' she said, seated opposite him in his overcrowded office. 'I'm sick of obscene phone calls, and now this . . .' and she pushed the photo across the desk towards him.

It had seemed that a visit to the police had been her only option. There wasn't a station near Plants Galore, and she'd driven into the suburbs, ending up at one near the Ace Productions headquarters. She had considered phoning Michael: she was his star after all, and it was in his interests to protect her, but the whole thing had embarrassing overtones. She smiled crookedly and remembered how much easier it was to talk to someone who didn't know her from Adam.

First mistake, she realised, when, on giving her name and being ushered from reception into his presence, the inspector had practically genuflected. 'Miss Maddox. I've seen your programmes. You could say I'm a fan,' he had begun, his face going red, his big frame in the dark blue uniform leaning towards her, his burly legs almost dancing in his eagerness to please. 'Inspector Warren, at your service. Now, what can I do for you?' He'd ordered coffee to be brought in and, as they sipped at the surprisingly palatable instant brew, she had told him about the phone calls.

'Were they recorded? Have you any evidence?' he asked, elbows on the desk top, his hands steepled together as he gazed solemnly at her.

'Only the first two,' she said nervously. He made her feel guilty and the bustling atmosphere of the station exacerbated this. But I've not done anything wrong, she told herself. I'm the victim.

Last night's call was too incriminating and she had erased it. No one must know that she had co-operated with the intruder. It made her hot all over to think of Inspector Warren listening to her climaxing.

He glanced at the photo, then his eyes lingered on the bronze woman's breasts. Rosemary wondered if he was getting hard, looking at the frank print, and maybe already excited by her arrival in his stuffy office. It was another scorching day, England sweltering under a heat-wave. And, as usual, no one was prepared for it – no air-conditioning, not even an electric fan.

Was Warren married or single? He was still an attractive man, even though he was putting on weight and balding. Rosemary's pussy twitched in response to his authoritative mien. He was *somebody* in the force. He had worked his way up, dealt with criminals, put men away, women too. The streets were safer because of him, or men like him.

He leaned back in his swivel chair, tapping the desk with the end of a pencil, as fidgety as only a reformed chain-smoker can be. 'Well, now, Miss Maddox, I'd better send a plain-clothes officer to your home. He can have a look around, ask your staff a few questions, listen to the tapes and advise you on security. Don't worry any more.'

She rose to her feet, and he got up, too, coming round to stand close to her. He patted her shoulder, his touch far from avuncular. He smelled of soap and freshly laundered underwear. It made her long to do some investigating of her own, like measuring the size of his tool. Would it be anything like the truncheon he had carried in his humble beginnings on the beat? She wanted to undo his crisp blue shirt, rub her face in his chest hair, tweak the small male nipples, and then open his trousers. His air of complete control made her think of Neil and the way he had spanked her.

'Is that all you can do to protect me?' she asked, stamping down hard on her sinful impulses.

'I'm afraid so, unless this man actually attacks you,' he said, and instinct told her he was enjoying this interview, wanted to prolong it, was possibly wondering if he dare make an advance.

'Oh, so I have to be raped or half-killed first.' She couldn't contain her sarcasm.

'I'll do my best, Miss Maddox. The man I'm putting in charge of your case is highly efficient. I'm sure you won't be harmed.'

'And that's all the great British police force can offer me? I should have thought you'd make it a priority,' she challenged, slipping the photo into her bag.

'I can't do more, given my limited resources,' he replied apologetically, and saw her to the door. Once more in reception, she could see heads turning in their direction. Word of her identity had obviously spread.

'Goodbye, Inspector,' she said, giving him her hand.

'Goodbye, Miss Maddox,' he responded, holding it a

shade longer than was necessary. 'Rest assured, the man I'm sending will take care of you.'

In what way? she wondered as she left the station and headed for her car. Will he be a lecherous old goat like you, Inspector Warren? How would it be to have you stripsearch me? As she slid into the driver's seat she realised that the crotch of the tanga, drawn up tight into her crack, was more than a little wet.

Rosemary didn't go straight home. Instead, she parked up and wandered round the Soho sex shops, venturing inside one and browsing without being hassled to buy anything. This meant that she did, making several purchases of provocative, slit-crotch knickers and bras with peep-holes.

Scott will like them. His cock will get stiff, she thought as she handed over her Switch card, her cunt pulsing with heat. I'll get him to stay behind after work. He can shower at my place. I'll even wash him myself, get under the spray with him, soap him all over, then rinse his balls and lather his cock. After this, I'll pat him dry, dust him with talc and put these on to tantalise him.

But, as with all the best-laid plans of mice and men, when she strolled into her kitchen, Fran was there, getting a drink of orange squash from the fridge.

She poured one for Rosemary, perched her butt on a corner of the table, and announced, 'There's a bloke hanging around. I thought you ought to know.'

'A customer?'

'I don't think so.'

'What's he like?' Rosemary's wits sharpened. Could he be one of the stranger's sidekicks? It was obvious that he must have someone spying on her. She parked herself on one of the rush-seated, ladder-backed oak chairs.

'A big guy, rough as fuck,' Fran opined.

'Is he outside now?'

'Could be. Last time I saw him, he was talking to Scott.' Fran gave her a worried glance. 'Are you OK?'

Rosemary passed a hand across her eyes. 'Tired, that's all. It was like an oven in town.'

The stranger's spy. His private investigator, reporting on her movements and those around her. She yearned for Inspector Warren's strong, comforting arms and steady head. She wanted to turn tail and run. Back to him? Or to that other surrogate father, Michael?

'You should take a holiday,' Fran advised, her minute skirt rising as she crossed her bare, brown legs. 'I can manage here, and Robert will take care of the house.'

'I can't go far, not until everything is settled.'

'The split, you mean?'

'Of course. I can't leave all this and have Terry coming in and helping himself to anything he fancies.'

'Nor her either. The bitch. I'd like to pin her up against the wall and give her a right going over.' Fran had never liked Belinda much and now made it clear she detested her. 'You've had the locks changed?'

'Some of them, but I can't keep him out entirely until the property is finally mine. He still has a right to come into the nurseries, shop and office. Partnerships are a pain to dissolve, nearly as bad as a marriage.'

Glancing round the kitchen, once ruled by a cook and her minions, Rosemary had never felt more possessive. She had planned and overseen the renovations that had modernised it without losing its old-world ambience. Just as she had done in the rest of the house. No one, certainly not Terry and his bit on the side, was about to take it away from her. She knew it was going to cost her an arm and a leg, but no matter. She was riding high on a wave of fame and had a canny accountant who would battle with the taxman and ensure she had a steady income.

If only this recent nuisance could be dealt with so easily. She was tempted to tell Fran about it but, maybe later, she decided, saying aloud, 'Is the man around now? Can you see him from the window?'

Fran craned to look, standing on tiptoe in her clumpy, stack-heeled shoes. Her skirt rose higher and her bikini panties showed, the thong disappearing between her taut buttocks. Rosemary envied her, wishing she was eighteen again. Fran even had an affair going with a pale-faced, androgynous friend, who she swore was male. She was clued-up and feisty. Not like me, Rosemary concluded. I'm too trusting, too gullible.

She got up and joined Fran near the white Belfast sink, beech drainer and dishwasher set in front of arched windows that faced a cobbled courtyard. She gulped as Fran seized her hand, saying excitedly, 'There he is. What d'you think? Lean, mean and tasty.'

Rosemary nodded, wishing circumstances were different and she didn't have to be suspicious of him. He was coming across the yard towards the back door, the distance giving her the chance to observe him. He was tall, wearing faded blue jeans and a ragged, once white T-shirt. He had scuffed trainers, and a baseball cap that part covered his collar-length dark hair.

Her heart leaped into her mouth. 'He's coming here,' she gasped, poised for flight.

Too late. He was standing at the stable door, leaning in at the top half. She heard him rap on the wood and call out, 'Hello. Anyone at home?'

Get a grip, she ordered herself, turning to face him. 'Can I help you?' she asked politely, in her best upper-middle-class accent.

'I'm looking for Miss Maddox,' he said with a smile that would have tempted a nun into sin.

She stared, momentarily speechless, assessing his aquiline nose and high, verging on Slavic, cheekbones. He even had a dimple in his chin. Too handsome by far, not classically handsome, but craggily handsome. The type that men hate and women cream their knickers for. He was having just that effect on her.

'I'm Rosemary Maddox,' she managed to blurt out, annoyed at her loss of cool. Going to pieces over a man. Ye Gods, Fran was watching! What an example to set her!

'Can I come in?' His broad hand was already on the latch.

'Well, yes. I suppose so. It depends on what you want,' she said steadily, rather proud of her recovery, though her nipples had peaked and were rubbing against her cotton dress. A quick glance down and she could see them. So, without doubt, could he.

He smiled again, and drew a wallet from his hip pocket. He flipped it open and she wondered if he was a gasman, electrician or someone from the Water Board who was bound by law to show his credentials.

'DC Holland. CID,' he informed her briskly. 'I've been sent by Inspector Warren to investigate your complaint concerning nuisance calls, obscene post and general harassment by an unknown person.'

Fran's astonished gasp was audible. 'You're a pig?' she shouted.

'I'm a policeman. That's right.'

'God, you could've fooled me. You don't look like one. On plain-clothes duty, are you?'

'Shut up, Fran.' Rosemary's stomach was a home for fluttering butterflies. The way he was looking at her sent a tingle through her lower regions.

'Have I put my big, fat foot in it?' Fran asked, grimacing.

'You have rather,' Rosemary said, then dared to look at him and add, 'You'd better come in.'

He did just that and it was as if he'd never been anywhere else. He fitted the place perfectly. 'Now then, Miss Maddox, you'd better tell me all about it. May I sit down?'

'Oh, yes. Sorry. Would you like a cup of tea or something?' She avoided his steel-grey eyes. He breathed out sex appeal from his very pores. She was achingly aware of his darkly furred forearms and stubbled chin, smelling him even from a distance. She wondered if his skin would taste salty.

'Thank you, Miss Maddox. Is it all right to talk in front of the young lady?'

'She's my secretary. She may as well know. Fran, put the kettle on. We've a lot to discuss.'

Chapter Six

'Weird!' exclaimed Fran, when Rosemary had finished recounting her recent experiences. 'So who is this guy? A nut-case?'

'That's what I'm here to find out,' Dan Holland said grittily. He had changed dramatically, no longer a scruff, adopting his policeman persona, and Rosemary's heart sank as he added, cynically 'If there really *is* anyone.'

'What d'you mean . . . if?' she sparked up.

He rocked on the back legs of his chair, his thighs braced, muscles straining against the denim. He was so adept at interrogation that she had found herself answering, willy-nilly. All the time he had never taken his hard grey eyes from hers. As when with his superior officer, she had lusted to feel his mouth on her cunt, and his hands cupping her bottom, fingers buried in the deep crease between.

'This could be nothing more than a publicity stunt, Miss Maddox,' he answered tersely, an austere inquisitor, skilful at trapping the unwary.

Her nerves jangled. She was scared and melting with desire all at the same time. I'd hate to be really guilty, she thought, shivering. Would you? jeered her other self. Aren't you getting all wet round the pussy when you imagine him chastising you?

'You've got to be joking,' Fran shouted, coming to stand behind Rosemary protectively, warm palms resting on her shoulders. 'You can't be so stupid as to believe it's a con? She doesn't need publicity. Don't you read the papers or watch TV? She gets a massive amount of coverage.'

'And you would know about this, being her Girl Friday?' His question was laced with irony.

'She doesn't have any secrets from me,' Fran said, stubbornly out-staring him.

Can't she feel the steel-to-magnet pull? Rosemary wondered. It's drawing me to him. I can hardly contain the desire to reach out and touch him.

She thought of Scott waiting in the greenhouse, and of the risqué underwear nestling in the discreet plastic carrier. Her vision blurred. All she could see was herself wearing the sluttish outfit for the young detective. She imagined the scratchy feeling of the cheap black lace that edged the crotchless knickers and the way it would frame her wet pink lips.

His voice brought her back to the present. 'She didn't tell you about the calls, did she? Nor the photograph?' he reminded Fran. Her face puckered and her eyes switched to Rosemary.

'Why worry you over nothing?' Rosemary faltered, struggling with the ache in her clit. Her panties were soaking up the increased moisture sliding from her sex.

'But it wasn't nothing, was it? Important enough to get the filth involved. You should have told me. I thought we were friends,' Fran ranted, tears threatening to ruin her mascara.

Rosemary vented her frustration on the young detective. 'I didn't organise it. It's no publicity thing. As Fran says, I don't need it.'

'You do realise I shall have to talk to the men you've named?' He cocked an eyebrow at her, then consulted his notebook. 'Business associates, I take it? Michael Pendelton, Neil Kemble and Jonathan Flynn. I've already had a word with Scott Bradbury.'

'You didn't tell him you were from the police?'

He shook his head. 'He thought I was looking for a job.'

'Don't forget Terry Veney, my one-time partner.' There was no way Rosemary was going to let him off the hook.

'Ah, yes. He's left you for another woman.'

'I kicked him out.' Her pride wouldn't have it any other way.

He cast her a shrewd look, eyes crinkled at the outer corners as if he was forever combing the horizon in search of criminals. 'Quite,' he said. 'Are you sure you've told me everything?'

The sunlight on his dark hair distracted her. He'd taken off his hat and his curls were untidy, but in contrast to the disreputable clothing, his hair had a clean, wholesome sheen. She liked its raffish, swashbuckling look. Not many men wore their hair long these days. There was a plethora of cropped heads, short-back-and-sides, executive cuts, pudding-basin styles, parted in the centre and flopping over the brow. Only people like Jonathan flouted the rules – Jonathan the designer – and Detective Holland the law-and-order man, scorning fashion. Only they were individuals in their own right.

But in spite of her hunger to run her fingers through his hair, invade the rips in his shirt and circle his wine-dark nipples, practical considerations had to be addressed, so she said, 'I've told you all I know. Is that it then?'

'Not entirely. I want to hear the tapes and examine the photo. I shall be here some time. In fact, I could stay tonight, keeping an eye on you and being there if he phones again.'

'So you do believe me?' This was suddenly of tanta-mount importance.

'I'm not saying yet. Give me time to have a sniff around.'

You can sniff round me any time you want. The words poised on the tip of her tongue, almost spilling out. I'd say them if I was a right old slapper, she decided, or someone as confident as Melanie.

'And what will Inspector Warren think about that?' she countered, re-filling his coffee cup and allowing herself a tentative peep into the evening ahead. Would it be an earth-moving fuck, or a let-down? It depended on his mood. She had already formed the opinion that moody he most definitely was.

'He's given me my orders, and bodyguard duties feature strong. I think you scored a hit with him, Miss Maddox.' His eyes were no longer flinty. Now they twinkled, flustering her.

'Can I go now? Craig and me are clubbing tonight. Seems like you've been coping fine without me,' Fran said sulkily, and Rosemary could tell she'd taken umbrage.

'Run along. I'll see you tomorrow.'

When Fran had flounced out of the door, he shifted his chair closer to Rosemary's and said, 'I'll be off duty soon. You'd better call me Dan.'

'Are you sure this won't transgress police regulations?' she replied acidly. 'And why are you staying in your free time?' She could feel herself blushing as his steady regard changed into something more potent. Tiny flames blazed in the depths of his inky pupils.

'The case interests me. You interest me, Miss Maddox,' he said, and raised his hand to touch her cheek. His smile broadened, and he was so sexy that her pheromones went into overdrive. 'I've never spent the night with a TV star before, not that I watch much telly. I certainly haven't noticed you on it.'

'You're not a gardener?' she ventured, almost paralysed by his caress. His fingers strayed so close to her mouth that she could have licked them, sucked them, used them as a substitute until the moment she could fasten her lips round his cock.

'Nope. I live in a flat over an Indian restaurant, not too far from the nick. There's a flat roof outside my kitchen window, and I sit there sometimes on warm evenings, breathing curry smells and pretending I'm in Bombay.'

'You could grow plants in pots, brighten it up a bit,' she said primly, trying to suppress the rude thoughts playing mayhem with her.

He gave a quick laugh. 'No way. I shan't be there long. I like to move around.'

'That's no reason for neglecting it.' Oh, Jesus, stop preaching, will you? She chided herself. Not everyone is as obsessed with greenery as you. 'Are you married?' she added.

He must be. No one with his striking looks could possibly have remained single. It was against all the laws of probability.

'Not any more.'

She was glad there wasn't a wife now but there was a smidgen of bitterness in his voice. 'She couldn't cope with your unsociable hours?'

'Something like that. I'm no nine-to-five man.'

'Nor am I. Terry didn't like that either, and he envied my success. But that's no reason to neglect your living space. This is important, good for the psyche if it's balanced and in harmony. Gardens are a refuge, safe havens without threats.'

His alert gaze riveted her. 'There are so many things to do, and I don't have much spare time.'

'What do you like? Propping up the bar in your local? Watching football?' Most men were into drinking and sport, two pastimes that bored her rigid.

'No. I read, and study movies. I've my favourite directors . . . Alan Parker, Neil Jordan and Peter Greenaway.'

An intellectual policeman who looked like a New Age traveller and wore several studs in his ears? This was becoming more and more surreal, just as he was becoming ever more attractive. 'I may have something here you'd like to watch later,' she offered, suddenly shy. 'Have you seen *Shakespeare In Love*? It's one of my favourites. So romantic.'

'I have. What about Kenneth Branagh's *Hamlet*? Now

there's a film and a half. Or the most recent *Romeo and Juliet*? Baz Lurhman's a fine director.'

'Both videos are snuggled up together on my classics' shelf,' she answered, watching the play of light and shadow over his mobile face. He was wired and totally enthusiastic. It was thrilling to have found his Achilles' heel. She suspected that he didn't talk like this with just anyone. No doubt he got his leg pulled down at the station.

Yet there was that other side of him, stern, authoritarian, and his manner changed again as he said, 'I don't think you've been absolutely truthful with me. These men you've mentioned. Have you been intimate with them?'

'I suppose you mean have I slept with them? Frankly, I don't think that's any of your business,' she rejoined smartly, but wanted to talk to him about it, describe each lurid episode in detail.

'I need to know, Miss Maddox,' he said firmly. 'It could throw an entirely different slant on the matter.'

'I don't have to answer that,' she retorted, fighting the urge to fall on her knees at his feet and confess, confess, confess, even make up stories so that he'd despise her as a filthy, twisted tart.

'You can tell me in confidence, if you like. It needn't go any further,' he murmured and his fingertips touched hers on the table's flat surface. The contact shocked through her like a bolt of lightning.

'Terry was unfaithful,' she stammered, staring at the back of his hand, the strong fingers, the sun-browned skin, the tendons and sinews. 'So I instigated an affair with Scott.'

'Where was that?' His voice deepened, and his hand came to rest on hers, turning it over and tickling her heart line with his thumb.

'In the hothouse, on a bed of pallets hedged in by plants. He was my first for ages, a virile young bloke who really wanted me. I'd never done it with anyone else since I'd been with Terry.'

110

'He made you come? Did things to you that Terry didn't?'

'Oh, yes,' she gasped, the breath catching in her throat. She snatched her hand away. This was just too much.

'You're in love with him?' he carried on calmly.

'No, I don't think so. I can't be, because I've had others since then. He freed me. Terry couldn't hurt me any more.'

'And the other men? Your colleagues? Did you have sex with them?' His voice was huskier, his breathing quicker.

He's aroused, she thought and glanced down at his crotch. The thick stem of his penis was pressing urgently against the fly buttons of his jeans.

'I saw no reason not to, now that Terry and I were finished. First there was Michael, my director, then Neil, who I knew at college, and then Jonathan.' She pressed her hands into her lap, surreptitiously grinding her lower lips against the chair seat; her clit was swelling.

'May they have something to do with the calls? Are they jealous of each other, perhaps? Think you should be punished?' he said very low, and the way his lips formed around the last word launched an icy avalanche into her groin.

'I don't know,' she whispered helplessly.

'Several sexual partners in quick succession. Do you always sleep around so easily? I hope you practised safe sex, Miss Maddox.'

'I did, and I'm not an easy lay, and if I'm to call you Dan, then I'm Rosemary. OK?'

Formality seemed pointless. The tigerish look on his face, and the burgeoning lump in his fly, made a nonsense of anything but ripe and raw fucking.

'Do you want to know what I think?' he growled.

'Not much, but I suppose you're going to tell me anyway.'

'You're a hot piece of arse, Rosemary, and used the break-up as an excuse to fuck men brainless. If I was in Vice, I might arrest you for being a mucky little hooker.'

111

She gulped, stood up and backed away. Like the stranger, he was talking dirty and her knees weakened, juices spreading beyond her panty crotch to dampen her inner thighs. He followed her, loomed over her, dark and menacing. Sweat glistened on his face, and his erection was forced painfully high by the tightness of his jeans.

'You said you'd help me. There was nothing about giving me a load of verbal. I could report you to Inspector Warren,' she managed to squeak. Her back was pressed against the roughly plastered wall. It dug into her spine through her dress. Dan braced his arms on either side of her, caging her in.

'You could, but you won't,' he said smoothly, his smile even more feline, his eyes narrowed to glittering slits.

'Don't be too sure. I could make trouble for you,' she threatened, fighting the desire to reach down and press her palm to his dick.

He stepped back, spreading his arms wide and grinning. 'I shan't do anything you don't want me to do. I'm not going to rush this, Rosemary. I like to take my time, get to know a woman before I fuck her. You smell as if you work in a perfume shop. I want to clean up before I come any closer to you. Can I use the shower?'

This stopped her in her tracks. A fastidious cop, when she'd been expecting a rough ride to bliss. Right, she thought. Two can play at this tantalising game.

'I'll show you to one of the guest-rooms. It has an *en suite* shower. Make yourself at home,' she said, recalling how she had planned to wash Scott, but this seemed aeons ago. Now her body was ripe to experience Dan's hard prick, and he was making her wait, the bastard.

'I've brought a change of clothes. They're in the van. I thought I might be in for a long night, but didn't anticipate meeting someone as gorgeous as you.' His compliment made her blush.

'I'll prepare a meal. Something light. We can eat on the terrace. I'm going to take a swim first.' She was gabbling, her pulse racing, like a girl on her first date.

When she had shown him to his room, she rushed

down to the kitchen again, grabbed up the phone and dialled the hothouse. Scott answered, saying jauntily, 'I'll lock up and come right over.'

She cut him short. 'No, please don't. I'm busy this evening.'

'But, Rosemary . . . we arranged . . .'

'Sorry. Something's cropped up. See you tomorrow,' and she pressed the magic red button that removed him instantly from her ken.

After plundering the freezer and tipping salad into one bowl, and rice mixed with fish, olives and capers into another, she carried the meal outside and round to the terrace. There were several loungers, and a teak table under a striped umbrella.

It was that still time of late afternoon. There was a breathless hush. Nothing moved. Even the birds seemed too enervated to sing. The heat that had beaten down all day seemed to coagulate, and the sun, hanging like a molten coin in a milky sky, sank lower, throwing off final, fiery flares. The shadows of the trees were elongated, stretching across the lawn, but not reaching the shimmering turquoise pool.

With the portable CD player switched on and the first, ominous chords of *Tosca* booming out, Rosemary left the food in the shade and the wine in an ice-bucket. She dropped her sarong and, wearing the briefest of silver bikinis, padded to the wide, tiled, half-submerged steps.

The tepid water crept up her legs, parting her thighs like persuasive fingers and chilling her entrance. She could feel it lifting the flimsy triangle, supported by a jewelled chain at either hip-bone, that barely covered her pubis. Sighing with the sensual wonder of it, at home in this element, she lowered herself, the water touching her breasts, each concealed behind a further minute scrap of glittering fabric, fastened by thongs at the back and nape.

Just for a moment, she leaned against the steps, eyes closed in ecstasy as the music swept her away, with its story of sex, sadism, religion and art. She hadn't got to Act II yet, with the compelling rape scene that fulfilled her darkest desires and almost brought her to orgasm every time she listened to it. It was the height of luxury to relax like this, pleasured by water, sun, and her favourite music drama.

'Glorious!' she said aloud, as the tenor and soprano hit the high notes in a love duet, their voices soaring effortlessly.

It brought happy tears to her eyes and rekindled her faith in the human race. She struck out, still listening as she enjoyed the warm, liquid embrace. The water caressed her skin, and she relished the play of smoothly working muscles and the sheer physical enjoyment of using her body, shaping and exercising it in the most sensual way. She did a length then floated on her back, her nipples clearing the water, twin peaks lifting the bra. She looked down her body, admiring her tan.

Where was Dan? She wished he would join her, two Water Babies frolicking in the sunshine. It was her idea of heaven. The man of her choice, this perfect setting, delicious food to eat, marvellous music to listen to, and a new body to explore.

He's probably reporting in to his boss, she thought and, reaching the steps, climbed out, dripping. She liked to swim and sunbathe nude, and now that she was certain the garden centre was closed and the staff departed, she untied her soggy bikini and hung it on a chair to dry. She had already prepared a lounger, covering it with a large beach towel. It was positioned to catch the sun's rays.

Little drops of moisture beaded her skin; her nipples were hard and the dark bush at her fork was curling and wet. She rubbed her hair with another towel, then stretched out, one leg straight, the other bent at the knee, waiting to dry so that she could apply screening oil.

Act I thundered to its dramatic conclusion, and Act II began, deceptively gentle, but with threatening undertones.

She put on her sunglasses and adjusted a wide-brimmed straw hat to shield her face. The sun was burning; it was gloriously hot; the music was transporting her to another world, and any lingering worries were drifting away. She dozed, though never losing the thread of the opera, then became aware of a coolness. Someone was blocking out the sun. She pushed up her glasses and hat, made a grab for her sarong, then thought better of it. He'd already seen her naked, must have been standing there for some seconds. It was useless to pretend that she minded.

'Sorry. I didn't mean to disturb you. Were you asleep?' Dan said, hands on his hips. He was taller than ever with his chest bare and his clean blue jeans so tight they might have been moulded on him.

He was seriously attractive, and she wanted to nibble his neck, leaving the blood-red bruises of love bites. She slowly perused his long legs, slim hips, narrow waist and broad, hairy chest.

'Did you enjoy your shower?' she asked lazily. Why hurry or push things? They would take their natural course without any prompting from her.

'I did indeed, but would have come down to swim, had I known you were serious about it.' He dropped into a wicker chair, and lit a cigarette. He passed it to her and ignited another for himself.

'We should eat,' she said idly, reluctant to move, while Act II entered its melodramatic conclusion.

Rosemary breathed in the soothing smoke, seeing in her mind's eye the darkened stage with the villain's body laid out, and Tosca, who had just stabbed him as he tried to rape her, placing a crucifix on his chest and two lighted candles each side of his head. Sonorous notes from the orchestra and a drum roll. Somehow it was all getting mixed up with Dan. He was tough, something of a bully, yet her nipples crimped and she yearned to have him pulsing, driving and possessing her slick wet sex.

It was as if he could read her like an open book, knowing what she wanted but making her wait for it.

'That's heavy,' he commented, jerking his head towards the stereo.

'Opera is immensely sexy. Do you like classical music? This is by Giacomo Puccini. You may know him from the football song made popular by Pavarotti years ago. That was taken from one of Puccini's operas.'

He was listening intently, nodding and saying, 'I like it. I can see what you mean about sexy. Very passionate stuff, and it keeps rising higher and higher, just like an orgasm. You'll have to teach me.'

'But what do you really like?'

'Things that stir me, like this piece, but I have to be familiar with all manner of music in my work. Mostly hip-hop and dance. Sometimes I'm ordered to go to the pop festivals, working with the Drug Squad. Can't be convincing unless I can talk rave with the kids. But yes, I could really go for some of this.'

Rosemary reached out and clicked off the CD. 'We should have dinner,' she said.

'When you're ready. Though I must admit I could eat a horse, saddle and harness and all,' Dan said slowly, feet propped up on a spare chair, his crotch thrown into greater prominence.

He's doing it on purpose, Rosemary thought. He wants me to see he's getting fruity. Moving in a leisurely manner, she sat up and wound the colourful cotton sarong round her, knotting it just above her breasts. She took a seat at the table and he moved his chair round to face her, stubbing out his cigarette in the ashtray.

He ate with enormous relish, though she merely pushed the food about on her plate, famished to have him satisfy her other bodily needs. He had a second helping of salad, and munched his way through the crusty bread. She noticed that he drank sparingly, refusing a second glass of chilled white wine.

'You don't like to drink?' she questioned, unable to stop watching him, her breasts thrust upwards under the Indian cotton, nipples greedy for his touch.

'On the contrary,' he said, with a quirky smile. 'I like it too much. When my wife left me, I was very depressed for a while and thought I could find a solution to my troubles at the bottom of a bottle. I was turning into a drunk, till I took a long hard look in the mirror one day. What I saw shocked me into going on the wagon.'

'That took guts.' She was gradually unravelling his past, wanting to know more. 'And you never had another partner?'

'Nothing serious. One night stands. Typical single male stuff. I didn't want to go through the mill again. Besides which, I haven't met anyone who appeals, until now.'

This was getting out of hand. 'Look here, Dan,' she began. 'You're my self-appointed bodyguard, that's all.'

'Say again?' he queried, teasing her. 'Like the Kevin Costner film?'

'You know very well what I mean,' she snapped and stood up, pushing back her chair.

He rose, too. Somehow, they were standing close together, and she caught the smell of him. His face became sombre, mouth hardening, and he suddenly reached down and slid a hand into the front of her sarong. She gasped as his fingers landed unerringly on her pussy, parted the lips, and cruised along the damp cleft. She tried to pull back, but his other hand clamped across her lower back, hauling her against his rigid cock. He slipped a finger into her, then another, rotating them, going deeper, and her lower mouth sucked them in.

Her blood rushed and her skin prickled, and she couldn't help writhing against those artful fingers. 'Hmm, you like that? I told you we'd take it slow,' he murmured and then bent to kiss her.

His lips were hard at first, but they softened as hers did, his tongue tasting her, first the outer corners of her mouth, then the cushiony centre. She sighed, leaning into him, as his fingers stroked her clit and his kiss deepened, his tongue exploring every part – her teeth, her gums, her palate.

She went limp, wanting to do it now, on the ground, among the flowers cascading from baskets and terracotta urns. There was something primitive and uninhibited about screwing in the open air. An element of danger added an extra buzz: Terry might come striding round the corner at any moment; he was always making up excuses to call in, and Scott may not have taken her brush-off seriously.

'Go on, make me come,' she begged, lifting one of her legs free of the sarong and wrapping it round his thigh. She gyrated her hips, the pressure against her bare quim making her clit throb.

'Not here,' he said. 'You're worth more than a knee-trembler. We're going upstairs.'

The bedroom was like something out of *Homes and Gardens*. Dan, even though his hard-on was making it difficult to walk, couldn't help staring round him.

Fuck! he thought, the guys down the nick were right. She must be getting on for being a millionairess. Only someone rich could afford a proper conservatory built on an upstairs balcony.

'Lucky sod,' they'd said in the canteen. 'You always were a jammy bugger, Holland. How come you get this job while we're dealing with drunk drivers and spotty oiks beating up old age pensioners and giving us GBH of the earhole?'

Dan had shrugged and raised his wide shoulders. 'Put it down to my good looks and charm,' he quipped. 'I'm obviously the right man for Miss Maddox.'

He hadn't given it much thought, till he'd walked into the kitchen and seen her. In a blinding flash, he'd realised why she had caused such a furore on the box. That moment was his Road to Damascus. This woman was beautiful, but it wasn't only that: there were many with more perfect features and better figures, but there was something about her, coupled with the sudden chemistry that had flashed between them.

He hadn't betrayed it, not at first. He had a job to do and was a stickler for duty, though considered to be something of a maverick among his superior officers. But once they were alone, his desire had fired, powered not only by lust but by admiration. She was a cool customer and honest with it. She saw no reason to lie, was maybe too outspoken for her own good.

He no longer distrusted her. She'd given him the tapes when he went to shower, and he'd carefully studied the photo and its message. He didn't like it. In his book, men who stalked and terrorised women were the lowest things that crawled. But, mulling over the evidence, he still had the sneaking feeling that she was holding something back.

She had stumbled on her skirt as he propelled her up the wide, curving staircase and his arm had come round her, pulling her into his side, never getting enough of her pliant body that fitted so well against his. The house amazed him, as did the extensive grounds. A massive hall, with the stairs rearing up gracefully, the light falling in rainbow shards from the central dome. Marble statues in alcoves; landscapes in gilded frames; wall-brackets holding lamps with crystal drops, and long sash windows, each offering a breathtaking view of the garden.

They had reached her bedroom and he kicked the door shut with his bare foot. He kissed her again, exploring the softness of her mouth. He was rewarded by a tremor that passed through her body, and her fingers burrowed into his hair, holding him close. He was extremely aroused, his cock pressing urgently against her belly. Now she clung to his shoulders and surrendered, letting him use her mouth as he willed. He wanted more, releasing her, and undoing the knot that held her sarong in place. It slithered down between them, forming a multi-coloured puddle at her feet.

His cock jumped and his hands formed cups for each high, golden-brown breast, his thumbs grazing the corona round the nipples, darkened by the sun, crimped by passion. She looked down, her breathing shallow as she watched the circular motion, her ribs lifted, her teats straining for more fondling.

The heat was lessening, a breeze stirring the wind-chimes hanging at one of the open windows. But Dan was getting hotter; his cock was iron-hard and his balls

119

tense. He wanted Rosemary as he'd never wanted a woman before. Her breasts felt soft and warm and the scent rising up from her betrayed her desire. He could smell it on his fingers, that strong, unmistakable odour which tells a man when the woman is receptive.

'That's not fair,' she murmured, and writhed against his hidden cock. 'You've seen everything I have, but shown me nothing of yours.'

'You want to see it?' he teased, spreading his fingers and rubbing the front of his jeans.

He watched as her eyes opened wide in anticipation. Then he unbuckled his belt and slowly slipped each metal button through its hole. He had deliberately left off his jockey shorts, and as the gap extended, he lifted out his cock. She made a small, helpless sound. He knew he was big, was proud of being well-hung, and he pushed down his trousers, untangling his feet. Now he was as naked as she, and, unable to control her hands, she touched his solid erection, the feel of her fingers making the thick, meaty stem arch up from his heavy balls.

Its colour deepened to rusty-red, and it stood clear from his thick thatch of dark hair, curving like a scimitar. The mushroom-shaped helm was substantial, a dribble of pre-come inching down from the slit. He held it, wanking it with firm precision. He wanted to make it even bigger, wanted to plunge it into her mouth, then her cunt, a warm tight place that would help him forget the irritations of daily life, to lose all his problems as if nothing else mattered.

She dropped to her knees and took him in her mouth, her lips sliding up his shaft, her tongue lapping under his cock-head, pleasure sweeping through him in waves. What he found most exciting was staring into her green eyes as she looked up at him. He held the back of her head and pistoned with his hips, hearing her choke as the engorged helm butted the back of her throat.

'I'm too big for you?' he asked.

She withdrew, shook her head and smiled. 'No, but I'd like to feel it inside me.'

Then they were on the mahogany, canopied bed, fully six feet wide and longer than average. It was draped with muslin, and had a handmade crocheted bedspread. He lay on his back and Rosemary flung herself on him, her breasts pressing against his chest, fingers working his nipples, her mouth, too, leaving his skin wet and sending shockwaves to his eager cock.

She left him for a moment, leaning over to the bedside cabinet. Upright now, he heard the packet tear and watched as she nimbly covered his cock with the flesh-coloured protective.

'How big you are,' she said, and her eyes smouldered. 'The rubber only just fits.'

Then she was up and over him, riding his face, filling his nostrils with her smell and his mouth with her cunt. She sat back, and her breasts jiggled above him. She leaned her hands each side of his head, arms straight, taking her weight. Buried in her heat, he licked and sucked, his tongue massaging her hungry little organ. He heard her shrill cry as she reached orgasm, felt the clit throb against his lips, then she slid away, as if unable to endure another second of pleasure.

He ran his tongue round his mouth, tasting the salt-sweet essence of her. She had not left him, merely wriggled down, agile as a kitten. She spread her thighs and straddled his torso. His eyes met hers as she poised tantalisingly over his cock-head. He jerked his pelvis, and felt her hand guiding him. He pushed with his cock, her cunt parting to receive him. She bore down, and he slid in deeper till he was fully sheathed, his black pubes mingling with hers, his cock base driving against her clit. Gripping her round the bottom, he plunged on, chasing his orgasm, and she grunted and jerked, her rhythm matching his, bumping up and down, her head flung back and her eyes closed.

They rolled over with Rosemary on her back, her legs high. He put her ankles on his shoulders and lunged. He had to have it, focused on nothing else but the imperative driving him. Now he had reached the point of no return.

The ecstasy increased. He was being consumed by fire. He was coming in long, slow jerks, the semen pumping out from him.

She sighed, and when he looked down at her, she was smiling. Lowering her legs, she eased out from under him, but did not move away, cuddled by his side. They didn't speak, and afterwards he shifted so that he could put his arms around her and cradled her head on his shoulder. It was like holding a precious child in his arms, or a wife of long standing. Her breathing became even and he was satisfied. This signified that she trusted him, was able to go to sleep in his arms.

All his years of training in the force, pounding the beat in uniform, then going into the local crime squad under the supervision of a CID officer, now seemed to be paying off. He'd had serious doubts, had even considered taking the sergeants' exam and giving up plain-clothes work, exciting though it could sometimes be, but Rosemary had changed all that. If he hadn't been a detective, the chances of them ever meeting would have been remote, and though women were attracted to policemen as a rule and there was never a shortage of them, she was exceptional.

He had as yet no plan how to go about it, but was determined that having found her, he'd never let her go. He buried his face in her hair and breathed in her wonderful odour and his limp cock stirred, rising to press against her thigh, and he was ready to penetrate her again. He grinned to himself, hoping she had a stock of condoms in store. If not, he'd have to go shopping PDQ.

It was waiting for Rosemary when she eventually came downstairs. Breakfast in bed with Dan had proved to be delightful – sexy and delaying. He had seemed amused by the variety of rubbers she kept in readiness, wanting to spend the day trying them out, and she had given her new underwear an airing.

On waking, she had been immediately aware of two

things: Dan was sleeping at her side, and the telephone had remained silent. Had the mysterious caller decided to cry off? Was he aware that she'd reported him to the police? Or, and this gave her an animal sense of being hunted, did he somehow know Dan had spent the night in her bed? It was hard to believe he had surrendered. What was he planning next?

'Parcel for you. It was left on the back doorstep,' Fran said, casting her a look of disapproval.

Oh, dear. I haven't been forgiven, Rosemary thought, saying, 'Thanks. Did you have a good time with Craig?'

Fran sniffed. 'It was OK. And you? Did the pig stay?'

'He did, and please don't call him that. His name's Dan.'

'He's still part of the Bill.'

Rosemary didn't feel like arguing. She was in far too contented a frame of mind, tingling as she caught the scent of Dan clinging to her, although she'd showered with perfumed gel. She took the package, which consisted of a light, oblong box. She carried it into the lounge, a grand, thirty-foot-long room where once she and Terry had entertained. Fran had been filling the vases with flowers.

I'm being unkind to her and she really is a gem, Rosemary thought guiltily. And I'm neglecting Robert. He looked quite shocked when I ordered breakfast for two. I used to confide in him, but no more.

'What's that?' Dan asked, coming in through the french windows. He'd been patrolling the grounds.

'It arrived this morning. It's addressed to me,' Rosemary said.

He was at her side in a couple of strides. 'Be careful. It could have a timing device,' he warned, and took it from her gingerly. 'I think the best thing to do with this is drop it in the pool.'

'But whatever is in it will be ruined,' she protested.

'Either that, or I call in the bomb squad.'

'How ridiculous! All right, dunk it, if you must.'

Taking it up, he moved at a run, and Rosemary tried

123

to keep up with him, the situation seeming more and more bizarre. What's happening to my life? she wailed inside herself.

The garden sparkled with dew, misted with that slight haze that promised another hot day. Dan reached the pool and dropped the parcel into the deep end. It sank in a cloud of bubbles. Rosemary leaned over, looking down at what was now a faint smudge in the blue depths.

'Oh, dear,' she said sadly. 'It might have been a present. Now I shall never know.'

'Yes, you will,' he answered crisply, his warm smile dragging pleasure sensors along her nerves. 'Give it half an hour, and I'll fish it out for you. It should be perfectly safe by then. Amateur devices rarely stand up to water. Trust me. I know about these things.'

They went indoors and drank coffee and she was wondering if they had time to go upstairs for a repeat of their dawn performance, when he put down his cup and said, 'Let's get it out.'

'Are you sure it's safe?' She was jittery, no longer doubting that he knew what he was talking about.

'We'll soon see. You stay here, just in case.'

She opened her mouth to argue but he put his hand over it, then kissed her, and went out into the sunshine. Rosemary was on tenterhooks, dying to look out of the windows, but he was right. There might yet be an explosion. The moments dragged by and nothing happened. Then she saw him coming towards the house, carrying an extremely soggy parcel.

'Is it all right?' she cried, and went out, pausing when he laid it on the teak table.

'The wrapping paper's disintegrating and the Sellotape's a mess. Apart from that . . . take a look.'

Beneath paper which tore at the touch, Rosemary found a cardboard box, protected by a plastic bag and sealed with more sticky tape. Dan produced a pocket knife, slitting it open for her. She lifted the lid. More plastic, but inside this the contents were unharmed.

'What is it?' she exclaimed, and drew the object out. She gasped with surprise.

'I kind of thought it was Christmas last night. Least ways, that's how it seemed to me,' Dan said suggestively, trawling a pack of cigarettes from the breast-pocket of his denim shirt. 'Or maybe your birthday. Someone has given you a doll.'

Rosemary's fingers tingled and she came out in goose-pimples. It was a doll all right, a very beautiful doll, about fifteen inches tall and dressed in a black robe sparkling with sequins. But when she looked closely at the face, her heart missed a beat, then raced on again. She almost flung the thing down.

'It's me!' she cried. 'Look, it's just like me, and that's my hair!'

'So it is,' Dan said, frowning as he took the doll from her and examined it carefully. 'I wonder who made it. Is there a letter in the box?'

Rosemary searched, then said, 'No. Nothing.'

Dan, meanwhile, had peeled off the doll's silk robe. 'Look at this. But at least it hasn't got pins sticking in it. I don't think the sender is ill-wishing you.'

Rosemary stared, her slow wits taking time to register what her retina related.

The doll was wearing an exact replica of the torn clothing belonging to the statuette in the photograph – a girl of the Roaring Twenties, wielding a riding whip.

'But she's like me,' Rosemary repeated, icy cold yet filled with an erotic charge.

'She is, and it seems to me she's into bondage. You've got yourself a weird admirer somewhere, Miss Maddox,' said Dan reflectively.

Chapter Seven

'*I*'ll have to report it. Inspector Warren takes this sort of harassment very seriously,' Dan said, laying the doll down on the table.

'No,' Rosemary replied, still shaken by its arrival. It should have been pleasant, even beautiful and collectable, but she found its painted stare sinister. It was like looking in the mirror on an off-day. 'I don't want to discuss it with anyone. Not Fran, or Scott, or the people I work with. No one, only you.'

'But it's risky. The person who sent it, and I can only assume it was the same man who made the calls and mailed you the photograph, may be a harmless crank, or a dangerous pervert. I'll be demoted if Warren finds out. He'll have me back in uniform pronto.'

'He won't find out, if we both keep shtoom.' Her voice was steady, as if the incident hadn't reduced her to jelly. It proves I'm a trouper. The show must go on, no matter what. But this self-congratulation offered scant comfort. 'What shall I do with it?' she asked, glancing round the room nervously. Her first reaction was to throw it out with the garbage or stuff it into the back of a cupboard.

'You'd better look after it, tend it like a baby,' he advised, and he was serious.

'Why?' She was becoming increasingly uneasy.

'I said who sent it didn't wish you harm, but if it's anything like a mommet – a voodoo doll – then you may as well take precautions, and one of them is to care for it.'

'You don't believe in that mumbo-jumbo, surely?' she scoffed, though icy fingers crawled down her spine. 'You're a hard-bitten cop who's afraid of nothing, aren't you?'

'I've seen some strange things during the course of my duties – particularly among some ethnic communities. Voodoo's a religion created from Catholicism and the beliefs of Africa, in the days when the slave ships brought their human cargoes to the West Indies. The science of the jungle, if you like.'

'But didn't witches use waxen images to hex their victims here and all over Europe in the olden days?' She shivered and rubbed her hands along her bare arms, her flesh chilled even though the morning was warm.

'Perfectly correct, and they probably still do. "By the pricking of my thumbs, something wicked this way comes,"' he quoted, and she couldn't tell if he was serious or just winding her up.

This is crazy, she thought, trying to be rational. I've spent the night with this man, enjoyed the most satisfying sex, and here we are, standing in this sunny room on a midsummer morning discussing black magic.

'Well, I'm a sceptic,' she vowed. 'It would take a lot to convince me.'

'Is that right?' He sounded as if he didn't believe a word. 'I think your doll is harmless, apart from the fact that someone has concentrated powerful energy in its construction. It looks craftsman-made to me.'

'It's horrible. I feel like throwing it on a bonfire,' she shuddered.

'I shouldn't do that.'

'Why not?'

'Well, it rather depends on how much you believe in it. I've seen big-built, iron-pumping guys reduced to a pulp if they think someone has put a spell on them. Auto-suggestion can be a killer.'

'So, I damage the doll and something horrible will happen to me.'

'I'm not saying for sure, just telling you what I know about these things.'

'I still think it's bollocks!' she shouted defiantly, but a bottomless pit seemed to be yawning at her feet.

The phone rang and she jumped violently.

'Shall I get it?' Dan said.

Rosemary was already there, snatching it up. A heart-warmingly familiar voice spoke into her ear. 'Hello, darling. It's Michael. I've called a meeting for noon today. Can you make it? It's important.'

'Yes, I can. What's this about?' She was so relieved to hear him that she would have agreed to swim the Channel if he'd asked her. For the first time in years she wanted to see her father, wanted to cry and say, 'Daddy, I'm frightened.' She'd always recognised that she almost looked on Michael as a parent. Most of the team did. He took charge of them and, grouse though they might, they carried out his orders.

'The next show,' he answered crisply, the director not the lover at that moment. 'I think you'll find it intriguing. Melanie will be there casting her beady eye over the contract, and Wesley Brown.'

'Why him?'

'Because Jonathan Flynn is involved.'

'Again? You're turning us into a double act,' she answered crossly, professionally jealous of that tawny-headed Adonis: angelic, demonic, with the instincts of a predator.

She would never forget the warm, wet feel of the creamy libation he had shot over her face and breasts. Many a besotted fan would have died for the privilege, but she had been thankful for the Jacuzzi, dunking herself under the bubbly, cleansing water. Even so, and despite all her misgivings, the idea of meeting him again, sparring with him, testing her wits and skill against him and possibly entering his sexual fun-house, made her pussy tighten.

'I'll be there,' she promised. 'Where are we meeting?'

'In the Ace Productions office. Then I thought we might have a spot of lunch somewhere. What d'you say?'

Rosemary looked across at Dan. He was lounging on one of the deeply cushioned sofas. A part of her wanted him to return that night, to keep her safe and make her horny. Her thighs relaxed as she recalled the delirious sensation of his fingers sliding smoothly into her. But the other, career-oriented part, urged her to meet Michael and further her ambitions.

'Can't you give me a few details?' she asked.

He chuckled in that confident way which made her nipples rise through the peep-holes in her red satin bra. 'No, Rosie, you'll have to wait. Rest assured that you'll like the new proposal. It's a challenge. I'll say no more. Goodbye, darling, see you at twelve.'

'I've a business meeting,' she said to Dan as she replaced the phone.

'You want me to come with you?' he offered. 'I still have half a day's leave.'

He stood up and held out his arms and she went into them, his big hand stroking her shoulders. She felt safe there and wondered why she had doubted him yesterday. He was wearing baggy combat trousers, the drab olive repeated in his bush jacket. A man of action, ready to fight or fuck. His mouth fascinated her, the lower lip full and sensual, the upper curling as if impatient with anything that smacked of incompetence.

She looked up and met his gaze. His steel-grey eyes pierced her to the soul, and penetrated parts of her body that only his sex should reach. Hard eyes, self-willed and fierce. He would never give up on a project, hanging on in there till he turned it around his way.

'There's no need,' she said, her eyes fixed on his face – that mouth, that stubble which was no affectation but a way of life. He looked like the bad boy hero of a violent, blood-thirsty movie which the board of censors would quibble about putting on release to the general public.

'Are you sure? I'll go back to HQ, see Warren and tackle a couple of other jobs. Yours isn't my only case. I've a grass to meet. I pay him for info. I may not be able to spend tonight here,' he said, but didn't move.

'That's all right. I don't have to come home. I can stay with Michael.'

'He's one of your lovers,' he said flatly, his fingers digging into her spine.

'He's my director. Anyway, I've another friend who'll put me up, if I want. My agent, Melanie Hart.'

'That might be your best bet. Michael Pendelton is a suspect, isn't he?'

'Not really. Not Michael. I can't see him stooping so low.'

'You never can tell,' he said, then his expression changed and he added, 'Any chance of a quickie before we go?'

Her pussy contracted. She was wet for him. Pressing her breasts to the flat wall of his chest, his shirt and her crop-top chafing her hard nipples almost painfully, she teased him lightly, 'I thought you didn't do quickies.'

'Try me,' he answered, grinning broadly. 'I'll do anything with you, lady, at any time.'

He turned her till she was facing the back of the sofa. Her hair was caught up by tortoiseshell clips for coolness, and his lips caressed the nape of her neck, then circled one ear lobe, setting the jewelled drop swinging. She shivered and arched her neck, pressing against him. She could feel his hard prick nudging her buttocks, and parted her legs for better access. His hands came round to reach her breasts, stroking the undersides, then lifting her top. His thumbs contacted her erect nipples through the bra slits.

'Jesus!' he hissed, and his cock jumped against her hip. 'Bend over for me.'

Rosemary flopped across the sofa-back, bent from the waist, knees locked, thighs apart, her bottom rearing high. He moved in closer, and she heard the rasp of metal as his zipper slid down. She wanted to turn her head and watch his cock escape from his trousers, but his free hand was still exciting her nipples, pleasure rushing through her. She reached round, blindly searching with her fingers, finding the open fly, the thickness of his shaft, the crispness of his pubic hair and the heaviness of his balls.

'Be still,' he warned. 'Or this will be over before we've begun.'

His hands groped between her body and the sofa. He rucked up her skirt and dipped a finger into the open crotch of her panties. She spread her legs, imagining her lips protruding lewdly through the red gash and Dan's finger tangling with the lace edging. Her clit felt twice its normal size, a straining miniature penis that throbbed as he massaged round the swollen head, down the stalk and up again. She groaned and bucked as she neared her climax, and cried out when he tipped her into bliss.

He tugged her panties down around her knees and she pushed upwards as he eased his rigid helm into her. Draped over the settee, she was in the perfect position to take all of him, and he slid into her till buried to the hilt. Now he braced himself, upright, hands gripping her hipbones, the iron muscles of his thighs powering his pelvis in and out. Rosemary was buffeted by the storm of his passion, though the solid Chesterfield didn't as much as judder.

He felt so big inside her, and her muscles expanded to sheath him. He growled, pumped faster, made sounds of pleasure and she knew when he came, though he continued to move, but slower. It was then that she thought about a condom, cursing herself for her carelessness. However, when he had withdrawn and she was retrieving her panties, she saw him rolling one down his softened cock.

'When did you put that on?' she asked, admiring his organ. Even relaxed it was still formidable.

He smiled the satisfied smile of a man who has just

had a woman. 'You were too busy to notice,' he quipped. 'Just as well I'm around to look after you.'

'Just as well,' she agreed, catching sight of the doll again.

She had the eerie feeling that it was watching them.

Michael wasn't there when Rosemary arrived at Ace Productions.

Like similar organisations that provided material for the TV channels, its office was at the top of a tall terraced house in a narrow lane off the city's theatrical heartland. Whatever the company made, and she assumed it to be a significant sum, they certainly didn't squander it on decor. She wished Dan had come after all, but having followed his shabby van through a network of back-streets to avoid the traffic, she had lost him as he disappeared in the direction of the police station.

The senior crew-members, wearing jeans, shirts or vests, lounged around the boardroom table, smoking, drinking coffee and exchanging gossip. Melanie signalled to her, already ensconced, with Wesley on one side and Jonathan on the other. She was pristine in white. Her make-up was perfect, every hair in place, her eyes screened by glasses that were a fashion accessory rather than a protection from the sun.

'Morning all,' Rosemary said and occupied a chair at the wide table. It was dark with age and had probably been used for similar purposes for a hundred years or more. 'What's all this about? Does anyone know?'

Jonathan flexed his thin hands, then thrust them through his artfully rumpled hair, contrived to make him look as if he had just got out of bed. This image conjured a dozen stimulating computations.

'Michael's being his usual controlling self,' he opined, stifling a yawn. 'He must get a kick out of it, but I should have thought he'd have mentioned it to you, my sweet. Aren't you two as thick as thieves?'

Before she had time to voice a suitable retort, Michael swept in, accompanied by Helen Douglas from research, who was a pale, intense young woman, and his secretary, Mary Piper, super-efficient and dedicated to shielding him from life's petty irritations. She strode behind him, wearing a trouser suit in caramel linen and, like Helen, she carried a clutch of papers.

'Here we are then, boys and girls,' he began, and the very air seemed to crackle. Everyone sat up; cigarettes were extinguished and coffee cups pushed out of the way. Only Jonathan remained languid and unimpressed.

Michael took a chair next to Rosemary, and she almost forgot about Dan. He eclipsed every other man by his sheer size and personality. He was casually dressed, but rivalling Jonathan in expensive clobber. His lightweight cotton and silk suit had been made by a top designer. His shirt wasn't high-street chain store, neither were his leather Milanese loafers, which he chose to wear without socks. He had acquired a deep tan, no doubt on his boat, and his stints at the gym had paid off.

He cast an eye round his assembled team, leaned back in his chair, and said, 'As you know, we're often approached by private individuals with requests to send in our experts to improve their gardens. This has become a popular feature of our programmes. I had a couple in mind to do next, but then this arrived. Mary?' He held out a hand imperiously and she hurriedly pushed some correspondence across the table.

'Here you are, Mr Pendelton,' she said breathily. He had that effect on his entourage.

Michael rifled through and drew out a sheet. 'It's a fax from someone called Anthony Selby. He suggests that we film at his country estate. He claims to have a two-hundred-year-old hedge maze that wants sorting. He's sent photos of it. Have a look, Rosemary.'

She glanced at the pictures. The house was impressive, timbered and turreted, possibly Tudor in part. The maze had been snapped from several angles. It was huge and overgrown and high. She experienced a creepy feeling. She never had liked mazes much, preferring to know where she was going and what lay at the end. But other shots of the garden showed it to be a magnificent jungle, and her fingers itched to tame it, but only a little: its very wildness was part of its charm.

'You want to do it?' she asked Michael, handing back the material.

'I do. What a challenge for you and the team. Mazes are in vogue at the moment.'

'Where do I fit in?' Jonathan asked, casting his eye over the photos. 'I don't want to appear as Rosemary's drudge.'

'No fear of that, dear boy,' Michael beamed, his smile encompassing Wesley who was leaning forward, alert to his client's interests. 'There's a dilapidated orangery, apparently. Look, you can see it there at the back of the house. Mr Selby gives you *carte-blanche* to spend as much as you like on it. He'll want to see your sketches of suggested innovations, naturally, but once you get his approval, and I'm certain you will, then it's full steam ahead.'

'Who is this man?' Rosemary asked. 'Is he genuine?'

She hoped he was. This job was a godsend, the chance to get out of London she so desperately needed and, as Michael had so rightly said, a challenge she could hardly refuse. Such a romantic setting would rouse the viewers to an even greater frenzy of enthusiasm.

'Helen?' Michael nodded in the pale woman's direction. 'You've already run research on him, haven't you?'

'Yes, Mr Pendelton.'

'And what have you found out?'

Helen cleared her throat, adjusted her gold-framed spectacles and started to read. '"Anthony Selby has recently inherited Malvern Chase which has been in his family for generations. He shouldn't have done, by rights, because he was a long way down the line, but a series of freak accidents and a totally unexpected case of coronary thrombosis left him the sole surviving heir."'

'Some people have all the luck,' Jonathan commented, quizzing the photographs.

'Yes, indeed,' said Michael, watching the reaction of

his team closely. Rosemary could see he had already made up his mind.

'Is he young or old? Married, or does he live there alone?' Her curiosity was piqued, and she was always inspired by age-old gardens, with their well-established plants, sun-warmed walls, and orchards heavy with fruit.

'He's nearly forty,' Helen continued, the centre of attention for once, suddenly richly rewarded for those long hours spent ferreting through the backgrounds of prospective candidates for *In Your Own Backyard*. She had the nose of a Miss Marple, and never let go of a scent. Malvern Chase and its master were grist to the prying person's mill. 'He's not married and has spent most of his life abroad. He lives with his cousin, Carol Selby. Well, not exactly lives with her: they share the house. They keep themselves to themselves and don't socialise much.'

'Thank you, Helen,' Michael said, then turned to Rosemary. 'What about it? Will you suss it out?'

'I can do, but why me?' she asked. 'Can't Jonathan go?'

'I'm filming, duckie. Shan't be free for a week at least. Isn't that so, Wesley?' he answered, turning to his agent who nodded in agreement.

Michael leaned towards Rosemary, saying in that persuasive way of his, 'Selby says he particularly wants you to go initially. He trusts your judgement and respects your know-how. I shall follow when you've reported your findings.'

'Don't you usually send Helen first?' She got up and moved to the window which looked out on uneven tiled roofs, where grey, manky-looking pigeons strutted on their turned-in toes. Humid, smelly, dirty old town, with its heavily polluted air. A stay in the country sounded nothing short of heavenly.

'It seems to me, darling, that Anthony Selby is a very unusual man,' Jonathan put in. 'One of the great English eccentrics, I shouldn't wonder.'

'I think we should humour him,' added Michael. 'It'll make a stunning programme.'

'All right. When do I leave?' Rosemary said, spinning round and smiling at him. 'And can I take someone with me?'

'Naturally. Who d'you have in mind?'

'Scott,' she answered promptly. If she couldn't have Dan, then her stalwart young lover would do. On a practical level, she would need his assistance, already impressed by his botanical savvy.

'There are things to discuss before she goes,' Melanie reminded, sun-glasses pushed up to her forehead, eyes bright. 'The little matter of her contract, additional expenses, blah-di-blah.'

Rosemary sat down again, and Michael humoured Melanie. 'But of course. You're always so right. Wesley will want to talk about Jonathan's, too, I don't doubt, and I need to see the production manager. Are we all agreed that our next programme will be filmed at Malvern Chase?'

There was a unanimous show of hands, and Rosemary relaxed, delighted at the prospect of time away from Plants Galore, with its disturbing phone calls, packages and parcels. Even a break from the men in her life sounded ideal, particularly those she could no longer trust. As for Dan, she had the strong feeling that he would wait for her, a back-up whenever she needed him. Scott would be in the Seventh Heaven when she told him he was included on her trip. He would act as guard, aide and lover. She was looking forward to it, feeling as if a weight had been lifted from her shoulders.

'Trying to leave the house is like trying to escape from prison,' Rosemary grumbled. There were so many loose ends to tie up so that Fran could keep the wheels of industry turning, and Robert look after the general domestic management.

Not that either of them needed much instruction. Fran was the best possible secretary, and Robert the perfect housekeeper. On the morning she was due to leave, she had a last confab with them in the kitchen.

'Don't you worry about a thing, Miss Maddox,' Robert assured her. He was a small, dapper person of thirty-something, neat to the point of fussiness. The house had never been so spruce, the shopping so well organised or the meals cooked to such perfection until he arrived.

'I have absolute confidence in you, Robert,' she replied, sipping her last cup of coffee before setting out.

'I shall spring-clean,' he averred, so pretty that he should have been in cabaret, not taking on the running of a large establishment like Sutton Close. 'It's a little late, but no matter. There's a lot to clear out now that Mr Veney's gone.' The way he pronounced Terry's name left her in no doubt as to where his loyalties lay. It was heartening to know that Fran and he were on her side.

'OK, Fran?' she asked, making a mental note to raise both their salaries.

'Yes, leave the fanmail to me from now on. No more nasty parcels arriving to annoy you,' Fran replied with the enviable zest of youth. 'Will it be all right if I have Craig over sometime?'

'Of course, and don't hesitate to invite Carl, will you, Robert?' Rosemary said. Carl was his latest boyfriend. 'Feel free to use the pool. I shall be in touch by phone. Oh, and whatever you do, be careful if Mr Veney comes into the house. The solicitors say he's not to remove anything.'

'We will,' they chorused.

Scott walked in at the door, so bronzed and fit that Rosemary wondered how she'd be able to wait till they reached their first stop on the way. It would take them at least three hours to reach Waverney, the nearest village to Malvern Chase. She hadn't had him for what seemed ages and her pussy yearned hungrily. He picked up her suitcase and she kept hold of her hand luggage. The sun beat down on the yard as they went towards the car, and the morning sparkled. Rosemary's spirits rose. Even having to say goodbye to Dan no longer seemed so bad. He'd been with her for several nights, rousing a ferment of curiosity and envy in Robert, though Fran was still cool towards him. Craig, whose activities teetered on the edge of lawlessness, had taught her to distrust the police.

Rosemary had confided in Melanie over a bottle of wine when they'd spent a giggly, girlish night in her North London house after the meeting and lunch with Michael. He'd been rather put out, assuming she was going to stay with him on the *Daisy May*.

Melanie had gone all serious on her when she detailed the dirty phone call in which she had taken part, the one she'd not mentioned to anyone else, and had been very curious about the photograph and the doll.

'It's all right now,' Rosemary had assured her, sipping Chardonnay and feeling relieved at having confessed to coming while on the phone to a complete stranger. 'I've this horny detective who's taking personal care of me.'

'Really? Tell me more,' Melanie had insisted, and Rosemary had boasted about Dan, even preening herself a little. Melanie had advised her to hang on to that one.

Rosemary was inclined to agree, and it seemed as though her life was steering into calmer waters. There had been no further calls. In a fit of bravura she had bought a glass showcase, placed the doll inside and put it on an occasional table in her bedroom. She could almost kid herself that she'd started a collection and this was the first exhibit. Maybe I'll do that, she thought, standing four-square in front of it, eye to eye with its green painted stare. Maybe I should be flattered. Whoever sent it must admire me. But no amount of reasoning could alter her opinion of the creature.

Forget it, she cautioned herself, as the miles glided under the Golf's wheels and they left the town, the suburbs, even the motorway behind them.

'More then half-way there.' Scott was map-reading. 'Can't we stop for lunch?'

'I need to pee,' she admitted. 'Look out for a pub, a decent, olde-worlde one. I fancy eating in a panelled room with an inglenook fireplace, but most of all I want a loo.'

She had slowed now, the road too twisty, the hedges

too high. Then it opened out and they were driving between cottages set back in gardens, and a high-street that even had a supermarket. Beyond this, where the houses thinned again, stood an inn, its sign proclaiming that it was The Bell and Crown.

Inside it was all Rosemary had wished for, and more. Beams, horse-brasses, dark furniture shiny with beeswax and elbow-grease, the sparkling clean Ladies Room fragrant with pot-pourri. They ate in the lounge bar, and the Ploughman's Lunch ordered was more than sufficient; fresh baguettes, generous wedges of Cheddar cheese, yellow butter pats and home-made pickle. Scott had a beer, and she had coffee.

'This is great,' she pronounced, stretching her legs under the table and connecting with his desert-booted ankle. 'I didn't realise how much I needed to get away. What do you think about the maze?'

'We'd better wait till we get there and take a proper look,' he said, and she saw him wince slightly as she slipped off her sandal and walked her bare toes up the inside of his thigh and towards his crotch.

There were other people lunching, but Rosemary's table was set in a corner by the window embrasure. A chintzy cloth covered it, dangling down each side. She knew that no one could see what she was doing and she pushed her foot against the swelling behind his fly, gently prodding and playing.

He flushed to the roots of his hair, but did not try to avoid her touch, though he muttered, 'Bloody hell, Rosemary, lay off.'

'You don't like it?' she teased. It was refreshing to be with him again, his boyish naiveté so different to Dan's cynicism.

'Course I like it. You know I do. But I'll come in my jeans if you don't stop.'

She smiled and tormented him a little more, her own excitement dampening the gusset of her panties. She could feel the narrow strip easing between her crack as the lips swelled. Even the smallest movement brought pressure to bear on her clit. Her ankle-length, wrap-around skirt, her low-necked sleeveless vest, the fact that she only wore a thong and no bra, all contrived to arouse her. This was the glorious sensuality of summer, when near nudity broke down barriers and thoughts turned automatically to sex.

'Then we should find somewhere,' she whispered, big toe engaging with his foreskin. She could feel its heat through the denim. 'Have you finished eating?'

She beckoned to the waiter and picked up the tab. 'Let me pay,' Scott insisted, though he couldn't rise for a moment, as he was struggling to control his erection.

'It'll go on my expense account,' she said airily, sweeping a glance over the waiter. He was young, swarthy, probably an Italian on a work-experience scheme. She liked his fawn chinos and shirt, the fat finger of cock resting against his left thigh and his tight-muscled arse. She tipped him generously. Who cared? Ace Productions were paying.

The Golf was parked at the back of the pub, in a gravelled area surrounded by a low dry-stone wall. It was punctuated by a stile, and there was a battered notice erected by the committee of works for the area. It read: Footpath. Pedestrians Only. Stony Beck Long Barrow.

Lunchtime and the place was deserted, a drowsy heat holding everything in thrall. Only bees droned lazily as they dipped into hollyhocks and garnered nectar from lupins.

'Come on,' Rosemary said, and holding up her skirt, crossed the stile.

The path zigzagged, following a gentle slope leading to higher ground. She could hear Scott behind her, but was absorbed in the luminous light; she touched the soft, feathery grasses as she passed, inhaling the heady smell of crushed foliage. And all the time she was searching for a spot where she and Scott could be private she was throbbing with the urgent need to have him enter her.

The way levelled off and then she saw the barrow,

standing like a little island above the surrounding land. It was covered in short grass, and purple red heather massed in thick clumps, and a few tapering spikes of foxgloves. She headed for it and it grew bigger as she approached, a tumulus, a burial mound built thousands of years before by an ancient race.

She scrambled up, the wind lifting her hair as she stood on the top, shouting back to Scott, 'I'm the king of the castle! Get down, you dirty rascal!'

He reached her, panting and saying, 'You're bloody mad!' and hauling her into his arms.

They fell together into the shelter of the long barrow's earthen rim. Rosemary felt the springy turf at her back, and Scott lying half over her, one leg imprisoning her thighs. She pretended to struggle, till he seized her wrists and pinioned them over her head. He swooped, his mouth capturing hers, tongue probing roughly. She had teased him long enough and wondered if this possessive show of strength had anything to do with Dan.

It didn't much matter in that hot afternoon glow, when his lips bruised hers and his tongue delved deep, her own dancing with it. He was exceptionally good at kissing. His hands uncovered her breasts, the peaks hardening as the breeze caressed them. She was desperate to feel his mouth on her neglected snatch and gripped his thigh between her own as she ground herself against it.

'You're greedy,' he growled, laughing contentedly. 'You want me to rub you? Then fill you to the limit with my cock?'

'I do,' she purred as her skirt fell open, forming a carpet for their loving. He looked down at the scrap of black tanga that inadequately covered her mound. He inserted a finger round the edge, slipped it into her crack, located her clit and rubbed the swollen bead.

'Why haven't we done it lately?' he asked, very low, pushing the slither of fabric aside and exposing her dark floss. 'Was it the wrong time of the month or have you been with someone else? Dan Holland, is it?'

'Got to keep you on your toes, boy,' she mocked gently. 'Anyway, I'm hiring him as security. No need for you to worry, my pet. No one will oust you from my affections. Don't talk any more. Make me come.'

He undid his zip and his cock curled out, large and stiff, its single eye seeming to stare at her. She folded her fist round it, thumb rotating on the slit, easing the pre-come around it, making it slick-wet. Scott breathed hard and tore at the ribbon ties of her tanga. He dragged it off, the strip of material jarring into her slit, the friction rousing her painfully.

Scott had released her wrists and now he eased down, concentrating on the area between her legs. She spread them wide, and he parted her shining, sticky lips and massaged her clit. Moaning, Rosemary thrust upwards to meet his touch, seeking his mouth instead of his fingers. His breath tickled and roused her as he lowered his head to where she wanted it most.

'Ah,' she sighed, as his tongue lapped at her, sucking and teasing, flicking and nibbling. 'Ah,' she moaned again, as her eyes opened, seeing his closely cropped hair, like velvet or suede and, beyond that, the vast white-blue, hot sky, without a speck of cloud.

She wanted to make it last, but Scott took control, rubbing her fiercely till she came in a welter of physical sensation completely divorced from emotion.

He sat up and unlaced his desert boots, then wriggled out of his jeans. His T-shirt ended just below his navel, his cock curving aggressively from the forest of hair coating his underbelly. It seemed larger, ruder, more ugly than if he'd been completely naked, his big balls tight in the scrotal sac. Rosemary touched them, holding them in her hands as he kneeled above her. She was wet; she was satisfied, but he deserved as good as she could give in return.

Once she'd covered his cock in one of his favourite black rubbers, he pushed against her with his unwieldy weapon and she hooked her legs round his waist and took it. His bottom tensed, then relaxed, and she ran her hands over the smoothness of his skin, and dived her fingers into his crack, tormenting the dry puckered mouth of his anus. He groaned, moving his prick in circles, then backwards and forwards. He was breathing hard, sweat dripping from his chin as his movements became faster and faster. She relaxed completely, letting him enter as far as he was able. Now the base of his cock was touching her clit, but not regularly enough to bring her off. She worked her hand down there, her finger giving her the contact she craved.

He was beyond the point of no return – his breathing ragged, his heart thudding. His excitement communicated itself to her and her busy finger and she came again. Then, with a strangled cry, he let go, pumping and jerking and shooting spunk.

They came out of it in a leisurely way, lying flat on their backs and looking at the sky where larks vibrated so high that their song was inaudible.

'Is it true that they fuck on the wing?' Scott asked idly, hands locked behind his head.

'I don't know,' she said, and wondered if she had brought with her the CD of the Vaughn Williams tone poem for orchestra, *The Lark Ascending*. She'd indulged Scott so far, playing what he wanted to hear, but now it was her turn. He'd have to put up with it if he was bored. Not like Dan or even Jonathan, who shared her taste. 'Time to go,' she said, getting up and searching for her panties. 'I want to be there before the sun goes down. Hate trying to find places in the dark.'

She needn't have worried. The clock in the square tower of the Norman church was chiming four when they reached Waverney's market square. A pause for a cup of tea in a picturesque café, a quick look at the map, and then they were heading towards Malvern Chase.

It was a lonely stretch of road and, in a short while, Rosemary braked at a turning to the left. She saw a lodge house and a pair of wrought-iron gates and high stone walls. These stretched into the distance, broken glass set in concrete glittering ominously all along the copings.

There was a notice, too, which read: 'KEEP OUT. Trespassers Will Be Prosecuted'.

The gates were supported by pillars. Each was surmounted by a griffin, squatting on its hind quarters with a shield between its front paws. She didn't much care for their snarling lips and the suspicious look in their eyes. Spanning the gateway was an arch with a name carved in the stone in Gothic lettering: 'Malvern Chase'.

'Hello!' she shouted, approaching the lodge window. 'Is anyone there? I'm Rosemary Maddox from Ace Productions and I'm expected.'

No one replied, but with a grating sound, the gates slowly opened. Rosemary got into the car hurriedly, before anyone changed their minds, and drove through the gap. A glance in the rear mirror showed that they were closing again, and she experienced a thrill that wasn't entirely physical. She felt that she was entering an enchanted world where anything was possible.

Ahead lay a tarmacked road running through an avenue of beeches. It was hedged by a dazzling display of rhododendrons with leathery leaves and showy, pink or blue flowers.

'Wicked!' Scott enthused, his tanned forearm resting on the edge on the open window. 'This is super, Rosemary. I can't wait to see the rest.'

The beeches and bushes thinned out and lawns came into view, shaded by monkey-puzzle trees and Spanish chestnuts. Then they rounded a bend and, abruptly, Malvern Chase appeared. Rosemary slowed to a crawl, filling her eyes and mind with the scene. She had looked at the photographs and knew what to expect, but actually seeing it was something else.

It was built of dark-red brick and its frontage was timber-framed in black and white. The mullioned windows had diamond panes, gargoyles grimaced from the gutterings, the chimney-pots were twisted like barley-sugar and the stonework was scrolled and carved and exuberantly finished.

'It's like something out of Disneyland,' Rosemary

commented, drawing up outside the truncated tower of the main doorway. It had nine pinnacles rising from its roof.

At once a woman appeared from under the porch. 'Miss Maddox? How lovely to see you,' she said, her voice deep and mellifluous. 'I trust you had a comfortable journey. I'm Carol Selby.'

She held out her hands as she sashayed towards Rosemary who was standing by her car, struck dumb with surprise. Rosemary hadn't formed a clear picture of what to expect, but it certainly wasn't this glamorous woman. She was very aware that, despite the use of travel tissues impregnated with lemon balm, the smell of sex still clung to her. Her face grew hot as she wondered if Carol Selby would notice it.

This would be embarrassing, for Carol seemed so much the lady of the manor, gracious and graceful. It was difficult to access her age: she could have been anywhere between thirty and forty. There wasn't a trace of artificiality to be seen in the thick blonde hair piled high and twisted into a knot. Her figure was flawless. She was slim-waisted and agile-hipped as a boy, but her breasts were full, and her nipples showed through her pastel silk slip-dress.

'So nice to meet you,' Rosemary said, recovering her voice. 'We got here with no trouble. Let me introduce my assistant, Scott Bradbury.'

Carol smiled, and Rosemary saw that Scott was bowled over. She even experienced a tiny twinge of jealousy as Carol said, 'Have you appeared on television, too, Scott?'

'Not yet, Miss Selby, but I hope to,' he said, grinning down at her.

'I'm sure you'd soon have a huge following,' Carol murmured, eyes shaded by lashes thickened with mascara. The tip of her tongue came out to moisten her coral lips. She glanced back at Rosemary, and said, 'Don't you agree, Miss Maddox?'

'I do. He's extremely talented,' she answered, while

beneath the polite chit-chat ran a deep dark skein of something that had originated in the primordial forests. 'Please call me Rosemary,' she added, as sensitive to Carol's reactions as if a top layer of skin had been flayed off.

'I will, if you'll do the same. I'm sure we're going to get on famously, and Anthony is so eager to talk to you about the maze,' Carol replied, and linking arms with both of them, she led them through the door, past a panelled screen and into the large, lofty hall. 'This is the heart of the place,' she continued, dwarfed by its size but radiating pride. 'It was built first, you see, back in the eleventh century, that's why we call the manor a Hall House. Then, later, wings were added and another storey.'

'And the maze?' Rosemary asked as she inhaled the mellow odour of dust, polish, wood-smoke and time. Generations of people had been born, lived, loved and died in Malvern Chase and had somehow left a lingering trace of themselves in the ether.

'That was constructed during alterations to the grounds made at the whim of Percy Selby when he returned from his Grand Tour of Europe in 1780. He was inspired by architecture based on the buildings of Palladio, as were so many members of the aristocracy at that period. And, of course, the gardens, too, had to be made to look Italian. Anthony will show you round it tomorrow.'

She's as cool as the proverbial cucumber, Rosemary thought. She makes me feel grubby and uneducated, a right clod-hopper. I hope her cousin is a bit less patronising or he and I are going to fall out big style.

Then every thought was wiped from her mind when a voice spoke to her. 'Miss Maddox! How wonderful! I've been waiting ages for this moment.'

She turned to meet him as he reached the bottom of the flight of wide stairs that led down into the hall. Bathed in the light from the long, stained-glass window in back of him, he seemed almost mystical.

If she'd been astounded by Carol, then she was rooted to the spot and unable to utter a word, as he came towards her, smiling a beneficent smile and saying, 'I'm Anthony Selby.'

Chapter Eight

*T*here's a moment in most people's lives that remains with them forever, and this is it for me, Rosemary thought when she looked at Anthony.

He was tall and dark and lean, a mature man of around Carol's age, with silver-streaked black hair swept back in a ponytail. An intelligent face. An arresting face. A face without softness. He was wearing a tweed hacking jacket and jodhpurs, the beige stretch material clinging to him closely, emphasising the hollows at his flanks, the taut muscles of his arse and the fullness of his crotch. His shirt was open over a sun-browned, hairy chest. He carried himself haughtily, exuding power and a subtle aura of mystery, swishing a flexible crop against his riding boot and regarding her with a sardonic smile.

Poser! Rosemary thought acidly, and switched to 'TV Personality mode', giving herself breathing space to come to terms with the flagrant masculinity of the man. 'Mr Selby, I'm impressed by your house.'

'Wait till you see the gardens,' he said, his peat-brown eyes on her face, then wandering to her breasts and back again. This disoriented her even more. 'It was woefully neglected when I came here, but I've had local people getting it into shape. It's the maze that concerns me. It has reverted to the wild and is in desperate need of control. An expert touch is required, not that of a bunch of rustics, even though they've served the Selbys for years.'

His tone was dismissive, his arrogance off-putting, but Rosemary was responding to him; there was no denying his louche sexuality. In spite of red warning lights, everything about Anthony appealed to her physically. His height, his angular face, and the impression of power he radiated were so similar to Michael's. His eyes widened when they met hers and she read desire in them and a frightening, age-old cognition.

'I can't wait to see it,' she said, then included Scott in the conversation, grasping at the straws of normality. 'This is my assistant, Scott Bradbury. Hedge mazes are his speciality.' They weren't, but it sounded impressive, and she wanted to let Anthony Selby know that she wasn't tackling the survey alone.

'Pleased to meet you, sir,' Scott replied.

'I'm sure we're all going to have a very interesting, even educational, time,' purred Carol, and her smile changed, becoming warmer, even seductive.

She fancies him, Rosemary thought, and Scott's flattered. What's going on here? She felt a twinge of jealousy, though she had never thought of herself as possessive of him. She was aware of Anthony coming closer. He smelled of the outdoors, of horse and leather, of Calvin Klein cologne and masculine sweat. It was a brew too heady to ignore.

He was so close now that his arm brushed against hers as he said in that spine-tingling, cultured voice, 'This is for tomorrow, Miss Maddox ... Rosemary, if I may? Today you shall become acquainted with some aspects of Malvern Chase; it's too large to take in at once. I have invited friends to dinner. They're keen to meet you. We'll relax this evening. Tomorrow, however, I'll introduce you to the maze.'

'Yes. That will be fine. Thank you,' she burbled, reduced to near-incoherence by his proximity.

The fact that she had recently had sex did little to

alleviate her discomfort. Panties that were already damp became wetter still. Nipples that had peaked so readily at Scott's touch, now ached under her vest-top. A clit that had been fully satisfied earlier now enlarged. She knew she'd have no peace until she sampled what Anthony had on offer.

'Let me show you to your rooms,' Carol said and a manservant appeared as if by magic and took the cases. 'Dinner is at eight, but we'll meet for drinks in the library at seven thirty.'

'Formal dress?' Rosemary had no intention of being caught out by this sophisticated pair.

'Yes. It's so much nicer, don't you think? It gives women the chance to put on their glad rags, and men look so dashing in tuxedos. I'm sure you'll do justice to yours, Scott.'

Rosemary thanked her lucky stars that she had insisted he got himself an evening suit. He'd grumbled at spending the money, but she'd managed to convince him that it was an essential item for any young man who wanted to go far.

The house was a fine example of Tudor architecture. Rosemary's thoughts turned to Jonathan as she touched the heavily carved newel posts and followed Carol up the stairs. He would adore playing the Elizabethan courtier. They went along a panelled corridor, their footsteps muffled by carpet, their way lined with portraits in gilded frames.

'Our ancestors,' Carol explained.

The men were in doublets and trunk-hose, and the women wore farthingales and high-standing lace collars. Ones of a later period sported powdered wigs and cravats and the ladies displayed a great deal of cleavage. All seemed to stare at Rosemary with sly, knowing eyes.

'It must be great to be able to trace your forebears ... a family tree and portraits,' she said. 'So much better than a photograph album.'

'Oh, yes,' Carol agreed, pausing at a door under an elaborate architrave. 'It can be disconcerting, though, to find there were black sheep among them who disgraced the Selbys. They weren't all sweetness and light, nor necessarily honourable, though some were magistrates and Justices of the Peace. There was even a bishop, I believe. This is your room, and this –' she indicated a door to the right '– is yours, Scott. I hope you'll be comfortable. Don't hesitate to use the intercom if you want anything.'

Rosemary was impressed by her room with its stone canopied fireplace and walls covered in linenfold panelling. Rosy-bottomed cupids frolicked with ample-bosomed goddesses in leafy glades painted on the ceiling, spied on by horned satyrs with enormous phalli rearing from between their shaggy goat legs. The large bay-window had damask drapes, and its leaded panes looked out on a lawn with a border of standard roses. But where was the maze? By now she was eaten up with curiosity about it and its fascinating owner.

She prowled around, examining ornaments and a collection of snuff-boxes and wondering if they could possibly be genuine and, if they were, the premium demanded by Anthony's insurance brokers. And the more she handled these treasures, the more she envied him the richness of gold-leaf, chinoiserie and tapestries. Dominating all was a monumental four-poster bed.

'Shit,' she exclaimed, sitting down tentatively, almost afraid that she might damage the embroidered quilt. 'Who would I most like to shag in the middle of this?'

Try as she might to concentrate on Dan, Neil, Michael or Jonathan, all she could see were the dark eyes of her host, the haughty patrician nose, the lean hands grasping the riding crop. Her skin tingled and she wondered how much it would hurt if he lashed her backside.

The thought went through her like a sword, stabbing her sex. She pressed her hand into her lap. Her skirt parted and her fingers toyed with the damp heat of her mound. Sunshine streamed in at an opened pane, and the air was spiced with flowers and herbs. I could stay here forever, she thought. It's an enchanted place and Anthony is the sorcerer.

'Hello there,' said Scott, interrupting her reverie. 'This is neat. Our rooms are joined by the bathroom, one door leading from mine and the other from yours. This means we can get it on any time we like.'

Get it on! She suddenly found his slang distasteful. A man of Anthony's breeding wouldn't be so coarse. She was certain he was well educated and knew about world affairs, history and the arts. She trembled inside with eagerness to see him again. Scott obviously expected a different response, sitting on the bed beside her, reaching across and fingering her breast, then turning her towards him, his mouth already parted for her kiss.

And passion stirred in her. Might as well have the one that's here, if I can't have the one I want, she decided.

By now he was feeling her pussy through the cotton gusset, his touch extraordinarily pleasant. Thinking about Anthony had heated her to boiling point. She spread her legs for Scott and he worked a finger inside her panties, parting her lips and finding her clit, then rubbing it briskly.

She came in a trice, throwing back her head and gasping with the joy of it. Scott was at the ready, his penis prudently covered in latex. He kneeled over her, his weight forcing her back among the pillows of the four-hundred-year-old tester bed.

'Bet this could tell some tales,' he murmured breathlessly, pulling her panties down and off, then easing himself between her thighs. 'And it's solid. It won't shake no matter how hard I fuck you. Bet there's been loads of naughtiness gone on in here.'

'What a lovely couple,' Carol sighed, watching them on the monitor. 'A bonus, my darling. We weren't expecting two beauties.'

'We knew she was gorgeous,' Anthony answered, brooding on Rosemary as she appeared on the screen joined at the genitals with Scott, their movements captured by a minute camcorder concealed high up among the bed curtains.

'And now there's the boy. Can I have him?' Carol's eyes shone and her crimson lips drew back over her white teeth, giving her a vulpine look.

Anthony pressed her to his side, and she coiled into him pliantly, her body that of a ballerina. This had been her profession. But a dancer's working life is short, and though she could have carried on as a teacher and choreographer, Carol needed the limelight. He had found other outlets for her talents, ones they both enjoyed.

The monitors were wired to almost every part of the house, and the one connected with Rosemary's room gave Anthony complete access to every detail. He feasted on her, and on the well-toned muscles of the young stud plunging his cock into her. His taut, olive-skinned rump worked up and down at every thrust. When he withdrew a little, it was possible to see her wetness shining on his shaft. Anthony dreamed up a scenario where he mounted Scott and forced his length into that amber bottom crack, moving in unison with him as he plundered Rosemary's cunt.

This observatory was one of his secrets. Only Carol was permitted to share it. He had had the equipment installed in what had once been a dressing room off the master bedchamber. Now it was empty apart from a large armchair and a couch, placed so that viewers would not lose sight of the activities on the screens.

The close fit of his riding breeches squeezed his engorged cock painfully and made his balls throb. He ached for relief, but had trained himself to protract the longing, to bring himself to the edge, then control the surge, forcing it to die down until, finally, he could wait no longer. Watching Rosemary, hearing her sighs, seeing her legs wrapped round Scott's lean body, made it nigh impossible.

He grabbed Carol roughly, grinding his pelvis against her belly. He pushed up her skirt. She wasn't wearing panties. His finger delved between her shaven lips, then opened the cleft between her buttocks, finding her smallest orifice and worming his little finger into it. She groaned and wriggled, appreciating his attentions. And all the time, he pretended it was Rosemary he invaded, exploring her folds and exciting her clit.

Carol reached down, cradling his bulge in her hand, then tugged at the zipper. The breeches gaped, and he felt her grasp his swollen flesh. The rush of blood to his dick made him grit his teeth. He wanted both of them, his cousin and his guest. Soon, soon, he promised himself, we'll play a trio together, and Scott can turn it into a quartet.

He wouldn't object to Scott joining in, recognising him as a submissive. As orgasm gathered in his loins, so he visualised him wearing seamed stockings and a suspender belt, his feet crammed into stilettos, his cock strapped to keep it erect. And Carol implementing her commands with a flick of her tawse across his quivering arse. But though Anthony appreciated the tight rectums of both sexes, it was a woman's wet, hot core that he craved the most, promising oblivion and a return to the source of being.

He seized Carol's hindquarters in both hands, fingers tracing the welts left by his recent caning. She bruised easily, bearing the marks for days. Would Rosemary's skin be as sensitive? Positioning himself so that he didn't lose sight of his quarry writhing on the bed, he lifted Carol, then lowered her on to his upright cock. She wound her arms round his neck and scissored her legs about his waist. He took her weight, moving her on his slippery prick as if she was an inanimate, rubber pleasure doll.

'I can't come like this,' she muttered, her hair tumbling about her face. Loosening one arm, she pushed her hand down to where her mound met the base of his cock and used her fingers to stimulate herself.

'What you need, Carol, is to be tied to the crosspiece and given a thorough thrashing,' he grunted. His heart thumped as he quickened his movements and he kept his intent gaze on Rosemary, miniaturised yet perfect on the screen. And so do you, Miss Maddox, he added inside, and his climax took him and shook him and shot his spunk from him in quick-fire spurts.

After sending Scott back to his room to shower and change, Rosemary opened her suitcase. What to wear? Nothing too dressy. A simple little designer outfit which was bound to impress. Black was always a safe bet, and she had just the thing: a plain, cut-on-the-cross skirt, with a brief, V-necked bodice, spaghetti straps and no back to speak of. She always felt confident wearing it, confident and chic and slightly wanton. It didn't leave much to the imagination.

She joined Scott in the shower, but refused his invitation to play, her mind firmly fixed on the evening ahead. Yet she couldn't but be aware of how the water ran into the hollow between his pectorals, down across his flat belly, and tangled with the thatch at his groin. His penis was thick and sturdy and her pussy clenched as she recalled the feeling of him ramming into her.

There was something she needed to ask him, but wasn't sure if her mind was tricking her. She pushed both hands through her wet mane, plastering it close against her skull, as she said, 'Did you have the feeling we were being watched just now?'

'A Peeping Tom?' he said with a grin, his eyelashes spiky with water. 'No. I was too into what I was doing to notice. Why?'

'I don't know. I just had this weird sensation like we were in a goldfish bowl,' she said slowly, thinking, *déjà vu*. But I was hoping I'd left the stalker behind.

She had the sudden urge to phone Dan.

Pushing a reluctant Scott into his room, she wrapped herself in a fluffy white towel, went to the dressing table, dried, then dropped the towel and used a smaller one for her hair. She picked up her mobile and paged Dan.

'Yes?'

She started at the quickness of his response. 'Dan? Is that you?'

'DC Holland here. What's happening, Rosemary? You've arrived OK?'

She had forgotten that her number would have appeared on his screen. Nothing was sacred in these interesting times of progress and the Net and Big Brother. 'Yes, Dan. I'm ringing to let you know we're at Malvern Chase.'

'You and Scott?' He hadn't been enamoured of the idea.

'That's right. I'm going to call Michael and Melanie.'

'No heavy breathers in the vicinity?'

'Not to my knowledge.' How to tell him that she had felt herself the object of a voyeur's gaze while fucking his rival?

'Perhaps I'll become one. How would you like that? I could talk smut to you.'

'I knew it. It was you all along.' She entered into the joke. This was the longest of long shots; it wasn't in Dan's nature. Whatever else he was – hard-nosed detective, disillusioned cynic – she couldn't see him as a sneaky, hole-and-corner stalker.

'Whoops! You got me bang to rights, lady. When are you coming back to London?' He sounded crisp and controlled, and she wondered if, as he had said, he genuinely cared about her.

'I don't know,' she answered truthfully. 'It's out of my hands, and all depends on Michael. He could be straight down with the crew and start filming next week, or there may be a delay.'

'I miss you,' he admitted gruffly, and she imagined his prick standing stiffly, a drop of dew at its eye. Memory went into fast rewind, and she wanted to be impaled on his penis, sucking it into her depths. Her hand strayed to her breasts, the nipples rising sharply in response to her touch.

'And I miss you, too,' she whispered, seeing him so

clearly it was as if he stood in the room, her tall, muscular, hard-as-nails cop.

'You do? But you've got lover-boy Scott,' he said, with his customary irony. 'I'll bet you've already been a filthy little tart with him.'

'No one fucks me like you do, Dan,' she said, and she meant it – for the moment. Oh, dear, she mourned, the change that took place when I saw Terry with Belinda has made me as casual about sex as a man, and given me the ability to lie about it, too. Is this really me, or am I smothering my feelings to protect myself from pain?

She was interrupted by a tap on the door.

'I've got to go now, Dan. There's a dinner party,' she said hurriedly.

'I'll be in touch,' he promised and hung up.

'Who is it?' she called, putting down the mobile and shrugging her shoulders into her bathrobe.

'Carol. Can I come in?'

'Yes. One moment while I unlock the door.'

Carol wore a white gown that transformed her into a linten-haired Venus. The halter top clung to her breasts and the skirt fell in a straight, uncluttered line to her ankles, where it revealed sandals with high heels. Her nipples poked through the fabric, but there was no tell-tale knicker line. Not even a shaded area where pubic hair should have been; it would have shown up, no matter how fair. Her make-up was skilfully applied, drawing attention to arched brows and curly lashes, rouged cheeks and pouting lips. Her jewellery was plain but expensive: a rope of pearls and matching earrings.

'You have everything you require?' she asked pleasantly, drifting round the room like a gorgeous moth.

'Oh, yes, thank you. It's fine,' Rosemary answered, pondering on the purpose of her hostess's visit. She found her presence unsettling. It resurrected sensations she had experienced with Melanie, a desire to touch soft female skin and curiosity to taste a woman's lips and body.

I've no time for this, she told herself, too involved with

my work and the demands of my men. I've never yet tried lesbian love, and maybe I will, later, but just for now I've my hands full, literally, cocks all over the place.

But that ruthlessly honest little demon who sat on her shoulder said, 'Balls! You were convinced you'd never get off using a vibrator, but I see you've brought your noisy little friend with you. Hooked on it, aren't you? It's proved that men's cocks aren't the be-all and end-all.'

Rosemary hoped that her flushed face would be attributed to the shower. Above all, she wanted to appear cool and in charge of her emotions. She was aware of a sparkle in Carol's eyes absent until then. Perhaps she had hoped to find Scott with her.

'You're wearing black?' Carol remarked, her eggshell-blue lacquered fingers touching the dress that lay across the foot of the bed. 'It will complement your vibrant colouring. I've always longed to be a sultry Carmen, but all I can achieve is the traditional English rose.'

'And what's wrong with that?' Rosemary said, wondering if Carol intended to stay while she took off her robe and started to dress.

She rather hoped not, though her clit tingled as she imagined baring all to those lilac eyes, provocatively rubbing her body with perfumed lotion, and then putting on her only undergarment, a miniscule black thong.

'Nothing at all, and I suppose we're never satisfied with what life deals. Brunettes want to be blondes and vice versa. Are you pleased with how you look? You should be, for I've never met anyone so blessed by nature.' There was hunger in Carol's eyes and a slackening of her mouth, as she leaned towards Rosemary.

'You're putting me on,' Rosemary said, picking up her dress and withdrawing a little. 'I'm very ordinary really.'

'I don't call appearing on television on a regular basis ordinary. Oh, yes, I have watched you, although gardening isn't my bag. It's Anthony's though, and he admires your work tremendously.'

'Have you been together long?' Change the subject from me, Rosemary decided and, taking the bull by the horns, dropped her covering, sat on the dressing-table stool and started to apply body lotion.

'Oh, yes. Childhood companions, you might say. But we were apart for years. I was dancing on the stage and Anthony followed his own pursuits. Then he inherited all this, and by that time we were together again.'

'Do you love him?' Rosemary brought this out to confuse her, wanting to avoid the greedy way in which she was devouring her body with every glance. It was embarrassing yet arousing, and she was fumbling over the anointing of her flesh, leaving some areas, especially parts which would have meant exposing her sex.

'Of course I do. He's my cousin,' Carol replied airily, and inched closer, adding, 'May I help you with that? Let me do your back.' She trailed her fingers across Rosemary's upper vertebrae, her touch electric.

'I don't mean in that way.' Though Rosemary was convinced there was more to their relationship than met the eye. She was beginning to lose the thread of the conversation.

She didn't protest when Carol poured a little cream into one palm and smoothed it over her bare back, starting at the shoulders and working down and round, inadvertently brushing the sides of Rosemary's breasts. She drew in a sharp breath, wanting those knowing fingers to pinch her nipples, but Carol held back, going lower, working every inch of Rosemary's spine, knobble by knobble, and lingering where her buttocks pressed against the stool, the crease pronounced. She let a trickle of lotion enter there, and massaged it in, her fingers going deeper.

Rosemary gripped the edge of the dressing table, seeing herself in the mirror. Her mouth was open, her face flushed, her eyes heavy-lidded with lust. And Carol was behind her, exquisite Carol who was serving her, becoming her odalisque, prepared to do her bidding, silently begging to be allowed to pleasure her.

'You like that?' Carol whispered, her breath tickling

Rosemary's ear. 'Say the word and I'll give you a full body massage. I'm trained in aromatherapy.'

Rosemary sighed, breathing in Carol's exotic perfume crossed with her personal body scent. She wanted to yield herself completely and take the pleasure her hostess was so blatantly offering. A new experience? Why not? Any reluctance she might have had concerning making love with a woman faded into infinity. She was intrigued, wanting more, lifting herself off the seat as Carol's hands came round to play with the dark pubic curls, opening the cleft between them and rubbing each side of the clit, but being careful not to touch the tip.

Rosemary's eyes met Carol's in the mirror and one slender brow lifted enquiringly. 'You like this?' she whispered, leaning closer to lick round Rosemary's ear.

'Yes, but I'm not sure ... I've not done it before,' she confessed, hearing Carol's deep-throated chuckle, feeling her delectable tongue rasping against her lobe like a cat's.

'Never made love with a woman? I'm honoured to be the one to initiate you. Only a woman truly understands what another woman needs.'

Rosemary could smell herself, the strong odour of fresh arousal. Her sex was wet again, and Carol opened her vulva with her thumbs, then massaged the shaft of her clit, going deeper till she located its root, hidden away and joined to her pubic bone. The thousands of sensitive nerve endings attached to it fired up in response.

Standing now, resting back against Carol's breasts, Rosemary watched those expert hands manipulating her swollen bud. The image flung back by the glass was neither obscene nor graceless. The blue painted fingertips parting the slick folds and encouraging the clit to emerge from its fleshy cowl seemed beautiful. The natural grace of her body and Carol's clasped in close congress was nothing short of artistic. She could feel her lover's pubis writhing against her bottom, and her nipples, hard as cones through the chiffon, seeking stimulation in the curve of her spine.

Rosemary didn't have to instruct her. Carol knew

precisely where to touch her clit, and how hard or soft, quick or slow that caress should be. It was like doing it to herself. Without being asked, Carol dipped a finger in the juice pooling at Rosemary's entrance, then spread the slippery lubricant up her cleft, stroking it over the underside of her clit-head in just the right way. She didn't attempt to penetrate her, aware that she wouldn't want any distraction as she climbed to the plateau where she'd pause for a moment before forging ahead to reach her orgasm. Men had to be trained to do this competently. A woman did it through experimenting with her own ascent to that precious peak.

'Oh, that's so good,' Rosemary exclaimed, her voice sounding strained and harsh.

'I know,' Carol murmured, stroking the quivering clit, wetting it again and increasing the pressure by a whisper. 'It likes that, doesn't it?'

'Yes, it does.'

'It's a greedy little monster, just like mine. Time and place mean nothing to it when it gets the urge. Men talk about their cocks acting as if they have a life of their own, and I think the same applies to the clit. Let me see yours.' And Carol came round and dropped to her knees in front of Rosemary, lifting her hands and holding herself open. 'Put one foot up on the stool,' she encouraged. 'That's it, now I can see everything. Your pussy is so pretty, kind of Gothic looking. Every woman's is different and worthy of praise. I've an artist friend who draws them, her fabulous pencil sketches resembling lush petals. No wonder it's sometimes called a woman's flower.'

Rosemary's excitement increased as she exposed her private parts shamelessly, Carol between her stretched thighs, admiring the ripe, pink delta. She looked down and watched her, seeing her extend her tongue and gasping as it feathered over her enlarged clit. The intensity of it was enough to carry her to the crest, and she came, screaming. Hands resting on Carol's shoulders, she shuddered as the spasms passed through her. Her legs

161

were shaking and her heart thudding; the orgasm was so powerful that every particle of her felt rejuvenated.

Carol continued to lick her gently, washing her clean of juice. Then she rose, cool and elegant, gown and hair in no way disarranged.

'Now I must leave you,' she said. 'There are things to see to and people to greet.'

'But you . . .?' Rosemary faltered, priding herself on giving as well as taking satisfaction.

Carol laughed and said, 'Don't worry. My turn will come, and so shall I,' and when she kissed her, Rosemary could taste herself on her lips.

Later, she met Scott in the hallway and felt an almost maternal pride in his appearance. 'My God,' she exclaimed. 'You've scrubbed up nicely.'

'Is it all right?' he asked anxiously, fiddling with his collar.

'You look cute,' she said, taking his arm.

She meant it. A black jacket and trousers, a velvet cummerbund, a white shirt and black tie turned him into the fresh-faced boy-next-door beloved of Australian soaps. He could have been escorting her to an end-of-term college party, had she not been way too old.

They both made a hit downstairs, where Anthony and Carol introduced them to all who had turned up to meet Rosemary. Apparently Rosemary's fame had reached the county set who were normally only interested in point-to-point and hunting. They were a mixed crowd, ranging from thirty to fifty, the women lacking in dress sense, the men tending to be portly. There was the Reverend Raymond Chapman, who immediately started to rabbit on about his dahlias, and Bernard Trim, the local vet seeking her advice about a pond where the water-lilies had given up the ghost. Everyone remotely interested in cultivation seemed to think she was some kind of oracle. She turned most of them over to Scott.

The vicar was elderly, married and unattractive, but the vet deserved a second glance, and Rosemary decided that this project was wide open to opportunities for sexual dalliance. Carol had already established this fact, but Anthony was still an unknown quantity.

Rosemary found it hard to meet Carol's eyes, though that lady was behaving normally, the perfect hostess, putting everyone at their ease. Yet Rosemary could not help the heat between her legs when she remembered Carol's tongue exciting her. Was Carol thinking about it, too? Perhaps getting a whiff of Rosemary's juices that lingered on her fingers? She found the notion disconcerting, and had to concentrate hard to keep up her celebrity persona.

After a superbly cooked and presented dinner, people drifted towards the Great Hall. Latino music throbbed from stereo speakers and couples started to move to the sexy beat. Rosemary was besieged by a reporter from *The Waverney Journal*. It was obvious that the area was starved of news.

Eventually Anthony rescued her, looking down his nose at the man and saying in a voice that would etch glass, 'I don't recall inviting you.'

'But, Mr Selby, it's for the gardening page. Our readers will want to know what Miss Maddox has to say. Hints and tips for growing prize vegetables, and all that,' the reporter persisted, biro poised over his notebook, his sidekick aiming a camera.

'I don't do vegetables,' Rosemary averred.

'I may permit you to call and interview her for the *Journal*, if she agrees,' Anthony addressed him loftily. 'Phone the estate office in the morning. Now back off.' He signalled to a hulking, bald-headed individual in evening clothes who was leaning against the wall, arms folded over his chest. 'See these gentlemen are escorted from the premises, Higgins.'

'Your guard?' Rosemary asked. 'He looks like a heavy-weight boxer.'

'He was. Now he's on security.'

'Is it necessary?'

'Oh, yes.'

He took her arm. His fingers, though holding her

lightly, were like steel bands. All her senses were humming at a pitch that seemed almost supernatural. She glanced across the hall anxiously, but Scott was circled by women, revelling in his bogus star status, and Carol was engaged in conversation with Bernard.

Anthony smiled down at Rosemary, his eyes hooded in that dark face and said, 'We shan't be missed for a while.'

Without relinquishing his grip on her arm, he guided her to a door in the shadow of the stairs. The compulsive beat of salsa pervaded her senses. She wanted to dance, to run, to hide – above all, she wanted to disappear somewhere private with Anthony and have him explore her body and satisfy her hunger.

The corridor ahead was dimly lit and chilly after the warmth of the hall. Anthony closed the door behind them. The hairs on the back of her neck rose. She glanced at him as he moved easily at her side and found that he was watching her. She had seen that look in men's eyes many times before, but had never been so affected. She felt threatened and vulnerable and regretted not telling Scott where she was going. But she was excited, too, her nerves quivering, her black thong sticky where it cut into her slit. If he had suddenly flung her down in the stone-flagged passageway and taken her roughly, she might have made a fuss but would have been entirely willing.

Oh dear, she thought. I wish I'd been able to speak to Melanie instead of getting that frustrating answerphone, and it was no better when I tried Michael. She felt a sudden burst of unreasoning anger towards them – agent and director – for shunting her down here to deal with this situation. It wasn't fair!

'Are you cold? Here, take my coat,' Anthony said, and took it off, then laid it around her shoulders. He looked even more devastating in sleek black trousers with the dusky light falling on the open front of his shirt, a slash of dark skin showing against the white material.

'Where are we going?' she asked, almost running to keep up with his long stride.

'To a place I show only to close friends,' he replied, his voice tinged with a new, gritty quality.

She got a grip on her fear. He wouldn't dare harm her, would he? She was too well known and a lot of people knew where she was staying. Why should he hurt her, anyway? She was going to help him restore the maze, put his historic home on the map, maybe even encourage the tourist trade.

The corridor ended at another locked door. She began to enter into the game. Where would she find herself next? She was rather like Alice when she followed the White Rabbit into the tunnel. Anthony opened it, and switched on the lights. She stepped out into an auditorium.

It was an old-fashioned theatre, seating no more than one hundred, but exact in every way. Red plush seats, crystal mirrors and gilt carvings. Crimson curtains on either side of the stage, held back by cords with gold tassels three feet long. The smell of damp tickled Rosemary's nostrils, combined with size and greasepaint, cigar smoke and perspiration.

'This is yours?' she asked, clutching his coat around her. The atmosphere was strange, as if time had folded back, transporting them to a by-gone age.

'Part of my heritage,' he said, leading her down to the orchestra pit. 'It was built by an ancestor who liked to put on masques, with himself playing the leading female roles.'

'And you use it?' It was apparent that the place was kept in good order. Someone lovingly cleaned, dusted and polished it.

'Oh, yes. It's my hobby. Carol's, too, and we have friends who like to watch our shows and sometimes join in.'

'I didn't realise you were an actor.'

'Scriptwriter, scenery painter, props provider, costume and wig maker. You name it.'

'But this is amazing,' she cried. 'You'll put on a play for me, won't you? We can mention it on the programme.'

'If you wish,' he said, smiling, his hand at the small of her back as they mounted the short flight of steps that led to the stage.

The footlights were dazzling, the body of the theatre plunged into darkness by contrast. The backdrop represented a garden. The wings were painted to look like trees. There was a rustic bench under a rustic arch. Anthony drew her down on it.

'Everything looks so tawdry and artificial from this side of the proscenium,' she said. 'Like the inside of one's head. In reality, what the public see is what we project to impress them.'

'That's a profound statement, Miss Maddox,' he remarked mockingly, then added, 'Shakespeare had it in a nutshell when he wrote, "All the world's a stage and all the men and women merely players."'

'We should go back,' she said uncertainly, thinking: he's dangerously intelligent and observant and, God help me, I've never been able to resist his type.

'Carol will buzz me when I'm needed.' He leaned against the back of the bench, legs spread out in front of him, pelvis thrust forward so that she couldn't miss the fully erect cock tenting the black barathea trousers.

'You've shown me your theatre, and it's time to go,' she said, denying that she longed to have him go down on her and warm her sex with his breath.

'I say when we leave,' his said levelly, and, the curve of his lips more sensual, he reached over and flicked at her nipples through the thin silk. Then the timbre of his voice changed. He sounded harsh and domineering as he added, 'Open your legs.'

Without waiting for her, he pushed a hand between them, spreading her knees wide and lifting her skirt back till the black silk triangle appeared at her fork. An absorbed expression on his face, he arranged the folds against her thighs – black skirt and black panties contrasting with golden flesh.

'Stand up, Rosemary, and remember that next time, I want you to wear hold-up stockings. Later, we'll try a red garter belt and suspenders,' he whispered huskily, and her ears pricked. There was something about this hoarse command that made her uneasy.

'Next time?' she questioned, but she couldn't help obeying him. Both of them were standing, her skirt still crumpled as he fingered her hidden pubis. 'Who says there'll be a next time?'

'I do,' he rasped, turning her briskly and slapping her bottom.

The sharp pain was so unexpected and intense that she nearly wet herself, a few drops of urine escaping till she clenched her pelvic muscles. 'Ouch!' she exclaimed, fighting back tears of humiliation. 'What the hell was that for?'

'A reminder,' he answered blandly, his lips curving into a crooked smile. 'You're in my house now, and I call the tune.'

'Is that so?' she said, her voice echoing through the deserted stage.

Her body jerked as he slapped her again, then he thrust his finger into her wet panties, running over her crack and finding the thickened stem of her clit.

'You're defiant. All the better,' he purred, then abruptly let her go, raising his fingers to his nostrils and sniffing her scent. 'Ambrosia. Nectar for the gods. You smell like rare wine, like spices, with a hint of the sea.'

Rosemary pulled down her skirt and rearranged herself. 'Mr Selby,' she announced in icy tones, loathing him. 'You have a strange way of treating a guest. Don't forget that you're expecting my programme to do you a favour. One word from me and the deal is off.'

'I think not,' he drawled, so maddeningly condescending that she wanted to hit, scratch and kick him. 'It's costing me a packet. You know as well as I that *In Your Own Backyard* doesn't offer its services for free.'

'We meet a portion of the expenses,' she shouted, losing it completely.

'A portion, I grant you,' he agreed, 'but I pay the lion's share.'

He still held his fingers under his nose and this action disgusted yet excited her. The blood was thumping in her punished backside, and the heat of it communicated itself to her sexual regions. He appeared to be cool, but the hard stalk of his cock rising to his waist told a different story. The atmosphere was fraught. She felt the prickle of sweat on her back and realised how tired she was. She tried to move, then stumbled in her high heels. Anthony caught her and kissed her. It was a kiss to die for, tender and experienced, his tongue weaving magic circles in her mouth. And her bottom burned, and she wanted to relinquish control, letting him do with her what he willed.

He withdrew his lips, pushing his hands into her hair and holding her steady as he purred, 'You aren't going anywhere, Rosemary Maddox. And you'll carry out the contract. The professional in you won't be able to resist once you've seen the maze. You've met your match in me.'

The phone bleeped from his jacket lying on the bench. He dug it out, held it to his ear and spoke to the caller. 'Very well, Carol. We're leaving anyway. Tell the vicar I'll be with him shortly.' He replaced it and turned to Rosemary. 'I was going to postpone consummation anyway.'

'I didn't ... I wasn't about to. Christ, I've never met anyone as conceited as you!' she stammered.

'You've a lot to learn, but I'll take the greatest delight in teaching you, my dear,' he said, and fear rose in her again, drowning out the passion his kisses had aroused as he added, 'I know that Carol has already begun your training.'

'How do you know?' Her hackles rose, a purely animal response to danger.

He lifted a mocking eyebrow and said, 'Ways and

means. Nothing happens in and around Malvern Chase that I'm not aware of.'

'Master! Mistress! I'll do anything, anything,' drooled Raymond, on his knees at their feet.

'You have been a very naughty boy,' Carol said sternly, pacing round him. 'I saw the way you were looking at Miss Maddox. I expect you've been watching her on the box for months, rubbing your prick and wanting to give her a tit-fuck. Isn't this so?'

'No, goddess,' he whined, his naked arse raised, his only covering a leather apron attached by straps and buckles. His short pallid cock protruded from under the hem. His clerical dog-collar had been replaced by a spiked leather one to which Carol had attached a leash.

'Liar,' she snarled and whacked him across the buttocks with a springy white leather paddle. 'You've been jerking off, haven't you?'

'Yes, mistress,' he whimpered, squirming. 'Oh, please, don't tell my wife.'

'Poor old Joan doesn't know what a filthy pervert she married. I've a good mind to tell her about you. That would upset her flower arranging and charity work, wouldn't it? She'd never be able to lift up her head at WI meetings again.'

'You wouldn't? Oh, no, please. She's the chairperson,' he squeaked but even as he did, Raymond's foreskin retracted below his swelling helm, the ridge shining with moisture.

'What shall I do with him, sir?' Carol said, eyeing Anthony through the slits in her black velvet mask.

'He deserves a dozen lashes,' he answered, bored with this ritual, his thoughts returning to Rosemary and what he planned to do to her. But he couldn't resist the power that domination of the vicar afforded him. Even a man of the church had his fetishes, his sexual secrets, his fantasy world which Carol and Anthony re-created. Only they knew that he ached to be somebody's slave.

And it was worthwhile. Raymond had eased their

acceptance into Waverney's close-knit community. The only sins they had committed before Anthony's arrival in their midst had been a bit of harmless wife-swapping, well disguised and rigorously denied if any gossip was bandied about.

'Oh, master, thank you,' Raymond mumbled as he was conducted to the whipping-post standing centre stage of the cellar below Anthony's private apartments. He had turned it into a dungeon, replete with sombre drapes, the dim lurid light glinting on chains and restraints, and all the miscellaneous trappings associated with sadomasochism. His collection of whips and other instruments of chastisement were second to none. He had hand picked every one.

'Shall I do it?' Carol asked, taking up an insolent stance on the thin high heels of the black leather boots reaching her thighs.

A string covered her pubis, parting the labial lips and disappearing into her bottom crack. Her wasp-waisted corset was tightly laced and decorated with chains. It jacked her breasts high, the carmined nipples exposed. It amused her to wear outrageous costumes – the mask, the head-dress – and she had found that even in this enlightened day and age, submissives craved the conventional dominatrix gear.

'You may punish him,' Anthony said, and Raymond embraced the post, his face pressed to the wood, arms outstretched. Carol clamped his wrists above his head, forced his knees apart with a wooden truss and snapped leg irons round his ankles.

The paddle beat his flabby white buttocks, leaving a hectic flush. He groaned but hung limp and unresisting in his bonds. Half a dozen blows later, he was on the point of ejaculation, grinding himself against the post. Anthony watched him sardonically. We're all the same under the skin, he reflected. It makes no difference whether we're king or pauper, priest or gangster, there's corruption in all of us, the desire to flout the rules, and see just how far we can transgress.

'You love it, don't you, Reverend?' he muttered, standing close to the sweating man. 'What price your sermons now? Your congregation, small though it is, would never believe it, would they? Their pastor about to shoot his load while a woman flogs him? Mistress Carol, I suggest you use something with more of a bite.'

'Yes, sir,' she said, and replaced the paddle with a whip whose many leather thongs had knots at their tips.

Raymond yelped as it struck him, yelped and bucked and strained, but each time she stopped to lift her arm for another blow his expression was that of a saint undergoing martyrdom. When she had done, she flung the whip aside and released him. He fell at her feet, panting, welted, bony knees taking his weight on the cold stone slabs. His hands flew to his engorged and frustrated cock. One touch, and he had fountained his come over the toes of her boots.

'Filthy beast!' she sneered. 'Lick it off, every single nauseating drop!'

Anthony admired her artistry as the vicar grovelled, his tongue busy as he slurped his own secretion from Carol's foot. She could keep a submissive in torment for hours, having him or her perform the most menial tasks and, transported by the experience, begging for more.

He had seen her seducing Rosemary; there was more than one camcorder in the bedroom. Now he pondered on how she would react to Carol's expertise with the whip. More than that, he itched to give her orders to plug Rosemary's anus, stretching her for the time when he would take her that way.

He moved nearer as Carol barked a command, saying, 'And now, as a treat, you can suck my clit.'

She stood over the vicar, who raised his face to her as if she was some holy being who must be worshipped. Her gloved hands went down to her crotch and she pulled aside the leather thong, exposing the jewel in her clit. Raymond sighed and fastened his mouth there, his balding head with its fringe of grey hair bobbing up and down as he pleasured her. Carol stood stiffly. Anthony could see her thigh muscles bracing and the forward thrust of her pubis as she approached her apogee. His semi-erect cock uncoiled to its full potential under his evening trousers, and he rubbed a hand over it, eyes slitted as he thought of Rosemary.

Carol came noisily, and he did it in silence, feeling his come soaking his boxer shorts.

Chapter Nine

*S*top remembering those uncanny topiary animals in Stephen King's *The Shining*, Rosemary said, giving herself a good talking to. I know they moved around sneakily, but this doesn't. Don't be such a wimp. It's only an overgrown hedge maze.

'What d'you think?' Anthony asked.

He had got her out of bed early, rushing her here without any breakfast, not even a cup of tea. It was a humid, overcast morning. Thunder rumbled and soon it would rain. Now the garden was silent and utterly deserted. She found the absence of birdsong disquieting.

'They say there are no birds on the sites of Second World War concentration camps,' she said, fully aware of him standing beside her. This didn't feel untoward, for he had haunted her dreams all night.

'That's a macabre observation,' he replied, too impossibly attractive in black chinos and polo shirt, his bare feet thrust into sneakers. 'I asked you what you thought of the maze.'

'I gave you my first impression – doomy,' she said briskly, 'and here's the second. It's a mess. An untidy, derelict monstrosity. It must have been years since it was trimmed.'

'You're right, but don't you just love its fascinating air

of mystery? It's like the garden of Sleeping Beauty's palace. Who knows what will happen when we enter.'

She repressed a shiver and tried out a laugh. It fell flat. 'That's what I'm worried about. I'm not really into mazes.'

'It's easy to get through, once you know how.' His hand came to rest on her back, warm fingers dispelling the ice that seemed to freeze her spine. 'The ancients looked upon mazes as a journey to find the good and evil within us. It represents life, with all its setbacks; a tangled web to which there is ultimately a solution.'

'Aren't you reading into it more than was intended?' she suggested, as he led her to what appeared to be the entrance. 'Didn't the wealthy use mazes and man-made caverns and mock ruined temples as trifles to ornament their estates and amuse their friends? A kind of one-upmanship?'

'I'm sure they did, and these proved ideal for fornication, lovers invisible among the bushes,' he replied, his dark eyes shining. His hand trembled, and she was swamped by the desire that had brought her close to orgasm as she dreamed of him.

Staring into the tunnel formed by the hedge meeting overhead, she wanted to plunge into it, have him conceal her inside its maw, and fuck her till she yelled for mercy.

The air grew heavier. Thunder rumbled and the sky darkened, ponderous inky clouds rushing in. Rosemary's clothes clung to her sweatily and she longed to immerse herself in a bathtub of scented water. How dare this arrogant man drag her out at such an ungodly hour?

'Come on,' he urged, as the thunder boomed, the skies opened and rods of rain came hurtling down. He pushed into the maze and along a narrow path, dragging her with him.

It was like walking under the sea, murky light filtering between interlocked branches. The rain began to inch its way through. The smell of wet earth and the dusty odour of privet filled Rosemary's nose and, as they penetrated more deeply, she clung to Anthony's hand. She caught a glimpse of his face. It was beaded with sweat, and his intense expression was scary, yet caused a lusty throb between her legs.

'Which way?' she cried above the tumult of the storm.

'I'll show you,' he said.

She had the urge to tear off her clothes, though this would have been unwise. The sharp branches and briars tore at her jeans and shirt and would have played havoc with her sensitive skin. But this was undoubtedly a pagan spot, based on mazes constructed as sacred places in which to placate the gods, and then adopted by the Christians who turned them into a spiritual pilgrimage leading to salvation. Pagans are best, she thought, then pulled up short, facing a dead end.

'Where now?' she gasped, reminded of frightening games she had played when a child. Murder in the Dark. Sardines. Hide and Seek. She and her friends were always spooking each other. It was par for the course when growing up.

'This way,' and he darted off, letting the branches snap back behind him and leaving her to struggle through the undergrowth, terrified of losing him.

'How big is it?' she asked, bumping into him as she rounded a corner, the thunder retreating now, though the rain showed no sign of abating.

'It covers about an acre, and is of an unusual trapezoidal shape, like the famous one at Hampton Court.' He was breathing unevenly, and she stood quite still, waiting for him to touch her. He didn't. The chemistry flashed between them so fiercely that she thought it would set the hedge on fire.

'I'll use that in the intro to the programme,' she said, fighting to stay calm. 'Shall we go on?'

'You're eager to find your destiny at the end?'

'I don't know about destiny, but I'm going to draw a map so I can get in and out,' she continued briskly, trying to pretend that she wasn't aching to have him touch her as he'd done the night before – stroking her, rousing her, then slapping her bottom. It was still sore and, catching a glimpse of it in the mirror as she dressed, she had seen the imprint of his hand.

The memory of it made her fidgety, the tightness of her jeans dragging the seam into her crotch, while her nipples hardened under the thin shirt. I almost peed, she thought, longing grabbing at her loins. How humiliating. I've never, ever, passed water in front of a man. Or a woman, come to that. Of course, I got control of my bladder, but supposing I hadn't?

'Thinking about last night?' he asked with unnerving intuition, as they reached a junction with paths going in opposite directions. 'Your panties were sopping. You enjoyed that, didn't you? You wanted to relinquish control but stopped yourself. I'll let you do it. Make you do it. I'll order you to wet yourself at my bidding, torment you till you can't hold on any longer.'

'Why do you want to do this to me?' she demanded, her voice muffled and face flaming.

He touched the tips of her breasts, as his hard, beautifully chiselled face hovered above her. 'Because you must obey me, Rosemary.'

'I don't have to,' she declared, though her hips swayed towards the erection that distorted his trousers. 'I've never wanted to be anyone's slave.'

'Liar,' he mocked, and took each nipple between his fingers, pinching them firmly. Her pussy clenched and she imagined the feel of his cock in her, butting against her cervix till he came.

'Listen, Anthony,' she said and drew back, ashamed of her nipples that continued to poke hopefully through both bra-cups and shirt. 'I came here to look over the maze with a view to giving Ace Productions the go-ahead. I didn't expect that you'd make a pass at me, well, several passes, to be exact. I just want to get on with my job, make some notes, ring Michael Pendelton and tell him my findings.'

'I'm not stopping you.' His face was a picture of innocence, but his hand snaked out and cupped her mons, pressing the stitching just below the zipper. Her wayward clit jumped in response and she couldn't help rocking against his hand.

'Can we get on?' Her voice was strangled.

He smiled sombrely as he let her go, then took the right-hand path. She scurried behind him, darkness ahead and in back of her. The thunder was receding, and the rain slowed down, big drops hanging from the twigs, then falling on her head. All her old terrors rushed up, and she slipped her hand into his belt for reassurance, the heat of his body penetrating her cold fingers.

More twists and turns, the maze corkscrewing and doubling back on itself. I'm never going to get out of here, she panicked. This is the end of me, and she could almost hear the story read out by a solemn-faced newscaster. 'It was reported earlier today that Rosemary Maddox, TV gardening expert, has disappeared in the depths of a hedge-maze. No trace has been found of her. When questioned, local people said she had been stolen by the fairies, but the police are not ruling out foul play.'

And then, 'Thank God!' she shouted as the overpowering vegetation suddenly opened and they came to a moss-carpeted clearing. The rain had stopped and the sun appeared. Everything was steaming, swampy, verdant, gloriously normal.

But – and here she stopped going over the top with relief – in front of her was an arch, and below it steps leading down.

'What the hell . . .?'

'We're in the middle now, and I've another treat for you, Rosemary,' he smirked, then looked her full in the face, the directness of his stare robbing her of willpower. 'But first, what have you decided? You'll recommend the maze to your bosses?'

'It is very interesting, and the before-and-after shots will delight our viewers,' she said primly, wishing he'd give her more time. 'You want a decision now?'

'Why not?'

'I'll have to talk it over with Michael.'

'You can ring him from here.'

'Where?' Was he carrying a mobile?

He laughed and ducked under the ornamental arch. 'Down here,' he called.

Rosemary followed gingerly. The steps were worn, dipping in the centre, but there was a handrail to cling to. Anthony waited for her at the bottom, then slipped a key into a door. When he opened it, lights sprang on, illuminating the entrance like Santa's Grotto at Christmas time.

He smiled encouragingly and she went inside, dazzled by the shells and semi-precious stones rough-set in the uneven walls. Water trickled from a snarling lion's mouth into a basin. Ferns sprouted from its base. A paved path stretched in front of them. Anthony unhooked the wall-mounted phone and handed it to her.

She had to think hard before remembering the digital sequence, and it was a relief to hear Michael. 'It's me, Rosemary,' she began, peering around nervously. What next trick was Anthony the Magician about to perform?

'How are you doing?' Michael asked. 'I took your message when I got into the office this morning. It's a bit damned early, isn't it? You're lucky to have caught me, but I'm getting in at a ridiculously obscene hour these days. So much work to catch up on. Mary's a brick. She never grumbles about rising with the lark or whatever.'

'She's in love with you, that's why,' Rosemary pointed out, not for the first time.

'Balls,' he protested.

'Those, too, I expect. She worships you, mind, body, soul and testicles.'

'Humph! So the place passes muster? A suitable venue?'

Rosemary caught Anthony's eye and nodded. 'It's fabulous. When are you planning to arrive? Is it worth me coming home?'

'No, no. Stay put. I can get the team together by Wednesday at the latest. The chief cameraman will be back from holiday by then, and Jonathan can leave off filming his show for a few days while the rest of his crew do their stuff. His part can be edited in afterwards. You know how it goes.'

She did indeed, visualising the organised chaos that existed out of camera range. Programmes appeared to be faultless to the audience watching in their own sitting-rooms. The out-takes told a different story.

'So, I'm to stay here till you arrive?' She had hoped to pop back and spend a night with Dan.

'That's it. Only a couple of days, after all. I'm sure you can pass the time pleasantly enough with Scott. What are Selby and his cousin like?'

'Very hospitable,' she prevaricated. There was no way she was going to tell him the truth about the couple: so handsome, so sensual and so odd. 'You'll be able to judge for yourself.'

'Good. Tell Mr Selby to expect us. I hope he has plenty of guestrooms and food. You know working makes our people hungry, and thirsty. What's the state of his wine cellar?'

'I haven't a clue.'

'Keep in touch if there's anything else I should know.'

'I will,' she said and hung the receiver on its rest.

'That's settled. Now for the main business of the day,' Anthony said, and gestured towards the passage. 'You may tell Michael Pendelton when he arrives that there's an additional attraction here – a labyrinth.'

'That's put paid to breakfast outdoors,' Carol grumbled as the rain came down. She made a dash for the house. Scott loped after her, and one of the servants carried in a tray with a coffee-pot, orange juice and a rack of buttered toast.

'Take that upstairs, Chalmers,' she ordered and, as the young man passed her, she tweaked his bottom and mouthed a kiss.

Scott watched these shenanigans, and thought: There's more to Carol Selby than appears on the surface. She's been flirting with me ever since I arrived.

'Where's Rosemary?' he asked, following her through the hall and up the staircase.

'Anthony's showing her the maze.'

'They'll get wet.'

'I doubt it,' she said, opening her bedroom door. 'Anyway, wet clothes will cling, outlining her bottom. Oh, stop looking so uncomfortable, Scott. What's the matter? Does the thought of it give you a stiffy?'

Carol's outspokenness shocked, coming as it did from the cushiony red lips of such a ladylike person. But as soon as he'd met her, Scott had recognised a certain ambience which reminded him of his college lecturer. Her voice was precise and confident and she was mature. It was likely that she went riding. Now his erection became more abundant as he imagined her in form-fitting breeches and shiny boots, blonde hair in a snood under a hard, black velvet hat.

'Rosemary's great,' he conceded, obeying Carol's imperious gesture and sitting near the low table where the manservant had placed the tray.

'I'll bet she is,' Carol remarked, selecting a triangle of toast and transferring it to her mouth. A little smear of butter added extra gloss to her lipstick.

'I've learned a lot from her.'

'No doubt.'

He stared at her mouth, wanting to expose his affluent package, to have her tongue slide along his shaft and dart round his glans. Her perfume filled his nostrils – expensive, French, personal to her as soon as it touched her skin, mingling with her own intimate body odour. He had tried Rosemary's door last night, but found it locked. Frustrated, he had gone to bed and masturbated, his climax aided by visions of her and Carol teasing his balls and handling his prick.

He had come quickly, his jizz creaming his belly – warm, wet and sticky – but though he had slept he had remained unsatisfied, yearning for Rosemary – or this glamorous woman who he was certain indulged in games he had never played with his employer.

'I'd have liked to have gone with them to see the maze,' he said, accepting a cup of coffee and willing his rebellious member to lie down.

'Anthony wanted her first glimpse of it to be with him, on their own. He's been waiting for this moment a long time,' she said calmly, taking a cigarette from her pack. Scott leaned forwards to light it. 'Besides which,' she added, 'you and I must spend time together. It's obvious by the state of your cock that you need discipline. We'll start straight away. Take off your clothes.'

'Now?' Scott could feel his prick jerking.

'Yes.' As she spoke, Carol began to unbutton her blouse with agonising slowness.

Riveted by the delicate movements of her tapering fingers, Scott pulled his T-shirt over his head, glad he'd not neglected sessions at the gym. He was no weakling, his muscles toned by weights and the rowing machine, his skin browned by natural sunlight topped up with regular stints under solar lamps. He breathed in deeply, making his chest swell. Shoulders held back, he wasn't shy as Carol scrutinised him critically.

'Think you're Jack the lad, do you?' she sneered, and after crushing out the cigarette, paced round him, high-wedged mules clacking on the polished floor. Her blouse was open, exposing breasts that rose over the top of an underwired brassière. It was black, lace-trimmed and sexy. Her breasts weren't softly feminine. They had an aggressive thrust that thrilled him to the marrow.

'I keep in trim, watch my weight, take exercise,' he stuttered, reduced to jelly when she reached out and grasped his balls, lifting them as high as the restraining denim allowed.

'So I should think,' she said sternly, running a finger-nail over the line dividing the twin globes. 'I don't want anything but perfection round here. Do you understand?'

Scott was almost on tiptoe, trying to escape the pressure, but Carol refused to free him. She expected an answer. 'Yes, I understand,' he said, his voice tenor high.

'Is that the way to address me?' She squeezed harder.

'No, mistress,' he managed to get out. His teacher had liked to be called by that title.

'That's better. When you're with me, you'll do exactly as I command.' Carol relaxed her hold and started to stroke the thick bough surging behind his fly.

'Get it out for me, mistress,' he pleaded, pre-come leaking from him and spreading in a dark, give-away circle.

She gripped it hard and pinched his balls. 'Did I give you permission to speak?'

'No, mistress,' he said humbly, hanging his head.

With a change of tempo and mood, she jerked at the zipper, dragging it down, careless of the metal teeth catching tender skin or pubic hair. Scott's breath left him in a rush as she grabbed his cock and rubbed it vigorously, then let it go. It sprang up, tapping his belly, his balls rock hard. He was ready to come – very nearly losing it – till her fingers pressed firmly at the base of his cock. The zinging rush subsided, and he relaxed his thigh muscles. They would have to wait to empower his hips into that last, exquisite dance.

'Trousers down,' Carol ordered, circling him as he obeyed her. He kicked off his trainers and dropped his jeans.

The moment when he bared himself completely for a new woman was always thrilling. It never came again, not with her: if he wanted to repeat that heady sensation, he had to find a fresh love. He hoped that Carol was impressed with his tool. She was certainly examining it with a critical eye. The idea that she might be finding fault made it shrink a little.

He couldn't help asking, 'Does it please you, mistress?'

She measured it with her hand, then spanned it with her middle finger and thumb. They didn't meet round its girth. Triumph blossomed in him, making it grow a further inch.

'It'll do,' she answered casually. 'Stand there with your hands behind your back, head down, legs apart. That's good. I do believe you've done this before, Scott. Am I right?'

'Yes, mistress,' he muttered.

'With Rosemary?'

'With a college lecturer.'

'Ah, so I was right in thinking that Rosemary is inexperienced. But I've been working on her.'

'Rosemary?' He was astonished.

'Oh, yes. She came very quickly for me last evening. I think, with a little encouragement, she could swing both ways. Now, tell me about your teacher. How old were you and, more important, how old was *she*?'

'Getting on for forty. I was barely eighteen. She liked me to wait on her, take any beatings she decided to give me, ordered me about and used me to bring her off.'

'She sounds a woman after my own heart,' Carol declared, smiling grimly. 'Did she ever try this?' And she went to a drawer and returned with a jewellery box.

Scott watched, agitated and wondering, as she lifted out what at first glance he took to be earrings. She brought them over and pulled at his left nipple. Agonising pain bit deep when she attached the gold clamp. He yelped, but she slapped him into stillness, then sprang the other nipple clip.

'No, she didn't do that,' he muttered, longing to remove the things, then starting to experience a warm glow spreading from his chest to his groin.

Carol tweaked both ornaments, and said, 'I'd like to see your foreskin pierced by a ring. I'd fasten chains to it and lead you about by your cock.'

Scott couldn't repress a groan. He felt blissfully conscious that he'd found another ruthless mistress. Oh, he enjoyed being masterful with Rosemary, though both of them knew they were pretending: she was the stronger by far. But he had missed a dominating partner.

Carol had found another toy. 'You need to be punished,' she said sternly, running her hand up and down the dildo. It was a thick rubber strut, with realistic veins and a flange that circled the substantial head. 'Sometimes

I wear this attached to a harness and strapped between my legs, just like the real thing. I enjoy shoving it up a man's arse, letting him know how a woman feels every time she's penetrated. I climax, too. There are bristles at its base that rub against my clit while I'm thrusting like a man. But for today, I want other pleasures. Like your tongue making me come.'

'Gladly, mistress,' Scott said, the sight of the godemiche bringing back heated memories. He enjoyed anal penetration.

'Bend down and grip your ankles,' Carol continued, taking a scoop of butter from the breakfast tray and lubricating the vibrator.

He bent over, the nipple clamps pulling. He was aware that the backs of his thighs, the whole of his amber crack, the puckered hole of his anus, his defenceless balls jiggling in their hairy purse, were all brazenly displayed. He felt extremely vulnerable, and couldn't see what she was doing, but suddenly flinched as her buttery fingers eased themselves past his anal ring, first one, then two and finally three. His pleasure mounted as she slowly inserted the bulbous head of the mock phallus. He felt it at his rectal mouth, pressing home, forcing its way inside him, deeper and deeper, probing from his bowels to his brain.

He clutched his cock, but Carol shouted, 'No! I haven't finished with you.'

When she had lodged the dildo firmly within him, she moved away. Scott strained to listen, but was too aroused by the alien thing in his arse. His cock was dribbling moisture and was so swollen it looked as if it would burst. Then he heard the rustle of silk behind him and the air stirred.

Whack! Scott jerked under the force, the leather strap hitting his rear so hard that it made him dizzy. Again and again it struck his buttocks, and each stroke stirred the dildo, his clenching muscles holding it tighter and deeper.

Then Carol dragged it out, leaving him empty and bereft. 'Get on the bed,' she said.

He had already registered the magnificent couch, tented like an Arabian prince's, and, arse stinging, slithered across the vermilion chenille throw. His imagination was painting erotic pictures, but none were so arousing as the reality of Carol shedding her skirt and panties. His cock thickened as he saw her: the depilated quim, the naked cleft high and well defined, the clit poking forth from its diamond-studded hood.

'You're pierced there,' he said, wonderingly. 'I've read about woman having it done, but have never seen it.'

She smiled slyly, and wheeled over a cheval-mirror, arranging it so that he could see himself on the bed and get a double vision of her, too. Reaching round, she unfastened her bra, held the cups over her breasts teasingly, then let it drop. Naked, she seemed larger, even more dominating, and Scott gulped, his cock swaying as he lay on his back.

'It's like a cobra,' she remarked, pinching it. 'But we don't need a snake-charmer to make it dance.' Next she produced a pair of fur-lined manacles and snapped them round his wrists, saying, as she drew his arms out and up, linking the cuffs to chains fastened round the bed-head, 'My, my, what big bones and firm muscles. It must be all that gardening. I was meaning to ask you about the bugs that are eating my azaleas.'

'I'll take a look,' he whispered, in such sweet agony that thoughts of garden pests were far from his mind.

Like a child admiring a beautiful new toy, she stood with her thighs apart, balancing on those clumpy mules, and said absently, 'Yes, later, later.'

She freed his nipples, the blood running back into the sore tips. Then she secured one of his ankles with a silk scarf and knotted it to the footpost. He could have kicked and struggled but did neither, helpless to do anything but submit. His other leg was hobbled in the same way, his balls resting against the velvety quilt, his cock

185

pointing skywards. The tension doubled as he turned his head sideways and saw the scene repeated in the mirror.

Carol fingered her nipples to rosy peaks, then let her hand idle down to her satin-smooth slit, opening the lips, wetting a finger in her dew and then spreading it across Scott's mouth. He inhaled her strong, salty smell, and licked it in. She withdrew her hand and climbed on the bed, straddling him.

'Oh, God,' he moaned, his cock straining to reach her parted crack, but she skilfully evaded it, smiling wickedly, and her long nails plucked at his tender, reddened nipples.

'Not yet, young man,' she hissed, and worked a bright cerise rubber down his shaft, then wriggled higher, her wetness mingling with the sprinkle of hair coating his chest.

She slid closer and Scott, squinting down, could see all her secrets – the jewel crowning her clit, the twin lips, the bare mons. Her smell was like incense wafting from censers. His throat was dry with wanting, his cock wagging impotently in its red overcoat, denied its goal. He closed his eyes, engulfed by her as she stopped with her thighs wide open over his face. He stuck out his tongue, licking her labia and clit. She sank down on him, hardly giving him space to breathe. He guessed that she was playing with her nipples. Her sharp gasps of pleasure told him she was approaching her crisis.

His cock ached, and she swivelled round, her arse presented to him, the fullness of her pudenda, the dark-skinned crack where her nether hole pouted like a small, hungry mouth. He raised his head slightly and ran his tongue over it. He could feel her examining his balls, lifting them from where they sagged between his legs, weighing them, bending agilely to suck them. First one, then the other, was drawn into her mouth. She ran light fingers up his stem, and he groaned loudly as his jism wetted the condom's teat and glazed his helm. He wanted to do it so badly, and was joyous when she allowed him to brush over her vulva. He thought for one glorious moment that she was about to mount him, but she withdrew. Turning again, astride his chest, she picked up another toy, a vibrator, clicked the switch and aimed it at her clit. Her neck arched and her eyes closed; her lips parted in ecstasy.

Even she, his hard-headed mistress, misjudged her timing, unable to stop with the toy vibrating on her bud. She yowled her pleasure, and Scott watched her jerking, knowing she had come. In an instant, she impaled herself on him, her inner muscles convulsing. His climax tore through him as, humping and grinding, Carol rode him to the highest peak of sensation.

'Where are we?' Rosemary asked nervously.

'Under the maze,' Anthony replied, leading her down a corridor that turned at the end and snaked onwards. 'This is a legendary labyrinth, said to have been built by the druids, long before the Romans invaded Britain, and much, much older than the house. Remember Crete and the Minotaur? The labyrinth at Knossos was constructed by the technician, Daedalus, and was so complex that it was impossible to get in and out without a guide.'

'Didn't they sacrifice virgins every year?' She wished he wouldn't talk about it and was considerably worried as they went in deeper.

'That's right. Seven young men and seven young women. King Minos had ordered Daedalus to build it as a dwelling for the half-man, half-bull son of his wife, Pasiphaë. She'd indulged in bestiality with a white bull and the unfortunate result was this monster. He was eventually killed by Theseus.'

'I don't think I like it down here. Can't we go up again?'

'Not yet. In time, you'll learn to love it as I do.'

'I doubt that very much,' she said with a shudder. Warm and well lit though it was, she hated being underground. Even travelling by tube made her claustrophobic.

He, however, seemed in his element and, as they

turned another corner, she paused in amazement, staring at the figure of a woman in harem dress who began to gyrate her hips and swing the fringes clamped to her breasts in time to wailing flutes and throbbing tambours. She was so lifelike that it took Rosemary a second to realise that she was watching an automaton.

Anthony smiled lovingly at the creature, working the remote control and making her dance even more sinuously. Her flimsy skirt opened, and her perfect, hairless sex was revealed, one of her hands going down to rub over the jewel-encrusted mound.

'Isn't she lovely?' Anthony almost crooned. 'Nineteenth century. A rare example of Parisian craftsmanship. Clockwork when she was made, of course, but I've changed that. She now performs at the touch of a button.'

They passed on, and came to a tableaux where, against a back-cloth of sumptuous drapes, a pair of lovers were engaged in copulation. Her hooped skirt was lifted high and her beau had his breeches open and was thrusting his cock into her cunt. The sound effects were crude but effective, rousing Rosemary's blood, even as she gazed at the robot couple with something akin to disgust.

'By the same maker,' Anthony informed her, flicking a switch so that the creatures moved faster. 'I added the sounds: the squelching of his cock sliding in and out of her; her moans; his groans of pleasure.'

Further groups of figures confirmed her feelings of unrest. These were recently made, beautiful, sleek androids that moved as if alive, each engaged in a sexual activity – masturbating or joined at the genitals, male with male, female with female, or male with female. The scenes were fantastical – space-age, period, contemporary, whatever Anthony had dreamed up. Some of them were definitely dark, featuring bondage and punishment, leather-clad automatons meting out punishment to their helpless victims. And the sounds made Rosemary's spine tingle – the whistle of whips, the pleas and moans, the shrieks of pain that warmed into pleasure.

She frowned, though her cunt throbbed. 'You collect these things?' she asked.

'Another of my hobbies,' he said.

'And what are the others?'

'The theatre, as I've told you, and making marionettes to perform in it.'

'You've made all these?'

'Mostly, though I have friends who are into it, too, but the puppets are my babies entirely. Do you want to meet them?'

'Yes, I'd like that,' she said. Anything to get out of this gloomy, salacious place, whose inhabitants had sex to order and where Anthony was in absolute control.

He was excited, she could tell. There was a note in his voice, a quiver in his touch, and he touched her at any excuse, pressing his erection against her. Her response alarmed her, for she knew that she was losing control. There seemed to be no reason to resist, down there under the ground, surrounded by these mechanical dolls whose only purpose was to arouse. For an instant, he left her, and she knew pure terror when they were suddenly plunged into inky darkness and silence.

'My God! Anthony! Where are you?' she shouted.

'Here. Right by you,' he said, and his voice seemed different, distorted by the darkness, rich and resonant. The suspicion that had been forming in her mind for hours now became a certainty.

'It's you, isn't it?' she accused, trembling as he found her.

His hands caressed her throat and slipped over her breasts to her waist. In such thick darkness her senses were reduced to smell, touch, taste and sound. It was like being blindfolded, and she had an inkling of how exciting it would be if she were gagged and bound.

'What d'you mean, Rosemary?' he murmured, his breath warming her mouth.

'Someone has been stalking me; making obscene phone calls, sending me photos . . . and then this doll arrived.'

'A doll? And what did you think of it?' He controlled

her like one of his androids, gripping her hips and moving her groin over his.

'It freaked me out. It had been made to look like me.'

'How flattering. This unknown someone must admire you a lot.'

'Is it you?' She wasn't sure if she really wanted to know. If it was true, then it would shift the dynamics between them. If it wasn't, she would be unable to trust her male friends again.

'Does it matter?' he asked, and undid the button above her trouser zip and started to slide it down.

Oh, but he's a trickster, all right, a smooth operator, she thought, her awareness focusing on the pathway of his hands as her jeans and panties were pulled down about her knees. Giving her no pause, his fingers pumped into her liquid heat. The cool air hit the backs of her thighs and played round her crack as he stretched her bottom cheeks apart and lingered at her forbidden hole.

'Oh, ooh!' she wailed. 'Yes, it matters. If it was you, then you'll remember talking dirty to me over the phone.'

She felt rather then heard the chuckle reverberating through his chest. 'Soon you shall tell me all about it,' he promised. 'But for now, there's only the darkness and us.'

It was a foregone conclusion, but still came as a shock to find herself lying on the cold floor, naked below the waist, the cobbled path chafing her flesh. He was over her, hands pushing open her bra, pinching and squeezing, the sensation a thin thread of pain that reached her clit. His head went lower, his hair tickling her naked belly. He nudged her thighs open. She felt the rasp of his jaw, although he was closely shaved. It scratched her delicate membranes as he parted her lower lips and she jumped as he nipped at her bud, drawing it out and sucking it relentlessly. He didn't let up, anointing her anus with her own essence and pushing a finger inside.

It was as if an electric charge was building up inside her. When she came, it was so violent that she blanked out. Anthony rolled her over and lifted her to her knees. He cupped her pubis in one hand and worked his fingers into her wetness. Moving to his motions, she eased her pussy into his palm, wanting more. Then, in the complete blackness of that labyrinth womb, she felt his cock pulse against her. He thrust, and it entered her like a steel rod. She squealed and fought to break free, but he had her firmly by the breasts, his cock lodged deep inside her.

Her body urged her to rock on the thing embedded in her, despite her better judgement that she knew she should get him to stop. She rested on her elbows, her hands as if tied in front of her, the discomfort changing into a pleasurable sensation as he found her clit. He was panting, and this excited her. The cool Anthony was yielding to the demands of his flesh. Was he the stalker? At that moment it didn't matter a damn.

The closer he came to completion, so his pinches and scratches increased. Pain shot through her. She was held by his awesome power, and groaned as he moved within her. It was too harsh an invasion to permit her to orgasm. She was sure she'd never be able to do it, but his fingers slid through the slick folds, fastening on her clit, and her climax shocked through her without warning.

Then he pushed her lower, driving into her with brutal force. She heard him gasp and felt the heat of his ejaculation, and she shuddered as if she had come again herself.

Chapter Ten

*T*he lights came on. Rosemary scrabbled for her jeans and knickers. She was confused and angry, but the thought of Anthony's cock made her hips squirm and her belly quake.

He was calmly zipping his chinos and buckling the belt. Certain that he had engineered the powercut, putting her at a disadvantage, she went for the throat. 'How very convenient for the electricity to fail.'

'What's the matter, Rosemary? Haven't you had enough yet? I could have sworn you came at least twice.'

'You shouldn't have done it, especially without protection.'

'I was protected,' he replied calmly. 'It was too dark for you to see and, as you didn't touch it, how were you to know? But I can assure you, Rosemary, that I never take risks. Life's too precious. I even use a condom when fucking my robots, remembering that story about sailors at sea who made a rubber woman for sexual relief. They all used her, and she ended up giving them syphilis.'

'You do have a fund of weird stories. I doubt any of them are true,' she countered, wondering if he really made love to his androids. Men all over the world purchased inflatable dolls, so why did it make her horny to think of him having sex with one of his own design? He had probably made it up anyway, to shock her.

'When you've travelled as far as me, and seen things that would make your hair stand on end, then you'll collect a few yarns on the way.' His answer was cryptic, his casual manner riling her. It was as if, having discharged his load, she no longer mattered.

'I could sue you for sexual assault,' she threatened.

Anthony threw back his head and his laughter echoed in the labyrinth. 'My dear girl,' he managed at last. 'Have you any idea what you're talking about? Sexual assault? Good grief! It was on the cards that we'd fuck. You wanted it as much as I, probably more.'

Glaring at him, she buttoned her shirt and huddled into herself, rubbing her hands up and down her arms. 'I'm cold,' she complained, seeking a human response from this uncaring person.

'Poor baby,' he said sarcastically, reaching out and hauling her against his body, then kissing her full on the lips. 'We'll do it again later, but now I'm taking you to my workshop. There you can decide whether or not I'm the stalker.'

She wished he wasn't so bright. It was impossible to hide anything from him, and she admitted to herself that she did want to stroke his cock, cradle his balls and have him fuck her again. She was also fascinated by the mind of this enigmatic man. Now he was guiding her to another part of his domain, and her curiosity was at feverpitch.

She had expected to leave by the route they had come, but Anthony had other plans. He linked his fingers with hers and led her away from where his mechanical creatures performed libidinously.

'There are so many paths,' she said, praying that she hadn't allowed herself to be kidnapped by a mad axeman, serial killer, or someone equally deranged. Dan would have told her she was an idiot to trust him, but she had no alternative and would never have reached the surface by herself.

'The house is honeycombed, too. Secret passages, priest holes, you name it, we've got it.' He stopped at a blank wall, twisted the leaf of a carved stone acanthus plant and a section slid back, revealing a spiral staircase.

'It's like Bluebeard's Castle,' she commented, out of breath by the time they reached the top. 'Have you several wives languishing in cells, like Duke Bluebeard?'

'Perhaps,' he said, and pushed open a door, standing back so that she might step inside.

The room was large, with arched narrow windows. Anthony unfolded the shutters, and sunlight streamed in. It reflected on worktables, on racks of costumes and scenery leaning against whitewashed walls, on props, swords, spears and the hundred and one items needed for a theatrical production.

But everything else was eclipsed by the puppets hanging on specially constructed stands. Some were no more than twenty inches high, others three-quarters lifesized. And there were some, in a section to themselves, which were of near-human proportions.

'Rosemary, meet my children,' Anthony said, caressing them with more affection than she had seen him display to any living thing.

'I'm gobsmacked,' she replied, as unsure about these as the doll delivered to Sutton Close. 'Did you make them?'

'Not all. Some are antique. I've been a collector for years. Once, I just about survived by taking part in street theatre, using the skills learned from masters I'd trained under in Europe.' He took down one of the larger puppets, and it immediately became vitalised. 'This chap is an Italian marionette, Pulcinella. He was made in 1800, and his roots go back to the fourteenth century when the extempore drama known as the *Commedia dell'Arte* first appeared, performed by mountebanks up and down the country.'

The marionette moved as Anthony manipulated the controller to which the strings were attached. Dressed in a baggy white shirt and pantaloons, a conical hat on its head, Pulcinella became a hook-nosed Neapolitan peasant, foolish and sly, boastful and cowardly.

Rosemary shrank back as he advanced on her lecherously, saying in a guttural accent, 'Ah, *bella signorina*, kiss me, caress me, rub my prick and make me dance for joy.'

It wasn't the capering clown, of course, but Anthony who was speaking, his voice deeper and foreign-sounding. His skill was remarkable. Even without stage lighting, she wasn't conscious of the strings. Pulcinella had acquired a forceful, alarming personality.

'He likes you,' Anthony said, no longer a coarse buffoon, and the puppet made cow eyes at her, raised his hand and placed it on her breast with so insinuating a touch that her nipples crimped.

'You're very talented,' she said, addressing the man not the manikin.

'I studied hard. Hunger makes you learn quickly and I had nothing in those days, the drop-out of the family who wanted to make the stage his life. Now, thanks to fate, I can do that.'

'So this is what you use your theatre for, marionette shows?'

'It is, but with a difference. You won't have seen anything quite like it. Carol and I are puppet-handlers, and so is the vicar and the vet, and a few others you haven't yet met. D'you want to try it?'

'I might, but I don't think it's my thing.' Rosemary was now convinced that her doll had been Anthony's work. It was on the tip of her tongue to tackle him, but then he put Pulcinella aside, took down a ballerina in a tutu, and handed it to her.

'It's not easy,' she said, the strings immediately becoming a tangled cat's cradle. Far from dancing daintily, the ballerina sagged, elbows sticking out, feet thumping on the floor, knees pointing any which way.

'One has to be patient. It's worth waiting for. There's nothing to compare with the thrill of having a little, inanimate body come to life in your hands and under your command.' He took the puppet and at once it fluttered its arms gracefully, rising on its points and executing perfect steps.

His face was intense, and Rosemary could see that he revelled in the things he could make the puppet do; walk, gesture, back-bend, twirl. It looked so simple. He was omnipotent with the control bar in his hand.

'You remind me of Dr Coppelius, the old toy-maker who made a mechanical doll so lifelike that everyone imagined her to be a beautiful girl.'

'The ballet *Coppelia* was based on a much darker tale by the German writer, Hoffman,' he said. 'It's as light as air and has a delicious score by Delibes. Let's listen to some of it now.'

Handing her the ballerina, he slotted a CD into the portable player. At once the familiar music soothed Rosemary. She absorbed its melodies and even succeeded in getting the little dancer to follow the rhythm.

'That's it. You can do it,' he said. 'Hold the bar more like this,' and he stood behind Rosemary, his arms coming round her, guiding her fingers. 'Ah, yes. You're getting the hang of it. Can you feel the power you'd have over an audience? Few persons can resist the lure of a doll in motion.'

She felt the hardness of his cock pressing into her bottom, and her own answering need. What had happened in the labyrinth hadn't slaked her lust. It had been too quick. She thirsted to savour Anthony, to drain every last drop of pleasure. But there was a question she had to ask him before they went any further.

She rested her head back against his chest. 'I think it was you who pestered me in London. Tell me the truth, Anthony.'

He put the ballerina down and stopped the disc. 'You really want to know if I'm the big, bad wolf?' he teased, running his tongue across the nape of her neck, the erotic sensation making her sigh and press into him, seeking more intimate contact.

'I do. Tell me.'

'This should answer you,' he said, and let her go. In an

instant he had whipped off a dust-sheet. There hung another marionette.

Rosemary was unsure whether to be glad or sorry. The puppet was a copy of the rag-time flapper, with the same torn Charleston dress and wanton expression: a trollop with Rosemary's face and hair and a whip in its hands. But it was larger and its limbs were jointed. Anthony had it shimmy across to where Rosemary stood, stuck one of its hands on its hip in a harpy pose, legs spread, pelvis thrust forward, showing a patch of dark floss at its fork.

'Why?' Rosemary whispered.

'I want you, and what I want I always get,' he murmured close to her ear, and the timbre of his voice made her limbs tremble and her sex yearn; it was the voice that had seduced her over the phone.

His assumption that he had the god-given right to have his own way should have ignited her girl-power torch, but she didn't even question it. Melanie would throw up her hands in despair at such surrender, she thought guiltily, but even she, if faced with this remarkable man, might not be able to resist.

Anthony replaced the marionette and, behind her, Rosemary could hear the rustle of a condom packet being opened. She braced herself, dying to turn and look at him, but not quite daring. Her warm juices soaked into her panty gusset as she anticipated what he was going to do to her.

'Unzip,' he commanded.

She hesitated and he implemented his order with a crisp slap that made her backside smart.

'Don't,' she said, her voice quavering, her fingers flying to open her jeans and pull them and her panties down.

'Don't what?' he teased. 'Don't fuck you, or don't slap you?'

'I don't like being hurt.'

'No? I understood that at least one of your recent lovers had been a little rough. Neil Kemble, I believe.'

'You listen to everything your spies report?'

The front of his legs brushed against the backs of hers

as he moved into position. 'I take it all with a grain of salt, but, on the whole, my sources are reliable. It's all a matter of money, you see. You pay for what you get and I can afford the best. Get your pants off and come over here.'

He shifted books, papers and drawing equipment from the top of a table and laid her belly-down on it. Then he steadied himself with his hands placed either side of her buttocks. Rosemary bit back a moan as he started to knead her flesh, then went lower, sliding his fingers into her avenue and fingering her anus.

The sunshine struck sparks from the tinsel crown of a puppet king. Rosemary looked at him and at the other make-believe people. They seemed to be watching her with prurient interest. Pulcinella's head lolled, and his eyes bored into her like gimlets, his wooden hand resting at his crotch. It was as if they were a live, randy crowd who found the spectacle amusing.

Rosemary didn't care. She was wet and ready, longing for Anthony to lodge his cock inside her. She shifted position, raising her butt a little, praying for him to do it, hardly able to bear the tension as he eased his helm into her an inch or two. She bore down on it, taking it deep into her cunt. He grunted and gripped her harder, hauling her against him, buried to the hilt, his wiry pubic hair tickling her parted crack.

He moved slowly, rotating his hips rather than pumping them. She wormed her hand down to her clit, circling the tip, chasing the sensation. He stepped up the speed, ramming his cock into her, filling her with his solid length. She arched her spine as he reached under her and replaced her finger with his own. A massive orgasm racked her, then faded into tiny, irregular spasms. She fully expected him to come, but felt him spreading her juices up the cleft of her arse, then pushing the entire length of his finger into her tight anus.

'Don't fight it. Relax,' he whispered, and a breeze stirred the marionettes, making their heads nod in agreement.

198

'This is new to me.' She sensed what he was about to do, and scraps of conversation she'd had with Melanie echoed in her mind.

'Anal sex?' her agent had said. 'It's fun for a change, once you get used to it. You've never tried it? I don't suppose Terry was into anything vaguely perverted, was he? I wonder if Belinda will show him a thing or three? You can never be sure what these hamsters get up to in the privacy of their own warrens.'

And here she was, about to experience the unknown. It would be like losing her virginity all over again, and that hadn't exactly set the world on fire. Was she ready for this? Rosemary wasn't at all sure, but, in the afterglow of climax, she was willing to try. She hadn't yet crossed that line where she could simply use men for her own pleasure, then dump them. Her sense of decency and fair-play insisted that she satisfied them, no matter how weird and wonderful their requirements.

'The trouble with you, Rosemary, is you're too nice.' Melanie's rather strident voice seemed to reverberate in her head.

Nice was no use now, she discovered, as Anthony used her fluids to lubricate his finger, allowing him to slide it to the second knuckle in her arsehole. She protested when he added another and then a third, twisting them slightly.

'God! I don't think I want this. Oh, please. Let's do it the other way.' She squirmed on the table top, her breasts squashed, her bottom in the air, legs braced and feet resting on the floor.

'You're a perfect target, just waiting to be buggered.'

He replaced his fingers with the head of his cock. She felt it easing its way in. She clenched her sphincter, but failed to dislodge it. Like forcing a cork into a bottle, Anthony's shaft pushed inexorably into her virgin anus. Rosemary swore as he penetrated her, filling her loins and bowels with a shuddering sensation that felt distinctly odd.

'That's it,' he muttered, rocking inside her.

'You bastard!' she shouted and wanted to hurt him, longing to drag him into her cunt and snap off his cock. Let him experience the male nightmare of a vagina with teeth.

'Shut up! You know you like it really,' he growled and forced himself in and out of her opening. 'Jesus! You're so tight there. It's wonderful.'

Rosemary could feel her arse relaxing. The pain was nearly gone, and a strange pleasure took its place. She was accepting his cock and no longer wanted to expel it. The table was hard, but as she moved involuntarily, propelled by his thrusts, her nipples rubbed against her shirt, and she ached for him to touch her clit.

He was concentrating on his own release, using her as hard as he dared, for she was new to this and must not be injured. His fingers indented her flesh as he held her to him and thrust. She shut her eyes and endured, feeling her arsehole expanding to take all of him. Buffeted by his passion, gripping the edge of the table to prevent herself sliding off, she felt his orgasm seize him, then he collapsed on her, his weight crushing her into the wood.

She was panting, every delicate membrane in her loins seeming to be on fire, yet she trembled in response to the power of this man. He was like a drug that was too potent for her to handle, but she wanted to experiment, all the same.

He rose from her and, groaning, she sat up. He rolled off the condom, the teat heavy with his come. She looked at him as he stood watching her, and she instinctively recognised the expression of a dominating master carved on his haughty face.

'When you go to bed tonight, Rosemary,' he said, 'inspect your sore arse and masturbate to the memory of me. Don't inhibit your fantasies; imagine the wildest scenario, and tell me about it next time we fuck.'

'So you assume we'll do it again?' she said, gaining control of herself as she put her jeans back on. They felt too tight, even the soft silk of her panties irritating her stinging arse.

'Of course. We haven't even started yet. I've so much to teach you. Never doubt my ability to bring out the darkness in those I select as my disciples.'

'Everything's fine here, Miss Maddox,' said Fran down the phone. 'That cop friend of yours has been nosing around. Robert's all of a twitter. Says he's a pushover for men in uniform.'

Rosemary smiled, imagining Robert flirting with Dan and getting the cold shoulder. 'Dan doesn't wear uniform, except when ordered to.'

'Robert has a vivid imagination. Anyhow, your DC is cool. I give him coffee and, ever so politely, he asks if he can listen to that operatic thing you like so much.'

'*Tosca*?'

'That's right. It does my head in, but he seems to get off on it.'

'Not with you, I hope.'

'No chance. I've told you, I'm allergic to pigs.'

'Has Mr Veney been in?'

''Fraid so, but only in the office and the garden centre. You can't keep him out, can you?'

'Not till the place is mine. It's going through, but there's bound to be a delay.' A red-hot knife twisted in Rosemary's gut as she thought of Terry and Belinda poking about in her absence, but her solicitor had told her very firmly that she wasn't allowed to bar him while he was still part owner of Plants Galore.

'Are you having a good time? Is Scott behaving himself?'

'I guess so.'

Rosemary wasn't sure about Scott. Two days into the visit, and he had shamefacedly confessed to his session with Carol.

'She's so dominating and I enjoy it,' he'd said, a blush deepening his tan. 'I've always liked being a sub, Rosemary. When a woman bosses me around, I get a massive hard-on.'

'Why didn't you tell me before?' she had asked, staring

201

at the red ladder of whip marks on his muscular back. 'I had no idea you were into SM. D'you want me to thrash you?'

He had shaken his head. 'It wouldn't seem right between you and me.'

Two days in, and she was uneasily aware that, since fucking her arse, Anthony had been deliberately avoiding her. This was galling, for she was on fire for him, despising herself but in a constant state of excitation which neither masturbation nor screwing Scott managed to alleviate. Would he whip her, like Carol had done to Scott? She wanted it, yet was appalled, and couldn't wait for Michael to arrive. He'd soon snap her into line, make her concentrate on work and forget these flights of fancy. In retrospect even Jonathan was preferable, a pussy-cat compared to the moody Puppet Master General. Above all, she was desperate to see Dan. Even talking about him with Fran brought him closer.

'We can make it earlier,' Michael rang to say on Monday morning. 'The cameraman has had a row with his wife and curtailed his trip. Nothing quite like family holidays for breaking up the happy home. Expect us later on today. Melanie's asking after you, by the way.'

'I'll have to tell Anthony.'

'It's sorted, pet. Don't worry about a thing.'

'Which is your room?' Jonathan wanted to know as soon as he sauntered into the hall, superbly stylish in plum velvet, low-slung loons, a silk shirt opened down to his navel, showing fair chest hair and a thick gold chain.

'I'll show you when we go up,' Rosemary said, glad that she had made an effort with her appearance, for he was set to outshine her. There's nothing like the merest hint of a camera for bringing out the exhibitionist in all of us, she thought.

He was looking devastatingly handsome and Rosemary smiled inwardly as she introduced him to Anthony. Michael, too, was not the sort of person to be ignored – a large, expansive, extremely confident man who knew his craft inside out. Carol was obviously impressed by both men. She was wearing an expensive raw silk caftan with a revealing neckline and slits to the thigh on each side. Her jewels consisted of pendant earrings and a necklace that dangled to her middle, made up of amber in an antique setting.

'What a fabulous house,' Jonathan enthused, responding as she flirted with him. 'I think I'll move in.'

Helen from research was there, vying with Mary for Michael's attention, and Anthony came into his own, an expansive, generous host, captivating everyone, with the possible exception of Michael, who muttered to Rosemary, 'What's he like! I'm too long in the tooth to be taken in by his malarkey.'

'He's an OK guy,' she answered, and his knowing hand was at her waist, warm through the fine material. She smelled his aftershave and wanted him in her bed. She knew she'd sleep better with him beside her.

He cocked an eyebrow at her. 'Really? And you've done a study of him already, have you?'

'Talk to him. Ask him about the labyrinth.'

'The what?'

'There's an ancient labyrinth under the maze,'

'Can we film it?'

'Wait till you've seen it.'

After dinner, everyone trooped out to look at the maze, but it was too dark to see much. Back inside again, Michael and Anthony went into a huddle, and Rosemary decided to go to bed; it was going to be a long day tomorrow. But her mind was working overtime and she found it difficult to sleep. Restless and hot, she curled on her side, then flopped on her back. It was no use. She was wound-up about the shoot that started in the morning. Though the programmes looked impromptu and the jokes and bits of business seemed spontaneous, it was in fact carefully rehearsed, and they stuck to a script. If anyone made a blunder, Michael called 'cut' and the scene was done again. Any serious mishaps ended up on the floor during editing.

Michael had already handed her a rough, and they'd be working on it early, while the team of gardeners, led by Scott, reconnoitred the maze. Then the heavy artillery would be moved in. She had already opined that machetes, not diggers, should be used to hack through parts that resembled the Amazonian rainforests. Michael had laughed, thinking she exaggerated, but then he hadn't yet taken a proper look.

As for Jonathan? She had half expected him or Michael to put in an appearance in her room, but time passed and she imagined them deep in discussion, with Michael holding forth and Jonathan adding his opinion. Scott would be there, too, drawing attention to himself, driven by ambition. Probably Carol was absent, preparing herself to give Scott further lessons in submission.

Rosemary felt oddly left out. I should have stayed with them, she thought. Decisions will be made which I won't agree with. There will be arguments in the morning. I wish I was home, or in Dan's flat. I'd like to be a private person again, not a sideshow freak that people gawp at.

Her hand strayed down to her naked belly, and tangled in her bush. Without thinking, she slid a finger into her crack and started to manipulate her clitoris, tracing the stem back, deep in her fleshy mound, and deliberately keeping the head dry. The feeling was harsh and likely to last longer.

She tossed back the quilt and reached into the bedside table to bring out her vibrator. Its shiny surface glistened invitingly. Her mood had altered and she needed a change of pace. She switched it on. The buzzing tip touched her clit and she jerked, then inserted it in herself, pushing it deep, feeling the charge but knowing that she would never come unless her clit was stimulated.

Unable to wait any longer, she applied the dildo's rounded end to her bud. The friction was almost too much. She wetted it in her cunt, and rubbed the smoothly moving instrument of pleasure over her clit, lightly at first, then with more pressure. When she came, it was like a bolt of lightning blasting through her.

She turned the vibrator off, and slid its hard length into her, feeling her muscles contract round it. With it still inserted, her last thought before she fell asleep was: Who needs men?

'The maze was originally planted with hornbeam, but later additions were made of other species, including whitethorn, privet, holly, sycamore and yew,' Rosemary said for the umpteenth time. To her relief Michael stayed silent. The camera rolled. The soundman's boom remained stable, just over her head but out of camera range. She'd got it right!

They were recording the introduction to the programme. Jonathan had already done his piece concerning the architecture of Malvern Chase and had interviewed Anthony and Carol. There were plans for him to come back and continue working on the orangery. Shots of this had already been taken.

Besides the camera crew, lighting and sound, there was the continuity girl and best boy, key grip and Gary from make-up, as well as others essential to filming. Helen and Mary were much in evidence, and the horticultural assistants, all of whom had been housed, fed and taken care of by the butler and his cohorts.

Rosemary knew that although she would appear to be coping effortlessly with the work of maze clearing, making light of it, exchanging banter with Scott and Jonathan, the rest of the team would be carrying out her orders; they were the unsung heroes of gardening slots. One of her hardest tasks was making Scott chill out. The prospect of actually appearing on television was going to his head. She had enough to contend with ensuring that Jonathan didn't upstage her, let alone her apprentice.

Michael had his finger on the pulse. By the end of the first day, petrol-driven hedge-cutters and sheer muscle had cleared the way to the centre. The blind alleys and false paths would be dealt with tomorrow. Already some of the team had started to tidy up outside the maze, ensuring that the surroundings were immaculate.

Michael called a halt at the stone archway. 'Is this it?' he asked Anthony.

'Yes. That's the way down to the labyrinth.'

'You were telling me about it last night. Can we go in? I'm not saying that we can include it in this programme, but . . .'

'I could use it in my show, perhaps,' Jonathan interrupted. Though he had helped Rosemary, he managed to remain unruffled, apart from the delicate sheen of sweat that bedewed his make-up. His carefully rumpled tawny hair added to the illusion that he had taken his full share of the slog.

Michael shot him a stern glance; he was possessive when it came to items which might favour *In Your Own Backyard*. He preferred to keep Jonathan under his thumb, rather than have him pinching ideas and wafting off to incorporate them in his own weekly feature.

'Can I go in?' asked Scott, cocky now, feeling himself to be their equal.

'I don't see why not,' Anthony answered.

'Count me out,' Rosemary said, pushing back a lock of damp hair. She inhaled the ripe aroma of her body which no amount of deodorant could quite dispel – the scent of sweat and pussy juice.

Were the men aware? Did they pick up on these smells exuded by women to encourage a mate? Dame Nature is ruthless, she mused. Nothing matters to her but the continuation of the species. What a waste. I have no intention of producing a child. All that concerns me is pleasure. Even the search for this proves complicated. Maybe I'll stick to my own fingers and a vibrator.

The security guard stepped out from a side path.

'Conduct Miss Maddox to the house, Higgins,' Anthony ordered.

'Yes, sir,' Higgins grunted.

'It's not necessary, you know. I'm sure I can find my way now.'

'I disagree. We can't have our star lost or kidnapped

now, can we?' Anthony's tone was playful but his face determined.

'Do as the man says, Rosemary,' Michael chipped in, grinning.

'What about me?' Jonathan asked, brows raised.

'We'll take care of you. You're going to adore the labyrinth,' Anthony said and went down the steps.

Rosemary followed Higgins, secretly glad to have him there, still feeling hemmed in by the maze, though the path was wider now, the hedge controlled, no higher than seven feet. She smiled encouragingly at a couple of her stalwarts in safety helmets and goggles who were standing on step-ladders, attacking larger branches with chainsaws. Her spirits rose when she stepped outside, seeing the green lawn, the herbaceous borders, and the magnificent Cedar of Lebanon and pine trees.

'This is a truly splendid place,' she said to Higgins, who was matching his stride to hers, the sunlight glistening on his shaven head. 'No matter what trials and tribulations you're going through, step into a garden and its peace and tranquillity heals you. Flowers, trees, birdsong and, best of all, water. Don't you agree?'

Higgins looked down at her from his great height, a broken-nosed heavy with his face screwed up in thought. 'That's right, miss. My old dear loves her garden.'

'There you are then,' Rosemary concluded, and left him on the terrace, heading for her room and the powershower.

As the door closed behind her, someone rose from the armchair near the window, and she jumped three feet – at least it felt like that.

'Hello, Rosemary, I've been waiting for you,' Dan said.

'Good God! What are you doing here?' Her knees turned to jelly.

'Had a day's leave owing, so thought I'd come down and check that you were all right.'

The shaking feeling lessened as he came across and hugged her. 'I'm so pleased to see you,' she whispered, and lifted her face. It felt so right when he kissed her: a deep, searching, tongue-twining kiss that went on and on, till she was pushing her breasts up against him and gyrating her pussy round the long penis in his jeans.

Still kissing her, he half carried her to the bed. And then it was a tangle as they struggled out of their clothes, too eager to take it too steadily. She whipped back the duvet and they lay together on the sheet. Then, and only then, did they slow down a little.

She hadn't forgotten how good he was, but now it all came back tenfold. That dark hair and steely eyes, the crooked smile, muscular body and divine high bum-cheeks, the cynical turn of wit and gritty sense of humour. Dan. 'Your DC,' as Fran had dubbed him.

Early evening and the sun was lower, sending fiery darts between the drapes and the four-poster bed; the entire romantic chamber was ready for loving. She forgot Scott, but remembered the feeling of being watched. She placed her hand over Dan's lips and said, 'I think the room's bugged.'

'It was,' he growled, and pointed. 'A camera up there, at the top of the headboard. Don't worry. I've covered it. There's another in the bathroom, and I've blanketed that, too. Someone gets his jollies by looking at you. Who is it? Anthony Selby?'

'Who else? But I don't want to talk about that now.'

She rested back and played with her nipples, tugging them into peaks. Dan watched her, then said, 'Let me do that,' his broad fingers taking over, plucking pleasure from her like a lute player drawing notes from strings.

His cock was hard, as it pressed against her belly. It was perhaps the best one she'd ever seen – long, thick and veined, with a mushroom-shaped helm that begged to be touched. She went to close her hand round it, but he stopped her.

'Let me,' she pleaded.

'Not yet. I want to bring you to orgasm first, but I'm so ready to burst that if you touch me I can't guarantee to hold back.'

He went down on her, parting her legs and burying

his face in her pussy. Then he raised himself, taking his weight on his elbows and examining her. 'I want to spread you. I want to see everything.'

Heat surged through her. Her knees flopped open, and she helped him, sliding her hands down to between her legs, holding herself apart. Her pussy felt cold as if in a draught, but her clit was swollen and red, the tip a paler shade, like a pearl.

Dan moved closer, staring down at her, then he dribbled a morsel of saliva that landed right on her clit. He massaged it in with his middle finger and she wanted to come so badly. His lips followed, sucking at the little shaft and Rosemary's need rose higher. His tongue was magic, avid and powerful, and under his ardour, her excitement increased.

'Put your fingers in me,' she gasped and he reached under her bottom and inserted two deep inside her, curling them and holding them tight against her inner wall.

It wasn't like Anthony's invasion of her arse. That had been jarring, shocking, a conglomeration of pain and pleasure. This was entirely wonderful: Dan's fingers in her cunt, his mouth on her clit. She was rising, clawing at the sheet under her, clawing at him. Her head tossed from side to side, eyes tight shut, and she could feel the sweat trickling, adding to the dirt of the day. She hadn't showered or even washed her private parts, but Dan obviously didn't care.

He took a breather, smiled at her and said, 'I love the smell and taste of you.'

His words stoked her fire. When he returned to her clit, she pulsed against his mouth, the feeling rushing through her in surge after surge. He kept his lips there, but, sensitive to her heightened state, stilled his tongue. She descended slowly, passing from one lovely plateau to the next. Dan understood.

When her respiration returned to something approaching normal, she reached for his prick. It was stiff and high, a bead of clear fluid poised at the slit. Rosemary rubbed it, spreading the pre-come up and down, over and around. He worked his hips, rising and falling, matching the rhythm of her hand, then he suddenly withdrew. She was disappointed, but accepted that his care for her included sexual protection. When he returned, he pressed her down against the mattress and entered her in a single, slick stroke.

He was going faster now, flying towards completion, and Rosemary jerked at each successive thrust, so high herself that she arched her pelvis, seeking pressure on her clit, hovering on the edge of another orgasm. He was going for it, riding the whirlwind and she knew when he came, feeling the pulse as his semen pumped.

He relaxed on her for a moment, then rolled off and pulled her against him, his arm under her head. She closed her eyes, one hand moving over his chest as if she was seeing him with her fingertips. She sighed.

'Something wrong?' Dan asked sleepily.

'No. I just wish this could go on for ever,' she said, but inside she was bordering on panic, thinking: My God, I could so easily fall in love with him!

'I can't stay.'

'Why not? I'm sure Anthony wouldn't object to another guest. I could say you're one of my helpers.'

'This isn't a social call. I came because I couldn't keep away from you, Rosemary, but I've also been doing some ferreting into Anthony Selby's past. He's an oddball.'

She cuddled closer, breathing in his special scent. 'I know that. He's the one who has been phoning me and sent me the doll.'

His eyes narrowed and he thrust a hand into her hair, holding her head steady so that she couldn't avoid his eyes. 'That's the conclusion I'd come to. Be careful, Rosemary. Shall I arrest him?'

She shook her head. 'I don't think he's dangerous, just obsessive. He makes marionettes, and crafted the doll for me. He's a man with too much money and time on his hands.'

As Rosemary met his gaze candidly, so she avoided

telling the absolute truth that she was fascinated by Anthony and had already toyed with the notion of playing the submissive. Dan was quick off the mark, however, and she wondered if he had guessed at her intimacy with her host.

'I'd like to be able to hang around, but must get back,' he said, his breath warm against her neck, his fingers weaving patterns round her nipples.

'How did you get in without being stopped? He has bodyguards, you know?'

He laughed, and scooted his fingers across her belly to her mound. 'It's lucky there are so many strangers here, the film crew, the gardeners. I walked in bold as brass and no one asked me my business. Your room was easy. The lock is crap.'

'You'd better go before Scott sees you. He has the room next door.'

'I've already checked this out.'

'He's in the labyrinth with the others at the moment. I'll tell you all about it when I phone.'

His voice was husky, his cock already rising again, as he whispered, 'One more before I go. And this time we'll come together.'

'Anything you say,' she agreed, losing herself in him.

'And Rosemary?'

'Yes, Dan?'

'Be careful of Anthony Selby.'

Chapter Eleven

Jonathan had made up his mind. He wanted to feature the labyrinth on TV, not with Rosemary or Michael, but by himself. He was adamant about it.

Dinner was over, and he was sitting in the conservatory on a reproduction Victorian rattan chair. At his side, on a matching coffee table, stood a genuine Georgian silver teapot, sugar basin and milk jug, arranged on a solid silver tray. On his knee was a teddy bear called Marmaduke, wearing a tasselled fez and quilted smoking jacket. He was a recent acquisition, presented to him by a besotted fan. Jonathan had adopted him as his mascot, and had taken to carrying him around. Marmaduke was almost as good an attention getter as a dog or a small child, neither of which Jonathan had any intention of sharing his life with; nasty, messy, noisy things.

Bathed, fed and relaxed, he stretched out his seemingly endless legs in their natural-dyed, shantung trousers, appreciating the grandeur of this warm, glazed room filled with exotic plants. Carol reclined on a cane-work sofa, velour and chintz cushions in the small of her back. Her ankle-length dress resembled lingerie, and was of so fragile a material that her nipples lifted it with ease. Jonathan could see that her pussy was denuded of hair. His cock stirred and his long forefinger itched to push the fabric deep into her crack and wriggle it around, bringing her to a quick climax. He was more than sure she'd be a willing participant.

Carol lit a cigarette in a jade holder and touched it to her cherry-red lips. Her eyes regarded him, catlike, through the blue smoke. 'You like the maze, the orangery and find the labyrinth to your taste?' she asked, in carefully modulated tones.

'I do indeed, and so does Marmaduke,' he said, switching on his most beguiling smile, while thinking: She's gorgeous. A hedonistic, selfish bitch. But it might almost be worth marrying her to get my hands on this place. Of course, there's the cousin, but he looks as if he's into anything. He's been giving me the once over and I wouldn't say no. What an intriguing situation, one that's lost on Rosemary and Michael.

He gazed at Anthony, his eyelids drooping in that languid way which he knew would be appreciated. Michael was smoking a cheroot, and he hadn't bothered to dress for dinner, had merely changed into a comfortable sloppy sweater and loose trousers. Rosemary had gone for a walk, expressing an enthusiastic desire to explore the rest of the garden which Jonathan found boring in the extreme.

'I'd be keen to use the labyrinth, but with a few minor alterations,' Michael was saying to Anthony.

'Oh? And what might those be?' Anthony asked, his sensual lips curving into a slight smile as he admired Jonathan.

'Well, the automatons for a start. I find them fun but the programme controller may not. I agree that they're a collector's dream come true, but rather too near the knuckle. Couldn't you stop them indulging in such rude antics? A bit salty for *In Your Own Backyard*. It's a family show, you see, and goes out before the watershed.'

'I could modify them, but it seems a shame. Their charm lies in their vulgarity. Don't you agree, Jonathan?'

'Absolutely,' he answered at once, ever the opportunist. 'If you let me film there, I promise not to change a thing. I shouldn't offer it to my usual producer, but get in touch with someone I know at Channel 4.'

Michael glowered at him, and opened his mouth to argue, but at that moment Mary sidled in. 'Are you ready to look at the rushes, Mr Pendelton?' she murmured reverently.

Michael sighed. 'No peace for the wicked. I must have been very wicked in one of my former lives. We'll talk about this again, Anthony.'

When the three of them were alone, Carol leaned across and placed her hand flat on Jonathan's fly. 'We haven't shown you the other parts of the house,' she said, and something in her inflection alerted him.

'There's more?' He faked astonishment, thinking: Too right, there's more. You can't tell me they're not into the sub-dom scene. Wait here, Marmaduke. I don't want you corrupted. Rising, he sat the bear on the chair.

He wasn't disappointed, soon finding himself in a room built into the foundations. Jonathan suppressed a yawn. The decor was almost passé. He'd seen it all before in various fetish clubs up and down the country, mostly set in dank underground chambers such as this one. Even so, a frisson of excitement fired along his nerves and settled in his groin.

So, the Selbys led a double life, did they? He never could resist getting embroiled in other people's secrets – so sordid, most of them, no matter how bland their public face.

The dungeon was well equipped, and his eyes swept over the crosspiece and bondage-couch, the racks of whips, paddles, canes and flails. There were chains and handcuffs, leg-irons and manacles, masks, nipple clamps and anal plugs, all of which he recognised from personal experience.

'Well, well,' he commented and, picking up an elegantly crafted, ivory-handled riding crop, whacked Carol across the bottom.

She jumped, losing her composure momentarily. Jonathan swiped at her again. This time the tip of the whip

214

tangled in her dress. There was the distinct sound of tearing silk.

'Bugger it!' she shouted. 'That's new.'

'I'll buy you another. Half a dozen if you want,' Jonathan said carelessly and ran the whip through his hands, the feel of the pliant leather making his cock spasm.

'Don't be rude to our guest, Carol,' Anthony chided, and slipped the shoulder straps down her arms. In an instant the dress was off, and she was naked.

Jonathan fed on the sight of her slim body. The breasts were generous, the waist supple, the hips and buttocks large enough to give a man purchase, or sustain the blows of whichever implement he favoured. She stood there boldly, one leg relaxed, the other taking her weight, her hair coiled high, showing the graceful symmetry of her neck and shoulders.

'Do you want to try her?' Anthony said, propped against a crimson-draped pillar, observing them. 'She's that sublime combination of submissive and dominatrix, and will obey me. I think you need to get rid of the anger Michael's roused in you, and the frustration caused by Rosemary. The safe word is "Eldritch", by the way, but I doubt she'll use it.'

He led Carol to the couch, unpinned her hair, and had her lie flat on her back, arms outstretched and wrists fastened by cuffs bolted to chains. She raised her knees, and doubled them back against her chest, breasts bulging on either side. Anthony wound straps round her legs and ankles, holding them in place, then bound her eyes and stuffed a ball-gag into her mouth. She lay there motionless, like a trussed fowl. Jonathan paced round her, thinking, even if she does want me to stop, she'll hardly be able to say anything with that in her mouth.

His cock was so elongated and stiff that it seemed glued to his navel. The sight of Carol, helpless and exposed, her sex like a lewd offering to his lust, made him want to see her buttocks redden under the lash, to push ben-wa balls into her anus and himself into her hairless cunt. He'd torment her clit till she came, not once, not twice, but many times. She wouldn't be able to protest, even if she wanted to; she'd simply grunt and make animal noises. A peculiar bond would form between them, the victim and the dominator, till roles became muddled and he wouldn't be sure if he was mastering her, or she controlling him. The dichotomy of this always excited him and he'd achieved monumental orgasms when wielding the whip or under it.

He removed his jacket, replaced the crop and selected a Malacca cane, making it whistle and snap. Aware that Anthony was watching him critically, he took up a stance, his full shirt sleeves and tight pants turning it into a classic pose. He felt like a matador at the moment of truth, when he has to go in over the bull's horns and strike cleanly, severing the spinal cord. I'd like to do that, he thought, visualising the crowd, the arena, the hot Spanish sun and himself wearing a dazzling Suit of Lights, but this is more fun.

Silvery wetness escaped from Carol's pussy, her pudenda upward thrusting, purselike in that exposed position. She was swollen and ready, her diamond-adorned clit poking out at the top of her crease. Jonathan narrowed his eyes and measured the distance. To retain Anthony's respect, and Carol's, too, it was essential that he laid on the stripes correctly.

He stood back and waited till the room became absolutely quiet. Then with a quick swing he brought the cane down meanly on the undersides of her thighs. Her body jerked. She moaned into the gag.

Great skill was required to strike the backs of her legs and the lower half of her buttocks. The awkwardness of her bondage and the blatant exposure of her crack made it a prime target. But Jonathan held off; let her quiver in anticipation of a cut across the pussy, one which he'd probably never administer. Its redness and ample juices gave him other ideas, ones which involved his cock.

He repeated the stroke and Anthony leaned over her and unplugged her mouth, but she didn't voice the safe word. Jonathan's blows came faster, his arm and the cane fusing together, at one with her, absorbing her agony and arousal. Her response electrified him. Her mouth gaped, and tears ran back into her temples from under the blindfold, but still she didn't scream, 'Eldritch!'

The cane sang and red lines appeared, one after the other, on her thighs and bottom. Jonathan poured out ruthless energy on her and she wanted more. But he'd had enough, desperate for the next stage of the game, throwing the cane to the floor and advancing towards her, unbuttoning as he went.

Anthony stood at the end of the bench, close to her bent legs, and when he placed his hand on her cunt, she thrust against it as if seeking anything that would take her to orgasm.

'There, my dear, have it,' he whispered, parting her folds and massaging the pink stem till she bucked and moaned and came. Then he nodded to Jonathan, adding, 'She's ready for you.'

With his prick jumping in his hand, Jonathan took Anthony's place at Carol's entrance. He did what he'd been aching to do, fingering her wet folds and frilled opening, caressing the spent clit and feeling it harden again. He was spoilt for choice. Which orifice should he use? Both were available, and his cock was already wearing latex. His need was so great that when he pushed against her and felt her pussy pulsing, he couldn't help guiding himself into that welcoming channel.

'Yes, yes,' she sighed. Oh, yes, do it! Fuck me hard! she thought.

As his erection breached her to the root, he saw Anthony at her head. He had taken off the blindfold, and she stared up at him adoringly. Then she glanced at Jonathan between her raised knees, before Anthony buried his hands in the mass of her loosened hair, holding her firmly as he rammed his cock into her mouth.

Jonathan saw that thick stalk being tongued, Carol slurping and sucking it, while Anthony held her to him, his hips moving. The heat and pressure were mounting in Jonathan's loins, enhanced by the sight of Carol giving Anthony head. He could feel her inner muscles tightening round his cock, and was able to thrust very deeply with her legs stretched back. With every inward stroke the pleasure increased. With every outward drag it became near unbearable. He was close to the edge, his aching balls tight as a drum, and then he came with a cry and a shudder as he saw Anthony spending himself, his milky come spilling out over Carol's face and hair.

Rosemary had come in from her walk, found Marmaduke in the conservatory and guessed that Jonathan was somewhere in the vicinity. There was no sign of Michael, or their host and hostess. The crew and gardeners had taken themselves off to do a survey of the village pubs. Even Scott was nowhere to be seen. He'd probably gone with them, a star in the making who'd be wanting to pick their brains and also impress the local talent.

She was missing Dan already. He had done one of his disappearing acts while she was in the bath. She hadn't mentioned him at dinner. They might think it odd that her own personal detective was keeping tabs on her. It was clear that he distrusted Anthony, but she hoped he was wrong.

Listening for signs of life, she thought she heard something, faint and far away but distinct – the sound of a woman crying out in anguish or extreme pleasure. It was hard to define. She followed the noise, going in the direction of the tower where Anthony had his workshop. She knew that the theatre and labyrinth could be reached from there via a network of tunnels.

Although it was still daylight, the corridor was dimly lit, the windows no more than converted arrow-slits. Down, and down, she went, through another passage and then a half-opened door. It glowed with a murky red light, and the sounds were coming from inside. Obeying an animal sense that warned her not to be seen, she slipped in, hidden by the portière.

What she saw, as she peeped through a chink, sent the

blood rushing to her cunt. Carol was naked, strung up with her sex fully exposed, and Jonathan was beating her.

A surge of desire took Rosemary off guard, her body responding. Her hand flew to her mound. She lifted her skirt and pushed aside her panties. The need to come was too urgent to resist and, as she watched Jonathan drop the cane and penetrate Carol, while Anthony spurted in her mouth, so she came, stifling the cry that rose in her throat.

She escaped quickly, running as if the devil was after her. Is this what Anthony wanted of her? Did he intend to take her to the dungeon, chain and subdue her? What other erotic antics took place there? The mind boggled. Yet even while she denied it, heat spread across her backside as she remembered his hand slapping her. She hated it, but wanted it. Wanted to bare her arse for his punishment, feel the kiss of the whip, the force of the cane, the memory of Carol's welted thighs imprinted in her mind. She pinned the blame on Neil. He had spanked her and awakened her to the sexual power of pain. Neil, her bête noire from the past.

She wanted to rush into Dan's arms, to use him as a talisman against the evil thoughts tormenting her. This wasn't right. For some, maybe, but not for her – not yet. Maybe in the fullness of time when she was older and world-weary, when she needed something extra to revive her jaded appetite.

'And now, here we are. The third day of our restoration of the hedge-maze at Malvern Chase,' Rosemary began, walking along a path between neatly clipped green walls. The cameraman and soundman followed her, silent and steady. 'We have been on a voyage of discovery. That's what a maze is all about. You get to know its twists and turns and baffling cul-de-sacs, and find that you've learned a lot about yourself, too.'

'Cut!' Michael shouted.

'I don't have to go through it again, do I?' she grumbled.

'No, darling. It's fine,' he said, striding towards her, an authoritative figure, despite his shorts and terrain sandals. 'Come on, Jonathan. I want you and Rosemary standing under the arch in the middle, and doing those lines about the labyrinth. OK?'

Rosemary had been having trouble with her feelings towards Jonathan ever since she'd spied on him in the dungeon. At one moment she loathed him for his decadence, and in the next wanted to beg him to use her as he'd done Carol. She hoped she'd been successful in hiding this from him, but was finding it increasingly difficult to behave normally towards Carol and Anthony.

It was natural that, in this emotional turmoil, she'd turned to Michael, her sudden burst of passion surprising him. He had passed the last two nights in her bed, not all of them spent having sex. He was tired, always tense when filming, and she had been so drained that all she really wanted to do was curl up in his arms and sleep after a single bout of sex.

Dan had rung her, repeating his warning about Anthony. 'From what I've gathered, the bloke's a sun-dried tomato short of a full pizza.'

'Please don't worry,' she had said, the vision of Anthony ejaculating into Carol's mouth fresh in her mind.

'If he tries anything you don't like, I'll deck him.'

'I know. It's all right. We'll be out of here soon.'

And now, here I am, she thought, pretending to flirt with Jonathan and be deferential while he talks about gardens. He's a whiz kid when it comes to interiors, and has done an amazing job on the orangery, but put a spade in his hands and he's an amateur.

He tossed back his hair, looked straight into the camera and said, 'Malvern Chase has another secret. Follow me,' and he beckoned and went down the worn steps, stopping at the oak door. 'This is the way into a labyrinth, built hundreds of years ago. It's a place of mystery and no one knows its real purpose. Does it represent the Seven Circles of Heaven? Or is there a Minotaur at its very heart, a slavering, roaring, bull-headed man, seeking his full quota of virgins.'

'Cut,' Michael barked crossly. 'That wasn't in the script.'

'I know, but it makes it more dramatic. Does it really matter, as you've decided not to go in, reserving it for another time? Unless I get there first,' Jonathan replied coolly. They still hadn't settled their differences about this, and Anthony was keeping them dangling.

'Let's leave it there,' Michael said, and turned to the cameraman, giving him instructions for the closing shots.

'Have it your own way,' Jonathan replied with a shrug. 'If I'm not needed, I'm going for a swim. Coming, Rosemary?'

Michael nodded absent-mindedly, deeply involved in capturing film footage which would wind up the programme neatly.

The pool was kidney-shaped, not as large as the one at Sutton Close, but big enough to delight any sun worshipper and water fanatic. Rosemary went to her room, stripped, then donned her silver bikini, those three triangles that barely covered her nipples and bush. She had trimmed this to a tidy wedge and stood in front of the pier-glass, satisfying herself that no stray wisps of hair escaped the narrow gusset. She much preferred to bathe naked, thus gaining a seamless tan, but there were too many lecherous eyes about. She needed solitude to really enjoy nudity.

Watching herself, she poked a finger into the side of the tanga and stroked her sex. It was so raw and rude an action that she was impatient for more. She pulled the thong aside, her flushed sex lips protruding, the inner ones hanging a little lower than the outer, her retracted clit starting to stir. She pinched and rolled it, moving closer to the mirror to see better, the added visual excitement sweeping her towards bliss.

She wished it had been her, not Carol, chained to the couch, sluttishly displaying all her wares. Jonathan canning her with absorbed interest, then getting out his cock and shafting her. Anthony completing the *ménage à trois*, obviously the instigator, manipulating them as he did his puppets, and climaxing in Carol's mouth.

I want it. I want *him*, she thought, powering her finger with images of him fucking her in the labyrinth and, later, in his workshop. She remembered how bizarre and wonderful it had felt when he buried his cock in her forbidden hole. Lost in these fantasies, she rubbed her clit harder and groaned as the sensations peaked, her orgasm bursting in a euphoric rush.

She recovered quickly, washed her sticky fingers, slipped on a robe and sandals, picked up her tote-bag, checked that she had dark glasses and sun-screening lotion, then went down to the pool. She rather hoped Jonathan had changed his mind, feeling unable to face him with her body still buzzing from recently enjoyed wanking.

No such luck. He was stretched out on a lounger, basking in the rays like a sleek and pampered tom-cat. Rosemary could almost hear him purring. His hair was in wet tangles, tightly curled. 'You could easily grow dreadlocks,' she said, tempted to swim before she oiled up.

'The water's as warm as the Mediterranean Sea but without the sewage overflow,' he remarked lazily.

She scrutinised the hanging baskets and terracotta vases tumbling over with busy-Lizzies and trailing vines. 'Those flowers need dead-heading.'

'It's not your problem,' he reminded.

'Old habits die hard. I can't help being aware.'

'Chill out, Rosemary. Let it all go.'

He's right, she thought and came to a decision: indulge in her favourite hobby, soaking up the sun, then swim when she got too hot. She occupied a wheeled lounger near his, took out her bottle and started to spread coconut oil over her legs, thighs, belly and arms. The perfume was steeped in the smells of summer, of heat and water and blissful, idle days spent daydreaming and enjoying the weather.

'I wish I was alone,' she commented, undoing the bra straps and anointing her chest.

'Don't mind me,' he said, his eyes blanked by sunglasses. 'I've seen more tits than you've had hot dinners.'

He was practically nude, his genitals confined in a white posing pouch which, now wet, emphasised rather than covered his generous balls and thick cock. Lithe and well muscled, he had an enviable, all-over tan.

'You're very brown,' Rosemary said jealously, and throwing caution to the wind, took off her bikini top. Damn! He was already outdoing her in the copper stakes. She wasn't about to get strap marks just because he insisted on hanging around.

He lay back but still watched her through the smoky lenses. 'I've a villa in Spain. You should come and stay. It's a wonderful country – hot, passionate, with marvellous flamenco music that speaks of love and tragedy. It sends shivers down my spine.'

'I know. I love Spain. I'll think about it, and thank you,' she said, wriggling round and trying to oil her back.

'Allow me,' Jonathan offered and was soon crouching at her side, knees spread wide, his impressive package mesmerising her, cock uncoiled now, straining upwards. She could see the end of it pressing against the low-cut band of his pouch.

He poured oil into his palm and started to apply it, his hand coasting over her shoulders, her spine, the back of her waist, her bottom where the deep crease began, then her thighs. 'I've died and gone to heaven,' she murmured, sleepy but with every sense alert.

She heard him chuckle and then there was nothing. The sun poured its energy on to her prone body. She could almost feel her skin darkening. It was very nearly better than sex. 'Frying tonight,' she murmured, and laughed.

Head to one side, she stared across at his padded lounger. He wasn't there, and she became aware of him standing close, looking down at her. Not at *her* exactly, but at her bare buttocks divided by the thong that disappeared between the hillocks. Her heart thumped and she could almost feel the impact of his hand on her sun-scorched flesh. Her pussy clenched as if it was falling into itself and pulling the door tight shut.

'Chipmunks do that,' she said, sitting up sharply.

'Do what?' He seemed put out by this response.

'Dig a hole and bury themselves in it when they know their time has come. They even cover in the entrance. It's to preserve the rest of the colony, so that predators don't come to eat the living as well as the dead. I know, because I kept them when I was a kid.'

Why am I saying this? she wondered, the sweat inching down her face and joining that which covered her body, mingling with the lotion. Your defence mechanism has gone into overkill, her inner voice said.

'Do you remember that evening at my house, when you were in the Jacuzzi?' he whispered, dropping to his hunkers and taking off his shades. She could see right into his clear eyes, hedged by lashes that were dark at the base and gold at the tips.

'How could I forget?' she said lightly, propped on one elbow.

'You trusted me then. Why won't you now?'

'I don't know what you mean.'

'Yes, you do. You were watching us in the dungeon, if we must call it that, though I think it's just a cellar. I saw you hiding behind the curtain. Did you wank as you stood there? I believe you did, and have been thinking about what you saw ever since. I've talked with Anthony and know what you've been doing with him. He says you only need a tiny push to launch you into our world.'

'And what's that?' She had guessed, but wanted to hear him say it.

'A place were people with special needs can find others.' As he spoke, he dragged a finger over the rise of her breast and coaxed the nipple into a crest. 'We have to trust one another, and if it's our role to be a sub, then be prepared to hand over our will and accept the commands of a controlling man, or a fem/dom. They'll do all the work and all the deciding. It's a club, if you like, that operates nationwide. But you have to be in the know, or you may get involved in bad scenes, or maybe parties where newcomers are testing the waters. They're not serious people who need this lifestyle. They wear the right gear, lots of leather and studs, and naked bums, quims and tits. They're even tattooed and pierced in all the right places, but it's more a costume party. There's not a crack of whip on flesh all night. It's no use to me. I need sexual drama.'

Rosemary was silent, taking this in, his words conjuring up visuals that inflamed her and made her clit tickle. 'Anthony and his cousin are into this?'

'Old hands at it,' he said, smiling. 'We've talked about it and, apparently, they have quite a following in Waverney and district.'

'I don't know if I'm really interested.'

'You're curious.'

'Yes, I'll admit it.'

'Then give it a go. You won't be made to do anything you don't like, and will be given a word to say if you want it to stop. You could try it at Anthony's bash on Friday night. He's celebrating the end of the shoot, and is including a marionette show. Everyone's invited. No doubt the dungeon will be in use.'

Rosemary closed her eyes, seduced by the heat, his touch and his words. She felt him beside her on the lounger, felt his warm skin as his arm came round her. She hadn't realised how horny she was, turning into him, feeling his lips at her neck, his breath on her flesh. She ran her hand through his damp blonde hair, and he pressed his erection against her thigh as they kissed. It felt hot and she throbbed in sympathy.

She loosened the ties and his pouch fell away. His cock sprang free, eight inches of serpent power. A drop of clear fluid appeared at its eye. Rosemary spread it over the helm and the ridge of foreskin. Jonathan caressed her breasts, eyes slitted, concentration centred on his cock. He sank sideways on the lounger, knees bent, bare feet flat on the terrazzo tiles. She dropped on to her heels between his splayed legs. His cock challenged her, that pleasure tool which had been relieved in various ways by so many people.

I can do it, she thought, I can make him squirm and moan and beg me to let him come.

She wound his wiry pubic curls round her fingers and tugged at them, then lowered her face to his fork, breathing in the smell of lusting male spiced with chlorinated water. Hovering over the eager head, she put out her tongue and gave it a flick, so light that anything less sensitive might not have been aware. Jonathan's cock responded instantly, growing a further inch. It swayed, and Rosemary was fascinated by its hugeness. She wanted to see how much she could take in her mouth. He rocked his hips and she sucked him in, running her tongue over the silky smooth head, then choking as he pushed and the end of it touched her throat.

She pulled out, but continued to masturbate him with her hands, while she licked his balls and feathered her tongue round his anus. It tasted nutty. The tiny ring quivered and she smiled. As she had suspected, this had been used for satisfaction, either with a dildo or another man. Anthony, perhaps? She pushed the tip of her little finger in, and the puckered hole didn't resist as she rimmed it.

Jonathan's cock pulsed urgently in her hand and he sat up, clamped a thigh over hers and pinned her down. He was rough and she wanted him, the thrust, the relentless pounding of good sex. His hands were under her buttocks, lifting her against his erection. He was hurting her, his fingers digging into her flesh, and she wanted that, too.

'Yes, yes. More,' she begged.

In their struggles, the flat pallet slipped sideways and she ended up on the tiles, with Jonathan half on top of her. He laughed, and rearranged her, and she was content to have him do this.

He turned her over on to her stomach and said, 'Arms above your head.'

She shuddered, her sex thrumming as she experienced that mad feeling of being mastered and cared for. Closing her eyes, she listened for more orders from his deep voice that seemed to penetrate her to the bone.

'On your knees,' he commanded, and she presented her posterior to him like a bitch in season.

His slaps stung her bottom and sent waves of heat to her cunt. He grabbed at her mound, forced the lips open and rubbed her. His teeth nibbled at that erogenous zone at the back of her neck. She writhed under him, orgasmic spasms ripping at her. She couldn't contain or control it. The climax came abruptly, and fell away. Jonathan kept his hand there, tweaking her clit and pushing his fingers inside her.

After this, he turned her again and she hitched her legs high, her ankles resting on his shoulders, drawing him into her core. He was hard on her and she didn't want gentleness. As his passion mounted, so he scratched her skin and dug his nails into her breasts. She threshed and whimpered, bracing herself to meet his assault, grinding her clit against him in the hope of gaining another orgasm. It didn't happen, and he was gripping too hard for her to slip a hand down and bring herself off.

Too late now. She could tell that he was coming. His body jerked; he threw back his head, face contorted, the veins knotted at his throat. He grunted once, then slumped across her. The terrace righted itself and she was in a panic.

'Oh, God! Someone may have seen us!'

'The newshounds?' He was unconcerned, rolling off her and stuffing his towel under his head as a pillow. 'Surely Anthony's hit-squad deal with them? No one could get past the mighty Higgins.'

Rosemary knew one who had – Dan. But then he was a professional.

'Jesus, they'd give their eye-teeth for shots of us in a compromising position,' she said, back on the lounger now, as if intimacy had never taken place. She retrieved her bikini and covered her vital bits.

'So what?'

'Everyone seems to want to fuck me out of doors,' she complained, glancing round uneasily, expecting to see a reporter lurking behind each bush, and bemoaning the madness that seized her when she was randy. It made her forget everything else.

'It's your personal myth, darling.'

'The public won't leave me alone. It's as if they own me.'

'Tell me about it. Even in this backwater, the vicar's wife has been pestering me to give a talk to the Women's Institute in the village hall.'

'That would be worth hearing,' she said with a giggle. 'They'd go potty about you.'

Jonathan didn't bother to replace his pouch. He took off the condom and put it in a tub of begonias, covering it with soil. His bare cock glistened wetly. 'That'll give the gardener's boy something to think about,' he said, slanting her a wicked smile. 'He'll think it belonged to Anthony, no doubt.'

She became calmer, and they dived into the pool together. He was a strong swimmer, barrelling up and down, but after doing a length she sat on the steps and watched him. He was different, no longer so self-absorbed, showing another facet of himself, a man with the willpower and drive to have reached his present pinnacle. She was beginning to like him.

He swam over and bottomed it in the shallow end, saying, 'Let's do the labyrinth programme together. I wasn't going to include you, but I've changed my mind. It would be a laugh.'

'I'm not sure. It might contravene my contract with Ace Productions. We could ask Melanie and Wesley.'

'They're coming to the party. We'll discuss it then.'

'Everyone seems to have been invited, and I'm the last to know,' she said, angry with Anthony for this slight. She was sure he'd done it deliberately.

'Don't sulk, darling. He has plans for you. In fact, you'll be one of the most important people there. The main attraction. Just wait and see.'

'You'll help her,' Anthony stated flatly. 'We've only a few hours to get it right.'

'It'll be fine,' Carol answered soothingly. Anthony always suffered from stagefright, which manifested in foul moods and irritability. 'Have you told her yet?'

He smiled darkly. 'I want to do it when she's in a position where she can hardly refuse.'

'In front of Michael?'

'Something like that.'

Dinner was a useful custom, he had discovered. Not only a gathering where one lavished delicacies on one's guests, but had them more or less at one's mercy. The majority were too polite to get up and storm out, even if they felt like it. Yes, Anthony decided, dinner parties must have been invented by tyrants and politicians. And, if no one else had done so, then he'd have inaugurated them himself. As he stood at the mirror that evening, adjusting his bow tie, he could feel excitement warming his loins and stiffening his cock.

'I shall miss you all,' he said, after the dessert dishes had been removed and replaced by fruit, a cheeseboard and a selection of crackers. 'Malvern Chase hasn't known such a bustle for I don't know how long. The last time an heir was born, perhaps.'

He glanced down the table to where Michael was seated between Carol and Rosemary. Jonathan was on her right, and Mary and Helen had also been included. The rest had declined, though they were up for the party. As it was, they had booked in for a Chinese meal in the nearest town.

'It's been a straightforward operation,' Michael answered, tending to fall into military terms when discussing filming. He came from a long line of generals, brigadiers and admirals. 'You should see some of the sites we're asked to improve. Honestly, the majority have no idea.'

'I'm happy that you've enjoyed it,' Anthony said, touching his napkin to his lips. 'We love this house. Don't we, Carol? It means a lot to us, and we're thrilled to think it has now been recorded for posterity. We've already been approached by several newspapers with substantial offers if we consent to interviews. This should bring you even more exposure, Rosemary . . . you, too, Jonathan.'

He was so calm that no one, except perhaps Carol, would have guessed at the hard knot of lust and anticipation building in his gut. He could hardly bear to look at Rosemary, sitting there in all her matchless beauty. He could find no fault with her simple black evening dress, her hair tumbling about her shoulders, its darkness highlighted by the candelabra. He had the urge to get the family jewels out of the strongroom and bedeck her. Soon, he promised himself, very soon he'd do just that. When she had stripped for him he'd clamp her nipples and hang diamonds from them, wind ropes of pearls round her neck, clothe her arms in bracelets and weave gold necklets in her pubic bush.

Then, at a later date, but not too far ahead, he'd have her nipples and the hood of her clitoris pierced, so that every time she moved that sensitive bud would be stimulated by the ring he'd insert. When these wounds had healed, he'd apply weights to them, light ones at first, then increasing the load.

His breath came faster, and his cock was erect under the Savile Row trousers. He'd let her carry on working – while it suited him – as he rather liked the publicity and the thought that her fans would never guess that beneath the jeans and T-shirt that were her symbol, she'd be wearing his brand. It would never occur to them in a million years that such a sensible, knowledgeable and thoroughly *nice* woman would be his slave, needing discipline and restraint, allowing herself to be dominated by him.

She sat there demurely, yet she'd had everyone round the table. The exception being Helen and Mary who he knew, courtesy of his TV monitors, were a pair of lesbians who couldn't wait to hop into bed together, united as they were by their admiration of their boss.

People, he mused sardonically. How easy it is to use them. Anthony had never been above blackmail, emotional or otherwise. He'd filmed Rosemary in sexual abandon since she'd been at Malvern Chase, but had been frustrated recently, until examination of the camcorders in her bedroom had disclosed that someone had been tampering with them. Anger smouldered like a red hot ember inside him. Who had had the wit to do this?

Coffee time, and when they were installed in the conservatory he went over to Rosemary, saying, 'You know about the party, of course, but there's something I want you to do.'

She stared up at him, wary, yet excited. He could smell the arousal in her, and his fingers burned to touch her. 'I didn't know until Jonathan informed me. You should have mentioned it to me personally. And now you want me to do something for you. What is that, Anthony?' she asked, her voice level.

'I'm putting on a show. The marionettes will feature large in it, but several people have offered to join in. I want you to appear.'

'What a marvellous idea!' Michael exclaimed, twinkling eyes challenging her.

'Go on. Do it, Rosemary. I dare you. It'll be another string to your bow. Excellent publicity,' chimed in Jonathan, clapping Marmaduke's paws together.

'Me? But I can't sing or dance and wasn't much good with the ballerina puppet when I tried to work her.'

'You'll be fine. Come with me. Now.'

Anthony raised her to her feet, permitting himself to put his hand under her elbow, and the feel of her satin-smooth, golden-brown skin was like fire and wine to him. He yearned to press tightly, leaving the imprints of his fingers. He stopped himself. He didn't want her

231

backing off like a frightened deer. Time enough to hurt her, rouse her, pleasure her, make her wear his stigmata. He'd been planning this for so long that he wasn't going to ruin it now.

She looked towards Michael and Jonathan, but Carol was doing her part, monopolising them as only she knew how. Anthony played his fingers up and down Rosemary's arm. He felt her relax, her skin communicating her need, the fine hairs rising on its surface. Jonathan hadn't been wrong when he'd told him that she was fascinated by what she'd seen them doing to Carol in the dungeon.

He took her backstage of the theatre, into one of the changing rooms, where he made her stand in front of a dressing table, its mirror framed by lights, as befitted a star. The top was littered with sticks of grease-paint, pots of face powder, jars of cleanser, bottles of wet-white. There was even the traditional rabbit's foot with which to apply a dusting of rouge to the cheekbones, forehead and chin.

'Gary from make-up would adore to see this,' she said, her eyes bright.

'So he shall. I could do with his services on the night.'

She loves it, he thought. All the adulation, praise and public exposure. She's an exhibitionist, after all, no shrinking violet or she wouldn't be where she is today. Rosemary the entertainer. I can see it all now, and I shall be Svengali to her Trilby, or the puppeteer pulling her strings. Gardening? Not indefinitely, I think. I have bigger and better things in mind for her. I shall get rid of her agent and handle her myself. Hollywood? Maybe. We'll see how she goes.

'You're beautiful,' he said, and his hands closed on her shoulders, pressing her back against his body. 'I shall make you even more lovely. I've made your stage costume.'

'Have you? But how? I've never had so much as a fitting.' There was a trace of alarm in her voice that sent his blood pressure soaring.

'No need. You'll find it's your size.' He couldn't resist bending and placing his lips at her neck. The mirror flung back an image of a tall man in black kissing the woman in his arms. She was yielding yet alarmed, as if afraid of the force of her feelings, and her eyelids lowered and she sighed as his teeth nipped. He could have been Dracula and she Minna Harker. He was intrigued by the idea of vampirism, and had written a script and made puppets and scenery so that he could re-create the story.

Reluctantly he let her go and went to a wardrobe. Even his iron self-control couldn't prevent his hands shaking as he lifted a garment from the rail. He carried it over to Rosemary, then carefully eased the protective plastic covering from it.

He was proud of his achievement, never trusting costume making to anyone else; he was an expert pattern cutter and machinist. There, dangling from the hanger, was a satin dress from the first quarter of the last century. It was fringed and short, the hem dipping in handkerchief points. With it were flesh-coloured stockings, elasticated garters with sparkling paste buckles and shoes with Louis heels.

Rosemary started, her hand flying to her breasts as if to cover herself.

'You recognise it?' Anthony said, and the devils of passion and mastery within him chortled with glee.

'I do, but the others were torn.'

'That of the Charleston doll, who you didn't destroy but keep in your bedroom and the marionette I produced? The flapper with the whip?'

'That's right. But why have you made this?'

Desire surged through his chest and belly, and he lowered his voice to a throaty murmur as he said, 'You'll wear it tomorrow night, have your hair done like the doll's, and get Gary to make you up twenties' style. Then you'll appear on stage. By the time you've finished, this dress will be as ragged as the others and you will be as wanton.'

'And the riding whip?' she whispered.

'Ah, yes. We'll have to see about that, won't we? Either you use it or someone will use it on you, or maybe both. It should be an interesting evening.'

Chapter Twelve

Cars began to arrive at Malvern Chase during Friday afternoon. Anthony had invited people from near and far to see his marionette show. Old friends and new, who were conversant with his sexual deviations and shared them, arrived. Every bedroom in the house would soon be occupied.

He and Carol smiled a warm greeting as they came in, and he whispered to her, 'I wonder if I'll have time to peek at them on the monitors.'

She shook her head, knowing he'd have no opportunity before the performance, deep in rehearsals, drilling his live actors and making sure the puppets were put through their paces. She was in charge of organisation on the domestic front, marshalling her helpers, and coping with the outside caterers. The florists had done a first-class job, and gorgeous blooms and lush foliage filled porcelain vases from the Ming dynasty, and jardinières that had once graced Marie Antoinette's palace at Versailles. No expense had been spared.

When she wasn't being harassed by the butler, who was worried about the silver, the wine-cellar and the incompetence of the staff, Carol was backstage. She knew what Anthony wanted: it wasn't their first show by any means. But even so, she needed to ensure that the puppets under her control were strung correctly and their costumes faultless. He had also put Rosemary in her hands, and she was an absolute novice, in more ways than one.

'I'm scared to death,' she confessed, waiting for her cue in the wings.

'You'll be fine,' Carol cooed, itching to see her in the provocative costume Anthony had made, especially when the stage action hotted up. Rosemary didn't know about this, or the modifications to her frock which allowed it to tear easily. The surprise element would add to the realism.

'I wish I was as confident.'

'It can't be worse than facing television cameras.'

'It is. I'm not used to appearing in front of a live audience, apart from those invited to the studio to watch chat shows. But even those are recorded, so any gaffes can be edited out.'

All Rosemary had been asked to do so far was be on stage while Anthony worked the flapper puppet. They had gone through the motions and listened to the rag-time music and Rosemary had been taught a few dance steps. Raymond and Bernard had also practised, brushing up on performances they had given before; both were experienced puppeteers. Raymond had made it clear that his wife wouldn't be in the audience, which was as well considering the bawdy material he'd be using.

'I know you'll do your best,' Carol said, her hand at Rosemary's waist, then going lower to touch the little dimple at the base of her spine, just above the divide of her buttocks.

She had supplied her with ballet pumps, a shocking-pink leotard and tights, for rehearsals. These fitted snugly, showing off her firm breasts, slim waist and rounded derrière, and Carol fervently hoped there would be something left over for her when Anthony had taken his fill.

There were times when she envied him his penis, but thanked heavens for the godemiche. A strap-on dick enabled her to share male potency to some extent. As she imagined using it to penetrate Rosemary, her clit engorged, tightening the ring in its cowl.

Rosemary was surrounded by Anthony's friends. Those who hadn't already done so were clamouring to meet her. The reception room echoed with excited voices and bursts of laughter. Champagne corks popped, and alcohol flowed. A cold collation filled two buffet tables; canapés, *vol-au-vents*, smoked salmon, chicken, ham, cheese and great pyramids of fruit. But Rosemary was too nervous to eat.

Wearing a kimono over her costume, she managed to keep control, smiling and signing autograph books or scraps of paper and answering questions. But her sixth sense snuffed an oddness in the air, and the general attire was odd, too.

Some wore evening dress. Others had arrived in full hunting regalia – jodhpurs, black boots and red jackets – and it seemed they had brought their ponies with them – girls wearing nothing but reins, cruppers, bridles and with luxuriant tails dangling from plugs wedged in their back passages. They stomped, snorted, tossed their manes and plumed head-dresses, but only under their riders' orders. The chat was punctuated by the thwack of crops on naked flesh.

Several of the other female guests strode about in leather miniskirts and bustiers. Some took it further, with straps circling nude breasts, chains dangling from pierced navels to labia rings, and thigh boots with stacked heels and vicious-looking spurs. Blondes, brunettes, natural or not, their face-paint was lurid and their hair vigorously back-brushed.

'How trite,' Jonathan complained wearily, disengaging himself from a scrawny female who was insisting that he redesign her bedroom. 'Really, Rosemary, it's time the fetish market came up with something new. I've a good mind to settle down with a drawing-pad and pencil and have a stab at it myself. Have you seen Wesley? He's over there, wearing an awful dress. He looks like some-body's maiden aunt. I must have a word with him about the labyrinth. See you later.'

As soon as she could, Rosemary escaped to her dressing room. Melanie was waiting for her, exclaiming, 'Darling, I've caught up with you at last.'

Rosemary could feel herself grinning while they hugged. Her friend's presence was more than simply reassuring. 'You've been elusive. I sometimes curse the invention of the answerphone,' she said.

'Bad timing, that's all. But everything's all right? The shoot, I mean. Is Michael bullying you?'

Rosemary nodded and shrugged. 'Do bears shit in the woods?' It wasn't the right moment to enlighten Melanie as to what had really been happening in the shades of Malvern Chase.

She didn't take off her robe. Her costume wasn't to be seen until she made her entrance. The auditorium was filling up. She could hear the hum as people took their seats. It made her stomach churn.

'Some party,' Melanie commented, winged brows shooting high. 'I couldn't be bothered to find fancy dress, but Wes couldn't wait to frock up'.

'I know. I've seen him.'

'And this Anthony Selby character? What's he like? I didn't suss him out when we were introduced. He seemed in an awful rush.'

'It's been a rushed show. We've been rehearsing for hours. I'm completely pooped out,' Rosemary said, over-come by the weirdness of it all, having gone beyond exhaustion into that space where reality melds with other dimensions.

Her face in the mirror looked back at her. It was a stranger's face, carefully constructed by Gary. Her cheek-bones had been exaggerated by rouge, her eyes widened into a glassy, doll-like stare, her lips reduced to the Cupid's Bow so fashionable among the Bright Young Things of 1925. As for her hair? Her own dark locks had been pinned close to her skull and confined under a net, then Gary had topped this with a wig. It was the same colour but cut in a ear-length bob, with a fringe and kiss-curls.

She had been transformed into a replica of the statu-ette, the doll, and the marionette. With a shiver, she recalled the sinister phone calls, the uneasy feeling of being stalked, the fear and adrenalin rush, and Anthony had been behind it all along.

'I'll be glad when you're back home,' Melanie said. 'There's something not quite right about this place.'

'Home? Then I'll immediately get embroiled with solic-itors and unpleasant scenes with Terry. He has to accept that he's out of Plants Galore. It isn't negotiable,' Rose-mary said with a sigh. Did she really want to grapple with the real world again? Wouldn't it be better to stay in Anthony's enchanted kingdom?

Jonathan poked his head round the door, then stepped in so they could admire his costume. 'It's a ring-master's outfit,' he said, doffing his top hat and giving them a twirl.

White buckskin breeches so form-hugging that he might as well have been naked, a fancy waistcoat, a black jacket and the addition of a handle-bar moustache, turned him into a debonair showman about to compère a circus.

'I love the pants,' Melanie remarked, her sari-like silk dress clinging to every curve of her body as she went up to him and fondled his arse.

'You would, sugar,' he replied with that slight edge he reserved for her. Then he looked across at Rosemary, adding, 'Half an hour till the curtain rises.'

Rosemary stood up and, flouting Anthony's instruc-tions, discarded her kimono. 'Right then. We'd better go.'

Jonathan wolf-whistled and Melanie went, 'Oh!' when they saw her dress.

This was enough to unnerve her even more. The thought of the audience out there, of making a fool of herself and damaging her reputation beyond repair, was enough to make her slump back on the stool and bury her face in her hands, careless of ruining her make-up.

'I can't do it!'

'Yes, you can, darling,' Jonathan soothed, patting her bowed shoulder.

She shook her head. 'I can't go on. I won't.'

Jonathan grimaced, looked across at Melanie and said, 'We'll leave her. I'm going to tell Anthony. He'll talk her round.'

Convinced that nothing anyone could say would make her change her mind, Rosemary heard the door click behind them and then, in no time at all, Anthony was saying to her softly, 'What's the matter, Rosemary?

'I'm so frightened,' she murmured.

'That's good. Every artiste worth his or her salt suffers stage-fright,' he said, looking taller and leaner in a black jump-suit, black shoes, black gloves, a black balaclava with holes for his eyes and a slit for his mouth.

He was made up of darkness. The audience wouldn't see him as he worked against a black backdrop. They'd be dazzled by the clever lighting concentrated on the figure in the middle of the proscenium, unaware of its strings.

'You'll have to change the programme. Say I'm ill. Give any excuse. I'm not going on.'

She couldn't see his expression, only the flash of his eyes through the holes, but his posture betrayed his anger, the set of his shoulders, the way his gloved hands shot out to seize her.

'You will. You'll do exactly as I tell you.'

She could feel her will to refuse draining away, as powerless as one of his marionettes. Anthony would guide her through the ordeal. Anthony would see that it went without a hitch. All she had to do was bend like an aspen under a strong wind.

Silently, he picked her up and sat her on the dressing table, scattering pots and jars. He parted her knees and she felt his leather-covered fingers cruising up her inner thighs and arriving at their destination. He paused, glanced down at her bush and said, 'I'm pleased to see that you've obeyed me and aren't wearing panties. Your pussy is beautiful. I want the audience to get glimpses of it, not too much, just a tease.'

The leather was against her slit, different to a bare finger, firmer yet sliding easily. He pushed her back and she braced herself on her arms, then he opened her. The glove chafed her wet furrow and she bore down on it, gyrating her hips while he stroked and stroked, taking her to the peak and hurling her over into bliss.

'Ah, yes,' she said, seeing his cock protruding from the zip-front of his suit. Long and stiff, it jabbed against her slippery cunt. He pushed and it slid inside.

She closed her muscles round it and he grabbed her buttocks, holding her against him as he pumped fiercely, growling, 'Look at me, Rosemary. Watch my eyes as I come. You *will* do as I say. You *will* go on to that stage,' and with each word he rammed harder till her insides ached.

'I will,' she whispered, rejoicing in his power but mourning her lost freedom – even, it seemed, her lost innocence. She looked into his eyes. Then she flung her arms round his neck, burying herself, her fears and her desires in him, and his lusting cock impaled her once more, bringing on his orgasm.

'Right,' he said, removing himself from her almost before he'd stopped spurting. 'Now don't mess me about any more or it'll be the worse for you.'

He propelled her out of the door and along to the wings. Music was already blaring from loudspeakers and the smaller stage for average-sized puppets had been erected on the big one. The crimson velvet swags were part drawn on either side and a curtain draped above so the puppeteers wouldn't be seen.

Shivering, Rosemary waited, beginning to understand the fever that drove actors – the tension, the excitement, that feeling of never knowing whether one would be booed or deified by the public. She couldn't but help admire Anthony and Carol as, after being introduced by a swaggering Jonathan, their puppets acted out a sketch in which Pulcinella wooed a lively married woman,

241

Caterina. It was a racy performance, with Raymond controlling the strings of Alberto, her doddery old husband.

The Rabelaisian behaviour of the automatons in the labyrinth were as nothing compared to Pulcinella's bawdiness. His maker had given him an enormous wooden prick in a permanent state of erection, and Caterina was equipped with a hole in her rear where he could thrust it, when he wasn't fucking her hands or her mouth. Alberto protested, declaiming his concern regarding his wife's honour but ending up with Pulcinella's cock in his own arse. The whole thing was extravagantly humorous, robust, outspoken, coarse and indecent.

The audience were enraptured and aroused. Peering from the wings, Rosemary could hear but not see them, but it seemed as if the theatre was already in an uproar. Next Carol presented her harem lady puppet, complete with two male slaves in chains, crawling along behind her, their spiked collars attached to a jewelled leash. Rosemary could see Raymond and Bernard controlling these characters. They did it with so much verve and understanding that she wondered what went on when they were alone with Carol.

'Great, isn't she?' Scott murmured, coming to stand by her. 'And yes, the Reverend Chapman is one of her subs. And the vet, in case you didn't know.'

'I didn't,' she replied, not as surprised as she would once have been. Anything seemed acceptable here.

The scene ended with the curtains rolling back, and on the small stage, too. The three puppeteers appeared; Carol in a skimpy copy of her marionette's costume, tits and shaven quim on show, and Raymond and Bernard wearing nothing but chains and leather straps, their genitals forced high. They grovelled at her feet and she took the whip to their rumps. The applause exploded into raucous cheers and shouts of encouragement.

Now it was Rosemary's turn.

'Break a leg,' Scott said.

She walked on to the stage, head held up, determined

to acquit herself well. Michael was out there somewhere and most of the film crew and the team. She couldn't let them down. She started to dance the Charleston to the compulsive jazz beat.

The marionette appeared to join Rosemary of its own volition, but she knew Anthony was behind it. The spectators went quiet, watching this skilful display of puppet control. Even Rosemary almost forgot that she wasn't dancing with a real woman. The music died to a murmur. She sank down on the couch, pretending to be tired, as in rehearsal, but then everything went wild. The marionette raised its riding-whip and started to slash at her.

Rosemary was stunned, the lash smarting, and it was Anthony's strength that powered it. Her skirt tore under the onslaught. The shoulder-straps broke and the bodice fell down, exposing her breasts. She leaped to her feet, chased round the stage by the marionette and its manic master. The audience laughed, shouted, stamped, and she ran for the wings, blinded by rage, her whipped skin burning, her heart thumping.

How dare he? The bastard. Stripping her before everyone, making her a laughing-stock. Where the hell was he at? Was he deranged, as Dan had suggested? She determined to find out more about him.

Taking no notice of Scott who tried to apprehend her, she pulled up her bodice, held it in place as best she could, and ran along the passage that led to Anthony's tower. His workroom was normal enough, but the puppets on their stands seemed to move in the breeze, their grinning faces and shining eyes oddly alive. It resembled a creepy movie, but this time she was inside it, not watching it from the comfort of her own armchair. Trembling, she brushed past them, hearing them click and rattle. She found a staircase and went up, her knees trembling.

There was an unlocked door at the top. She stepped into a further room and stood stock-still, staring at the walls, a cold chill settling round her like a murky fog. They were hung with dozens of photographs of herself.

Recovering a little, she edged across the floor. Shelves lined with videos stood above a television screen. She took one down. It was labelled *In Your Own Backyard*. With shaking fingers she pulled out another, and another. The labels were the same and all neatly dated. Anthony must have recorded every single one of her shows.

The magazines and newspaper cuttings stacked on a bench were all about her, and there, too, she found the mould of the head he had used on her doll. He was obsessed with her; scarily so. Though the idea of him pursuing her so relentlessly and winding himself into the fabric of her existence was perversely exciting, it left a sour taste in her mouth, the taste of fear known by the hunted.

Not only had he photographed her, but also each of the men who had been her lovers. He had been nothing if not thorough. There was Terry, then Scott. Michael on his narrow boat and Neil in his roof-garden and Jonathan entering his house. She hoped he hadn't found out about Dan, but this was in vain: Dan was there all right, and she was with him. Anthony had written on the photo, 'DC Daniel Holland, Rosemary's latest piece of meat.'

The horror grew and solidified. He must have been stalking her for a long time and the invitation to film the maze had been the culmination of his plans.

I've got to get away, she panicked, but it was too late. He was in the room.

'Rosemary, what are you doing here?' he began.

'How could you?' she shouted, turning defence into attack. 'All these photos, all the stuff about me. You've lost the plot. You're insane! I'm leaving. Now!'

'You're not going anywhere,' he said, standing between her and the door. He had taken off his balaclava, his hair wet with sweat, his face set in hard lines, and an awesome glitter in his eyes.

'You can't keep me by force,' she retorted, but feared that he could.

'I don't need to use force, though you'd probably enjoy

it. When you've heard what I have to say, you'll think differently.'

'I doubt it.'

'Listen, Rosemary. When I first saw you on television, I was bewitched. You were the sexiest woman I'd ever seen. Don't ask me why. I've had countless lovers, but you were different.'

'So you wanted to reduce me to a nervous wreck?'

'Not so, but I felt compelled to keep watch over you, to meet you and have you fall in love with me.'

'You went the wrong way about it,' she said caustically. 'You can't go around treating people as if they're puppets. Get a life, Anthony!'

'Why do you defy me? I can give you so much,' he said reproachfully, as if speaking to a naughty child. 'I want you as my own landscape artist, and the model for my marionettes. You'll live here with me and Carol. I'll even marry you. Malvern Chase will be a paradise on earth. You'll be so much happier when you've accepted me as your master.'

'No.'

He touched her arm, his fingers burning into her flesh as if he would brand her with his own sigil. 'You'll change your mind. I don't expect you to forfeit your career, not yet. In fact, I have plans to extend it.'

'This is not up for debate,' she said, trying vainly to tug free, her bodice sliding down again, her nipples erect with cold and excitement.

He held her lightly but with steely strength. She looked around, hoping to find a weapon of some sort. There was nothing. She contemplated a move from her half-forgotten martial arts repertoire which could have emasculated him had her knee connected with his balls. But it had been fifteen years since she'd trained with her *sensei*. Besides, rob Anthony of his testicles? She didn't hate him that much. This was part of the trouble. She didn't hate him at all, but she had to escape his poisonous influence.

'I won't let you go,' he said with quiet menace. 'You belong here, with me.'

'How can you stop me? Do a Bluebeard? Chain me up and hide me? No, Anthony, too many people would come looking for me. You'd never get away with it.'

She spoke confidently, blessing Michael who had given her the ability to cover her emotions. No matter what state she was in when she arrived at a shoot, he had taught her to breathe deeply and maintain an outward appearance of calm. She did this now, and Anthony released her. Slowly she moved past him towards the door; her nerves were taut and she was terribly aware that he was an unbalanced man who lived out his extremes and found it impossible to divorce fantasy from reality.

'You're leaving me?' He sounded pained, making no attempt to stop her.

'Yes.'

'You'll be back.'

'Will I?'

'Oh, yes. You've tasted the forbidden fruit and, like Mother Eve, won't be able to resist another bite.'

'You think so?'

'I know so.'

Rosemary reached the door, yanked it opened and fled.

But later that night, when she was in her room, packing furiously as she recounted everything to Melanie, she suddenly paused and said, 'You know what?'

'What?' Melanie asked, curled up on the sofa, wine-glass to hand. 'The man's a lunatic. You should report him to the police.'

'No. Listen. Try to understand.' Rosemary flopped down beside her, back to normal with her hair unpinned and wearing jeans and a sweater. As normal as she'd ever be, post-Anthony, that is. 'He said I'd go back to him one day.'

'Jesus Christ! What is it with you? Haven't you been through enough?'

'I know, I know,' Rosemary said, then added, 'But I'm rather afraid he may be right.'

* * *

246

'I'm glad we're going,' Scott stated, as they drove away next morning. 'It was great, but I didn't see much of you.'

'Oh?' Rosemary replied, slanting him a glance through her sunglasses. 'I thought you were enamoured of the bossy Carol.'

'She's cool,' he muttered, flushing under his healthy tan. 'But I'd rather be with you.'

'With me or with Ace Productions?' she asked cynically, joining the motorway that would take them home. Michael, Jonathan and the rest were following later, but she hadn't been able to wait. She'd avoided seeing the Selbys and hadn't even said goodbye to them.

'With you, of course,' Scott avowed, and she couldn't resist teasing him.

'I can't see myself turning into a dominatrix overnight.'

'That doesn't matter, though Carol says she thinks you'd be good at it.'

'Does she, now? Well, not yet, Scott. I've a lot to see to when I get home.'

'Not at once, Rosemary. Can't I come back to Sutton Close with you? Seems like we haven't been together for ages.'

She smiled, and warmth spread through her crotch. After the darkness of Anthony, she needed someone fresh and untainted, even though Scott was unashamedly ambitious. She put her foot down on the accelerator, visualising an afternoon spent with this almost, but not quite, toyboy.

Fran and Robert were overjoyed to see her, and she couldn't avoid catching up on household news. Then, before she took Scott to bed, she wandered round the greenhouses and nursery acres, checking with the gardeners before entering the shop. The welcome she received from everyone was heart-warming, and the message left by her solicitor the icing on the cake. Terry had accepted her offer.

She went into a spin. The sum was enormous, but just as she was doing rapid calculations in her head and coming out in a cold sweat, Melanie called her on the mobile.

'Gemini Print want the new book,' she said joyously. 'We're talking telephone numbers here,' and she reeled off a staggering figure.

Then, floating on Cloud Nine, Rosemary celebrated with Scott, leading him to the balcony conservatory of her bedroom. It was covered in with glass on three sides and the sloping roof. She opened the sliding doors and stripped off her clothes. The air was warm and damp, her cacti were flowering ecstatically and her jungle orchids raised their stripy heads to the sun. The heated rays penetrated her skin as she stretched out on a rug and urged Scott to caress the tingling lines of her body and find the pulsing bud between her legs.

He was quick to respond, gently playing with her and kissing every part of her until she bucked and came against his mouth. She rolled over, her arse to the sky, wagging her bottom at him, letting him see all her secret parts, inviting him to feast there. And he did, then plunged his cock deep inside her while she rubbed her clit and brought herself to another climax under the hot sun.

Peace was short lived. First there was an irritating phone call from Neil asking when they were going to meet again and then, next morning, the headlines were blazing on the front page of every newspaper.

'ROSEMARY MADDOX, GARDENING DIVA, TO MARRY ANTHONY SELBY OF MALVERN CHASE. Our press representative was told by Mr Selby, that Miss Maddox, who has been working on the maze on his estate for her popular TV series *In Your Own Backyard*, has consented to be his wife. The marriage will take place later this year.'

'You never give up, do you, you sad git?' Rosemary screamed down the phone when she finally managed to get hold of Anthony.

She heard him chuckle and say, 'Oh, dear. Have I rattled your cage?'

'You certainly have. I was hoping for a few quiet days and now I'm being hounded by idiots wanting to know if this is true. I've had to let Ace Productions and everyone at the Television Centre know it isn't. What a bloody waste of time!'

'Maybe, maybe not,' he replied coolly. 'Your response tells me that you're overreacting and this gives you away. I predicted that you'd be back for more, didn't I?'

'Go to hell, and don't pull a stunt like this again,' she yelled and slammed the phone down.

One of the results was Scott coming to see her with a face as long as a fiddle. 'You're not going to marry him, are you?' he said, close to tears.

'Of course I'm not. Why?' Rosemary's patience was wearing thin. So much for a break.

'I was hoping that one day, not hassling you or anything, you might marry me,' he murmured. 'I'd like you to come and see Mum. She's dying to be introduced to you.'

'I'll bet she is,' Rosemary said, wondering how to let him down gently. 'She'll think I'm a right cradle-snatcher.' She put her arms round him tenderly and added, 'Thanks for asking me, but honestly I'm not looking for a permanent relationship right now. I've only just got rid of Terry. I'd rather go on enjoying you as a lover.'

Dan wasn't so easy to convince. 'What's this crap about you marrying Selby?' he shouted as he burst into her office later that day.

'Lies. He won't let go,' she said calmly, though her pulse was racing at the sight of Dan. He was so broad-shouldered and rangy, with his dark hair strangling round his neck and a four-day growth of beard on his chin.

'I told you to report him,' he snarled, straddling a chair, arms resting on the back. His jeans were stretched to breaking point over his thighs, and his bulge was prominent.

249

Her hackles rose. 'I'm sick of men telling me what to do. Why don't you all fuck off?'

He shot to his feet. The chair fell backwards with a clatter. 'All right. If that's what you want,' he shouted. 'I was going to ask you to come to a charity do our division is putting on, but I guess this won't appeal to you.'

'You wanted me to be your guest?' She was quaking inside. He really was a moody and magnificent beast.

'Not exactly. You're a celebrity, and it would help draw in the punters. I put your name forward.'

'Oh, did you? That was big of you. Don't you know the powers-that-be who pay my wages have a say in my public appearances? I can't do just what I like.'

'You seem to do that anyway,' he snorted and she was appalled by his lack of manners. 'OK. Forget it,' he ground out, and turned on his heel.

'No. Wait,' she said, rude and uncouth he certainly was, but his request was intriguing. 'Tell me what it's in aid of.'

He looked back, hand on the doorhandle. 'It's for the NSPCC. We do what we can for them. You should see some of the cases we're called out on. You'd never believe that a population like ours, who care so much about dogs, could be so cruel to their kids.'

'All right. I'll see what I can do. I might ask Jonathan Flynn to come along. He's a crowd puller. He can bring Marmaduke.'

'Who?'

'His latest gimmick. A teddy bear. They can draw the raffle. Put your organisers in touch with me.'

'That's kind of you.' His expression softened and he stepped towards her.

Her heart jumped and her cunt became juicy. More than anything else, she wanted to say to him, 'Put a hand under my skirt and give me a feel,' but she was still cross with him. He was almost as manipulative as Anthony.

Ignoring her hormones, which were urging her to cavort with him, then and there, on the rug, she became very brisk and businesslike. 'You'll have to excuse me. I'm snowed under with work,' she said crisply.

He gave her a piercing look, then said, 'Suit yourself. I'll call you later.'

She frowned, wondering if, having got her consent to appear, he'd now lost interest.

Three weeks had gone by and the gala night was almost there. Rosemary hadn't seen anything of Dan. He's angry with me, she thought; typical, possessive male. She was too busy to brood. Michael had called one of his famous meetings and announced that a young suburban couple with three children had put themselves forward for a make-over. He had sent Helen to interview them, and her research had shown they were eminently suitable.

It's in the hands of fate, Rosemary said to herself, sitting in on the meeting and listening to Michael. She visualised the task ahead; three young kids – which necessitated a play area and probably a Wendy House – a couple who wanted to entertain in the evenings when the brood were abed. Decking would be needed and a patio, outdoor lights and a water display. How unlike their last commission. Inevitably her thoughts strayed to Anthony. Since the bogus wedding announcement, everything had gone quiet on that front. She couldn't believe he'd given up.

The charity committee had been bowled over by her offer to attend the gala. Jonathan had agreed to take part and tickets were selling like hot cakes. It had been mentioned on the local radio and television. Dan had made no arrangement to meet her there, and she was hurt. She asked Robert to escort her, and he accepted, agog to see so many uniforms gathered in one place at a single time. He was disappointed. Evening dress was the order of the day. He went along anyway but Fran declined. Wild horses wouldn't have dragged her there.

Rosemary arrived in a chauffeur-driven limousine and found a large crowd waiting for her outside the Orion Rugby Club. It was newly built with a splendid club house which had been put at their disposal. Amidst cheers, she was met at the top of the shallow steps by the Chief Superintendent and Inspector Warren.

Having deliberated over her choice of gown, she had bought something new by an up-and-coming designer. It was made of layered chiffon in jewel hues, the bodice skimpy, the skirt falling in folds to her feet. She felt good in it, not over-the-top, but definitely glamorous. She didn't dare not to be, with the critical Jonathan beside her at the stall in the foyer where their photographs were for sale, and T-shirts and books, and all the usual accessories produced to advertise their shows. This time, however, the proceeds were going to the children's fund.

The press jostled, cameras flashed, and someone with a camcorder had arrived from Ace Productions. 'You arranged this, didn't you?' she said reproachfully to Michael.

'Naturally, darling. It's all grist to the programme's mill,' he answered urbanely. 'And Jonathan was for it. He's charging a quid a time for the privilege of stroking Marmaduke. The raffle tickets are going like a bomb.'

'Will you sign this for me?' said an instantly recognisable voice and she looked across the stall into Anthony's eyes.

'Why have you come?' she snapped, her pen poised.

'To support a worthy cause. Carol couldn't make it, but she's sent along a generous donation,' he replied and she was struck by how devilishly distinguished he looked in his impeccably tailored dinner jacket.

Her clit throbbed, his smile stirring up memories; of their first shag in the labyrinth, of their second in his workroom, of the quickie before the puppet show. He knew too much about her for comfort. She scribbled her name on the picture and thrust it back at him, snarling, 'Haven't you enough photos of me?'

'Never,' he replied, giving an ironic bow before merging with the crowd.

There was a live band, a buffet and the promise of entertainers. Rosemary danced with the courteous, reed-slim Chief Superintendent, and then with Inspector Warren, after he'd introduced her to his wife. Everyone pronounced the evening a roaring success.

'I can't see Dan anywhere,' she said to Melanie who had arrived late.

'It's no good asking me, dear. I've never met him. Try the bar.'

She stood in the doorway and saw him drinking with five other policemen. She was puzzled and upset for he'd told her he'd given up alcohol in quantity, yet there he was, knocking it back. He was looking so handsome, with his chin smoothly shaved and his hair cut shorter, but she didn't disturb him and felt infuriated by his rudeness. He had asked her to come. He might have had the decency to have met her.

Damn, she thought, damn, damn! The tuxedo and bow tie suited him. He looked super sexy, but was rapidly getting drunk, and she despised him.

She went back to her table near the stage, shared by friends and admirers, and was attempting to drag her thoughts away from Dan and begin to enjoy herself, when they were joined by Anthony.

'Why did he have to turn up like a skeleton at the feast?' she whispered to Jonathan.

'He fancies you rotten, that's why.'

'Wants to own me, more like.'

To her dismay, Anthony occupied the chair next to her. He was too close. She could smell his cologne and feel his thigh pressed against hers under the table. She was wedged between him and Jonathan, trapped as she felt Anthony's hand coasting over her knee, and upwards.

A northern stand-up comic took the stage, and his brand of humour was blue. He reminded Rosemary of a latter-day Pulcinella. People don't change much down the ages, she thought, trying to keep her mind from those long, lean fingers worming their way between her legs, seeking out her cleft. Anthony was watching the comedian, but his fingers were pushing aside her panties and burrowing into her damp cunt. Despite herself, she knew if he kept on much longer she'd come.

Gasping quietly, she tried to wriggle away, but this was impossible unless she wished to alert Jonathan. Just when she could feel waves of pleasure threatening to engulf her, the comic took his bow amidst a spattering of applause. He left the stage. The music changed as the band were replaced by a raunchy beat pounding from stereo speakers.

The master-of-ceremonies came forward, shouting above the noise, 'And now, ladies and gentlemen, give a warm welcome to our very own Full Monty!'

The music cranked up, the theme familiar – that sleazy, bump-and-grind theme associated with the film of the same name. Six fully uniformed police officers stalked from the wings and took up an aggressive stance. Dan was one of them.

When the cheers had died down, they went into their strip routine. Well rehearsed and deadly serious, their movements were synchronised as they removed their jackets, ties and shirts. The crowd went wild as their muscular, oiled torsos were bared, naked to the waist, hips gyrating suggestively.

Rosemary reached down and removed Anthony's hand from her pussy. She was wet and sticky, her panties soaking. Her eyes were on Dan, the sheer bravery of his actions taking her breath away. No wonder he'd found it necessary to imbibe a little Dutch courage. Were they going for the ultimate revelation? she wondered, along with a hundred other women. She longed that it should be so, eager to see his cock surrounded by its wiry hair, to glimpse his balls and know that she had been the recipient of his passion.

'*But you can leave your hat on,*' bellowed the voice of Tom Jones, and everyone joined in as the strippers drew belts from trouser loops with tantalising slowness, and then unfastened their flies.

The shoes and trousers came off and were flung away.

The six men now wore nothing but sapphire satin G-strings and their policemen's hats.

'Whoever choreographed this did a great job,' Jonathan shouted in Rosemary's ear. 'It's fabulous. Which one's your boyfriend?'

'The last on the right,' she said, standing up and pointing, ignoring Anthony's look of sheer fury.

The music thumped. The crowded roared. The song reached a crescendo. With a final pelvic thrust, the dancers whipped off their Velcro-fastened pouches. There was a flash of cock and balls, no more, before the caps swept down to cover their crotches. Then, bold as any Chippendale, they posed, spread-legged, and opened their arms wide, caps in hand. Amidst a pandemonium of cheering, whistles and cat-calls, women surged forward and tried to rush the stage. The strippers grabbed up their clothes and ran.

By the time Rosemary had elbowed her way through and into the side-room they'd been allowed to use for changing, Dan was already dressed again, enjoying a smoke with his mates.

'Well done,' Rosemary said, smiling at him, and including the others. 'Well done, all of you. That took some doing.'

'Especially in front of the top brass,' he replied, hugely pleased with himself. 'But I had to get drunk to do it. I've never been so scared. We've been practising for weeks. That's why you haven't seen much of me.'

She didn't care, understanding now. This supposedly hard-boiled cop and his buddies had put themselves out to raise funds for charity. 'You could do with a cup of strong coffee,' she said, but wanted to grab him up and strip him again. She'd never felt so hot for him as she did in that moment.

'Your place or mine?' he asked, grinning at the cliché.

'I've a limousine waiting outside. It has seats as big as beds.'

'What are we waiting for?' And his hand was on her shoulder, guiding her towards the door, stopping every

255

so often to accept congratulations and chat with his superiors.

They weaved towards the entrance, passing Michael's table. 'I'm going home now,' she said, running her hand down the side of his face. 'Will you take care of Robert for me and see that he gets back safely? I don't want to drag him away. He's having such a good time with that bunch of fledgling constables. I think I may lose him to the force.'

'You're not going, Rosemary?' Anthony barred her way. He looked angry enough to kill her.

'I am. Good night, Anthony.'

'But I've not finished with you yet.'

Dan squared up to him, drunk enough to be belligerent. 'Stand aside, mate.'

'I was talking to Miss Maddox,' Anthony said, glaring at him. 'I'm Anthony Selby.'

'I know who you are, and what you've been up to. Watch your step or I'll put you under arrest.'

'You can't do that. Tell him, Rosemary. Say that you're not pressing charges.'

Dan lost it then, shouting, 'If you don't piss off, I'm going to punch your lights out.'

'Leave it, Dan. I don't want you to get into trouble. He's not worth it,' Rosemary insisted, and managed to get him outside and into the limo.

The rear was like a warm dark boudoir; a smoky plate-glass screen hung between them and the chauffeur. Rosemary curled against Dan on the deeply upholstered seat, and it was like being a teenager again, snogging in the back of a car. He played with her through her dress. Her skirt rode up as she wound her leg round his thigh, rubbing her cleft against the roughness of his trousers. His mouth found hers in the streetlight-punctuated gloom, his tongue tasting the cavern of her mouth, dancing with hers, while his hands explored her breasts. First she felt his touch through the chiffon. Then he had bared her, head down, sucking at her nipples.

She sought and found the hardness of his cock but

didn't unzip him, nor did she permit him to fondle her clit. This was just an apéritif to sustain them till they reached Sutton Close.

The outside lights came on as the car passed between the sensors, and the gates opened. When it braked at the main door, Rosemary stepped out into the warmth of a perfect summer night. The house and grounds were deserted. They had it all to themselves.

Forgetting her promise of coffee, Rosemary took Dan upstairs, and pushed open the windows of her bedroom. Humid heat wafted from the balcony, the air rich with the pungent odour of stephanotis. She took the clips from her hair and let it tumble loose, glancing at Dan almost shyly. Her pulse raced as she watched him making himself at home, re-establishing his position in her house, her room and her life. He sat on the bed, shrugged off his evening jacket and loosened his tie.

Taking something from an inside pocket, he said, 'I've tickets for the opera. It's *Tosca*. Will you come?'

'Yes,' she answered, touched by yet another aspect of this extraordinary individual.

She moved over to where the doll stood and ran a finger over the glass dome protecting it. And now she could feel gratitude towards Anthony for sending her this gift. If it hadn't been for his obsession she would never have met Dan.

'You don't mind her?' Dan asked, and she felt him behind her, his arms sliding round her waist.

'No. But Robert hasn't been doing his duty properly. She's dusty.'

This was the last sensible piece of conversation they had. He undressed her and himself and then turned on the shower, guiding her inside and closing the door. She felt the warm water cascading over her as she clung to him for support, his chest hair abrasive on her breasts, his erection nudging her belly. He placed her hands on the chrome rail each side, then went down on his knees in the shower tray, and she felt his hands on her wet legs, sliding upwards and his face pressing into her thatch.

The water was reduced to a trickle and it was like standing under a gentle fountain, leaning back against the tiles while Dan tongued her and she pinched her wet, hard nipples and came within seconds. He rose, lifted her and, with her legs clamped round his waist, plunged his cock into her. She spasmed round him, shaken by deep contractions, wondering if he was protected, then not caring. She could leave it all to him. He wouldn't let her down, not now, not at any time.

When he'd climaxed, he wrapped her in a towel and looped another round his hips, then carried her into the bedroom. 'My, you are macho,' she teased, then said, 'No, not the bed. The balcony. It's a wonderful place to make love.'

'We've never done it there.'

'*We* may not have done, but I have,' she teased. He wasn't to become too sure of himself. No man would own her, ever again.

She let the towel drop, resting her hands on the balustrade and breathing deeply of the mingled scents. The moon was full, a great silver orb making the garden almost as bright as day. A magical night, yet whether it was because she'd just been satisfied, or due to lessons she'd learned with Anthony and the others, she found herself thinking about her future, not love. She was planning what she'd do now that Plants Galore was hers. There were several innovations she'd wanted to try but Terry hadn't. Now there was nothing to stop her.

'Penny for them,' Dan said, nuzzling her neck.

'Oh, I was just thinking about the nursery and the programme.'

'You're a workaholic,' he teased.

'So are you,' she returned, aware that his cock was lifting the towel and pressing it into her bottom crease.

'That's why we're such a great team,' he answered confidently.

She pulled cushions from the window-seat and lay

258

with him under the glass roof, the moon's huge face peering in at them. Looking up at it, Rosemary could see the reflection of their entwined bodies. Her second orgasm was brusque, and then she rolled on her back, legs raised so that he could drive deeply into her. She wanted to swallow him whole and her muscles grabbed at him.

Then they rested in companionable silence, pressed close from shoulder to hip. Rosemary was happy. He hadn't asked her to make any sacrifices or alter her life to suit him, but she knew that she very well might do it voluntarily.

He would fit it. She snuggled against his side, breathing in the warmth of him, feeling the air on her skin, the scent of flowers all around, lying there amidst the natural elements she loved so much.

The phone bleeped several times before Rosemary surfaced from sleep and reached for the receiver on the bedside table. She nearly knocked it off, grabbing at it and gasping, 'Hello,' into the mouthpiece.

Too late. The answerphone had kicked in. The message was simple, Anthony saying, 'Dan won't give you everything you need. No one will, except me. See you soon. Some strings can never be broken.'

BLACK LACE NEW BOOKS

Published in November

LEARNING TO LOVE IT
Alison Tyler
£5.99

Art historian Lissa and doctor Colin meet at the Frankfurt Book Fair, where they are both promoting their latest books. At the fair, and then through Europe, the two lovers embark on an exploration of their sexual fantasies, playing dirty games of bondage and dressing up. Lissa loves humiliation, and Colin is just the man to provide her with the pleasure she craves. Unbeknown to Lissa, their meeting was not accidental, but planned ahead by a mysterious patron of the erotic arts.

ISBN 0 352 33535 1

THE HOTTEST PLACE
Tabitha Flyte
£5.99

Abigail is having a great time relaxing on a hot and steamy tropical island in Thailand. She tries to stay faithful to her boyfriend back in England, but it isn't easy when a variety of attractive, fun-loving young people want to get into her pants. When Abby's boyfriend, Roger, finds out what's going on, he's on the first plane over there, determined to dish out some punishment.

And that's when the fun really starts hotting up.

ISBN 0 352 33536 X

EARTHY DELIGHTS
Tesni Morgan
£5.99

Rosemary Maddox is TV's most popular gardening presenter. Her career and business are going brilliantly but her sex life is unpredictable. Someone is making dirty phonecalls and sending her strange objects in the post, including a doll that resembles her dressed in kinky clothes. And when she's sent on an assignment to a bizarre English country house, things get even stranger.

ISBN 0 352 33548 3

WILD KINGDOM
Deanna Ashford
£5.99

War is raging in the mythical kingdom of Kabra. Prince Tarn is struggling to drive out the invading army while the beautiful Rianna has fled the fighting with a mysterious baroness. The baroness is a fearsome and depraved woman, and once they're out of the danger zone she takes Rianna prisoner. Her plan is to present her as a plaything to her warlord half-brother, Ragnor. In order to rescue his sweetheart, Prince Tarn needs to join forces with his old enemy, Sarin. A rollicking adventure of sword 'n' sorcery with lashings of kinky sex from the author of *Savage Surrender*.

ISBN 0 352 33549 1

THE NINETY DAYS OF GENEVIEVE
Lucinda Carrington
£5.99

A ninety-day sex contract isn't exactly what Genevieve Loften has in mind when she begins business negotiations with James Sinclair. She finds herself being transformed into the star performer in his increasingly kinky fantasies. Thrown into a game of sexual challenges, Genevieve learns how to dress for sex, and balance her high-pressure career with the twilight world of fetishism and debauchery.

This is a Black Lace special reprint.

ISBN 0 352 33534 3

To be published in January

MAN HUNT
Cathleen Ross
£5.99

Angie's a driven woman when it comes to her career in hotel management, but also when it comes to the men she chooses to pursue – for Angie's on a man hunt. For sexy, challenging men. For men like devilishly attractive but manipulative James Steele, who runs the hotel training course. When she turns her attention to one of her fellow students, Steele's determined to assume the dominant position and get her interest back. This time it's Steele who's the predator and Angie the prey.

ISBN 0 352 33583 1

DREAMING SPIRES
Juliet Hastings
£5.99

Catherine de la Tour has been awarded an assignment as writer-in-residence at a Cambridge college but her lover James is a thousand miles away and she misses him badly. Although her position promises peace and quiet, she becomes immersed in a sea of sexual hedonism, as the rarefied hothouse of academia proves to be a fertile environment for passion and raunchy lust.

ISBN 0 352 33584 X

MÉNAGE
Emma Holly
£5.99

Bookstore owner Kate comes home from work one day to find her two flatmates in bed together. Joe – a sensitive composer – is mortified. Sean – an irrepressible bad boy – asks her to join in. As they embark on a polysexual ménage à trois, Kate wants nothing more than to keep both her admirers happy. However, things become complicated. Kate has told everyone that Sean is gay, but now he and Kate are acting like lovers. Can the three of them live happily ever after – together?
This is a Black Lace special reprint.

ISBN 0 352 33231 X

If you would like a complete list of plot summaries of Black Lace titles, or would like to receive information on other publications available, please send a stamped addressed envelope to:

Black Lace, Thames Wharf Studios,
Rainville Road, London W6 9HA

BLACK
lace

BLACK LACE BOOKLIST

Information is correct at time of printing. To check availability go to www.blacklace-books.co.uk

All books are priced £5.99 unless another price is given.

Black Lace books with a contemporary setting

DARK OBSESSION £7.99	Fredrica Alleyn ISBN 0 352 33281 6	☐
THE TOP OF HER GAME	Emma Holly ISBN 0 352 33337 5	☐
LIKE MOTHER, LIKE DAUGHTER	Georgina Brown ISBN 0 352 33422 3	☐
THE TIES THAT BIND	Tesni Morgan ISBN 0 352 33438 X	☐
VELVET GLOVE	Emma Holly ISBN 0 352 33448 7	☐
DOCTOR'S ORDERS	Deanna Ashford ISBN 0 352 33453 3	☐
SHAMELESS	Stella Black ISBN 0 352 33485 1	☐
TONGUE IN CHEEK	Tabitha Flyte ISBN 0 352 33484 3	☐
FIRE AND ICE	Laura Hamilton ISBN 0 352 33486 X	☐
SAUCE FOR THE GOOSE	Mary Rose Maxwell ISBN 0 352 33492 4	☐
HARD CORPS	Claire Thompson ISBN 0 352 33491 6	☐
INTENSE BLUE	Lyn Wood ISBN 0 352 33496 7	☐
THE NAKED TRUTH	Natasha Rostova ISBN 0 352 33497 5	☐
A SPORTING CHANCE	Susie Raymond ISBN 0 352 33501 7	☐
A SCANDALOUS AFFAIR	Holly Graham ISBN 0 352 33523 8	☐
THE NAKED FLAME	Crystalle Valentino ISBN 0 352 33528 9	☐

------------✂------------------

Please send me the books I have ticked above.

Name ....

Address ....

....

....

.... Post Code ....

Send to: **Cash Sales, Black Lace Books, Thames Wharf Studios, Rainville Road, London W6 9HA.**

US customers: for prices and details of how to order books for delivery by mail, call 1-800-805-1083.

Please enclose a cheque or postal order, made payable to **Virgin Publishing Ltd**, to the value of the books you have ordered plus postage and packing costs as follows:

UK and BFPO – £1.00 for the first book, 50p for each subsequent book.

Overseas (including Republic of Ireland) – £2.00 for the first book, £1.00 for each subsequent book.

If you would prefer to pay by VISA, ACCESS/MASTER-CARD, DINERS CLUB, AMEX or SWITCH, please write your card number and expiry date here:

....

Please allow up to 28 days for delivery.

Signature ....

------------✂------------------